Dark Water

SHARON SALA

Dark Water

MIRA®

ISBN 0-7394-3030-0

DARK WATER

Printed in U.S.A.

Growing up the child of an alcoholic father,
I felt branded by his weakness. His shame became
my shame and, as I grew older, I feared his faults
would surely be my own.

It has taken me a lifetime to learn that,
despite what is often said, the sins of the father
do not visit themselves upon the child.

I am not less, nor am I more,
than the man my father was, or what he became
after twenty-one years in recovery. I am just me.
Responsible only to myself and to God.

And for all of my readers
who not only bore but overcame the mark
of someone else's shame, this book is for you.

One

If Avery Wheeler hadn't robbed an armored truck in Farmington, Maine, and taken a woman hostage, the state police would never have given chase when he headed north up Highway 27. He made it all the way to the outskirts of Stanton before taking a side road toward Flagstaff Lake. The police were only a minute or so behind him, and even though it was almost dark, he knew he wasn't going to make it to the Canadian border before they caught up with him. His plan, for the moment, was to get lost in the woods around the lake and hope for the best.

At that point he was wishing he hadn't dropped out of high school back in the seventies and had taken that job in his uncle's meatpacking business. Even more, he wished to hell he'd never laid eyes on the woman in the seat beside him. She hadn't stopped screaming since he'd shoved her in the car at gunpoint. Now all he wanted was to start this day over. But since that wasn't possible, he opted for making a new start, and to do that, he had to get rid of the police and that damned screaming clerk. As he rounded a curve in the road, he saw the opportunity to do both.

With the setting sun coming in through the driver's side of the windows and the dark water of Flagstaff Lake before him, he unbuckled his seat belt, lowered the window, then stomped on the gas. The force of the acceleration slammed both him and his hostage against the back of the seat. Gritting his teeth, he braced himself against the steering wheel while the decibels of her shrieks rose. Out of patience and time, he backhanded the woman into a state of semiconsciousness as the car went airborne.

The silence that followed was surreal. Even the sirens from the police cars seemed to fade. For Avery, everything began passing in slow motion.

The slight whistle of the wind coming in through the open window blew soft against his cheek.

The last rays of the dying sun glittered on the dark, mirrored water like broken glass on spilled coffee.

The soft moan coming from the woman's lips mingled with his own panicked breaths as the water grew nearer and nearer.

Then they hit.

The impact was sharp and jarring, and Avery

wondered how something so fluid could be so hard. The displaced water sent a ten-foot spray into the air, and then the car began sinking, faster than he would have imagined. When the water began spilling in through the open window, his heartbeat accelerated, even though this was exactly what he'd planned. He reached into the seat behind him and grabbed the bag with the stolen money. As he did, the woman he'd taken hostage began to come around.

A thin trickle of blood was coming out of her nose from where he'd hit her, and when she reached toward her face, it smeared across her cheek. She opened her eyes in blank confusion, then reached down for her seat belt, brushing at the water on her clothes as if it was dust. When it wouldn't come off, she looked up at him with a wide, frantic stare.

"Can you swim?" he asked.

She shook her head no.

"Sorry," he muttered, and pushed the front seat all the way back to give himself more room in which to maneuver out the window. She was going to drown. There was nothing he could do about that.

"Don't leave me!" she screamed, and grabbed at his arm.

He hit her with his fist. Her head snapped backward from the blow as she slumped down into the seat.

"You'll thank me later," he muttered. At least her death would be painless.

As he started out the window, the car began to flip. Panicked, he slung the shoulder strap of the bag over his head and began climbing out the window, desperate not to get caught in the sucking undertow. Twice the bag got caught—once on the gearshift and once on the side-view mirror on the outside of the door. Both times he thought about just letting go and saving himself, but he'd gotten into this mess because of the money. He wasn't yet ready to give it up.

Suddenly he was free, and the elation of the moment gave him renewed hope. He felt along the underside of the frame until he came to a wheel, climbed up on it and pushed himself off, praying that he was swimming up and not down.

The water felt thick, as if he was swimming in gelatin. He knew it was from the weight of the bag, but he was strong and a damned good swimmer. Moments later he surfaced, only to realize the sun had gone down. Treading water, he dared a glance at the shore. Although he could hear shouts from the police who had finally arrived, all he could see were the red-and-blue flashing lights and the vague silhouettes of the men as they ran back and forth in front of the cars. He didn't think they could see him any better than he could see them, but the knowledge that they might made him swim even harder. He swam and he swam, until his arms felt like lead and his lungs were about to burst.

Once again treading water, he stopped and looked behind him. The shore he'd come from was alive with flashing lights and the faint sounds of men's voices, shouting to one another. With a satisfied grin, he tugged the heavy wet bag to a more comfortable position and began to swim again. The opposite shore was nothing but a vague blur above the surface of the black water, but he could see one small light—probably someone's porch light— through the trees. He fixed his eyes on that light and began to stroke.

At first he didn't even feel the pain in his chest because the water was so cold. But when it spread to his arms and then shortened his breath, Avery knew he wasn't going to make Canada after all. Unable to believe it was going to end like this, he finally turned loose of the money, but it was a case of too little, too late. The sodden bag bumped against his knee and then his foot as it drifted toward the bottom. Moments later a pain seared his chest so severely that he shrieked aloud. The sound carried across the stillness of the lake, giving back an eerie high-pitched echo. In that moment, Avery knew he'd heard himself die. His eyes rolled back in his head as his body went limp. He sank into the dark water without another sound, following the money's descent.

Divers from the county sheriff's office were onshore when morning broke over the trees. The beauty of the impending autumn was lost in the cold, hard facts of why they were here. Amber-and-ruby-streaked leaves faded against the overwhelming task that lay ahead of them.

Deputy Danny Baldwin had been with search and rescue for over six years. He was proud of what he did but hated this part of his job. This time there was no rescue, only a search and recover.

His partner, Will Freid, was also his brother-in-law. Will had ten years on him in age and experience, but not in earnestness. Danny knew that the woman who'd been taken hostage had a husband and two teenage sons. The only way he could give her back to her family was to find her body and let them put her to rest. Will was as focused as Danny on the job ahead but kept his emotions closer to his chest.

"Here comes the sheriff," Will said.

Danny looked up, then went back to checking the pressure gauges on his air tanks. Within minutes the area was crawling with law enforcement, including an agent from the Federal Bureau of Investigation, who'd come to monitor the scene because money belonging to a bank insured by the FDIC had been taken. But none of it mattered to Danny. He let the powers that be do their pushing and shoving as to who was in charge, because ultimately, nothing happened until recovery was made.

"Looks like they brought in some other divers," Will added.

Danny looked up, recognizing the figures getting out of the vehicles as men he'd worked with before, and nodded.

"We'll need them."

Will turned and gazed out across the lake. "Damned big body of water."

Ignoring the obvious, Danny adjusted the neck of his wet suit and shouldered the air tanks. "You ready?"

Will nodded.

Danny waved the sheriff over. "We're ready, sir."

Ron Gallagher took off his hat and shoved his hand through his hair.

"You know the routine. Stick to the grid I gave

you, and I'll start the other divers to your south.'' Then he glanced at the sky. ''If we get any wind, I'm pulling you out. I don't want any more bodies in this damned water.''

''I ain't drownin' myself in no dark water,'' Will drawled.

Danny grinned. ''And I'm not drowning myself at all, so we're gonna be fine.''

Franklin sighed. He knew their lighthearted teasing was a cover for the grimness of the task that lay ahead of them.

''Just be careful.''

''Always,'' they said in unison, and headed toward the small motorboat tied up at the shore.

A few minutes later they were in the boat. With a couple of pulls on the rope, the outboard motor coughed to life. Danny steered the boat away from the shore and headed toward the place of impact. Even though the car that had gone into the lake was probably within twenty or thirty feet of where it had entered, there was no telling where the bodies would be. If they'd made it out of the car before drowning, they could have drifted away from the area. But there had to be a starting point, and Danny and Will were on it.

Moments later, Danny killed the engine and tossed an anchor over the side.

"You ready, Will?"

Will nodded, then glanced up at the sky, wincing against the glare of the new day.

"At least we got us some sunshine."

"Yeah," Danny said. "Now all we need is some luck."

They found the car within the hour and quickly began the process of hauling it out of the lake. The divers all watched from the shore until it was pulled onto dry land. The woman who'd been taken hostage was still buckled into the seat. Realistically they'd known she would be dead, but the sight of her lifeless body was depressing, as if they'd failed in what they'd come to do. But the driver was still missing, which meant their job wasn't over. Last night the authorities had feared the driver might have gotten away, but they had yet to find signs around the shore of anyone coming out of the water. So, operating on the theory that he was still in the lake, the divers went back in the water. Until Avery Wheeler's body was found, the search would go on.

It was about an hour before sundown when Danny found the bag. The moment he realized what it was, he knew that Avery Wheeler would be nearby. He signaled Will, who came quickly to his side, then motioned for him to surface, taking the bag with him. Will signaled an okay and began to swim upward, trailing air bubbles in his wake. Danny shone the light on his watch, checking the time against how much air he had left in his tanks. It would be dark topside soon. If they didn't find Avery Wheeler before long, they would have to come back tomorrow, which wasn't good. A cold front was predicted for tonight, and the water would be miserable tomorrow, even with the wet suits that protected their bodies from the worst of the cold.

His flippers stirred silt on the bottom of the lake as he turned in place, taking a complete three-sixty-degree turn and trying to decide where to look next. The underwater light Danny carried was barely more than a pale aura, cutting little of the darkness in which he floated, but the absence of light didn't bother him. He felt more at home in dark water than he did on dry land and wondered if it had to do with old memories of floating in his mother's belly before he'd been born.

Aware that time was running out, he resumed the search by taking five steps forward, then turning to his right and walking in a circle. Once he'd completed the circle, he took five steps farther out and began to circle again. It was on the third circle that he saw the foot. Even though he'd spent the bigger part of the day looking for the body, in the back of his mind, he had wondered if the man had gotten away. Readjusting the light, he moved it forward, painting Avery Wheeler's body in a faint, shimmering glow. For a long silent moment he stared, listening to the sounds of his intake valve and then his own breath as he exhaled beneath the mask, wondering how men like Avery came to be. It wasn't until he started to send a marker topside that he realized Avery was lying on something other than the bottom of the lake.

He moved forward, his steps slow and measured, then bent down and pushed at Avery's body. It floated sideways and then dropped into the mud, revealing a large oblong metal box on which Avery's body had been lying. One end of it was half-buried in the mud and silt, with the opposite end protruding a bit upward. Knowing the history of the area and the fact that three small towns had been sacrificed in the creation of Flagstaff Lake, he suspected it was nothing more than a remnant of someone's belongings that hadn't gotten moved. It appeared to be some sort of old metal footlocker, and heavily rusted at that. He was about to move on when he saw the padlock on the clasp. That piqued his curiosity in a way nothing else could have. It wasn't legal, but dumping in the lake wasn't unheard-of. However, he'd never seen anything that had been dumped that had been locked up first. Knowing that the marker he'd sent up would bring Will back at any moment, he took his knife out of the scabbard and jammed it into the hasp of the lock. It popped open like a ripe apple against a brick wall.

Just as he was about to open the lid, he felt a tap on his shoulder. He turned. It was Will, with a what-the-hell-are-you-doing? look that made Danny wink. He pointed to the body and then to the lock he'd broken off. Danny could see Will roll his eyes through the mask and knew he would hear about this later. He motioned to Will again, indicating he wanted to lift the lid. Will shrugged and then moved into place, bracing his knees against the metal box and lifted, but nothing gave. Danny motioned for them to try again, and again they pulled. But the hinges were frozen with rust, and the lid wouldn't budge.

Will motioned for Danny to stop, that their air was running low and they were losing light up above. Danny nodded, then dropped to his knees. Using all his weight, he tried one last time. Will grimaced and went down beside him. He knew Danny well enough to realize that he wouldn't quit until he'd accomplished what he'd started.

At first nothing happened; then suddenly they felt the lid give. Danny signaled a thumbs-up and resumed pulling even harder. Within seconds, the lid started to move. He stood and then slid his fingers beneath the lip and began to pull harder.

Even after he saw the skeleton inside the box, it took several seconds for the sight to register. But when a bony hand began to float upward out of the box, he slammed the lid down in sudden panic.

He turned and looked at Will, his eyes wide and filled with shock. Will's expression was blank, as if he couldn't believe what he'd seen, either; then, in unison, they reached for Avery Wheeler's body and headed for the surface.

New Orleans, Louisiana

Sarah Jane Whitman was late for work. Last night she'd stayed up late working on the books for her restaurant, Ma Chère, then forgotten to set her alarm. She owned the restaurant, so it wasn't as if she was going to get fired, but she liked being the first one there. She liked opening up—walking into the dining room and feeling the lingering energy of yesterday's customers, seeing the empty tables and chairs waiting to be covered in pristine white tablecloths and then set with fine china. It never failed to give her a sense of excitement. Even though the routine of feeding people was the same, the people were not. Each day at Ma Chère was like waking up in a new world, and she had her godmother, Lorett Boudreaux, to thank for it all.

She ran a brush through her hair as she stepped into her shoes. When she turned to toss the brush on the vanity, she felt the waistband on her slacks suddenly give. Running her hand along the band, she grimaced when the button fell away in her hand.

"Rats," she muttered, and headed for the closet to get her sewing basket. Sewing the button back on was faster than a complete change of clothes.

Slipping her pants down toward her knees, she sat down on the side of the bed, twisted the waistband toward her and began sewing the errant button back on her slacks. She was just tying off the knot when her phone began to ring. She glanced up at the clock and decided to let the answering machine pick it up, then changed her mind and answered on the third ring.

"Hello," she answered.

"Sarah Whitman?"

Sarah stifled a gasp. It had been twenty years since she'd heard an accent like this, and the memories it evoked made her sick.

"Yes, this is Sarah Whitman."

"Miss Whitman...my name is Ron Gallagher. I'm Sheriff of Somerset County, Maine."

Sarah stared down at the floor, noticing a small scuff on the seam of her left shoe, and took a deep breath. She kept trying to answer, but the bile in the back of her throat made speech momentarily impossible.

"Miss Whitman…are you still there?"

She shuddered, then wiped a shaky hand across her face.

"Yes. I'm sorry. Why have you called?"

"Franklin Whitman was your father, was he not?"

The palms of her hands were suddenly sweaty. She felt herself coming undone. This wasn't fair. It was over. It was supposed to be over.

"Can't you leave me alone?" she asked, unaware that the tone of her voice had risen to that of a child.

Ron Gallagher frowned. He'd been a rookie when the Whitman scandal had hit Marmet, but small towns were slow to forgive and forget. What had happened to the Whitman family as a result of Franklin Whitman's thievery and deceit was a crime in itself.

"I'm very sorry, Miss Whitman, but it's my duty to inform you that, two days ago, we recovered your father's body from Flagstaff Lake."

It was the last thing Sarah had expected him to say. Her father had been vice president of Marmet

National Bank for ten years—a well-respected member of the community and the most wonderful parent a ten-year-old girl could have. And then he'd robbed the bank, run off with a million dollars in unmarked bills, and left her and her mother to shoulder the blame. It had ruined their lives and, ultimately, killed her mother. If it hadn't been for her mother's best friend, Lorett, Sarah would have wound up a ward of the state. Now they were trying to make her feel sorry for the man who had caused them such pain.

"What do you want me to do about it?" she snapped.

"Miss Whitman...I don't think you understand," the sheriff said.

"What's to understand?" Sarah snapped. "I would think you'd be happy you found him. What does surprise me is that he ever came back to the scene of the crime."

Ron Gallagher sighed. What he was about to tell her had already caused a big ruckus in Marmet, but there was no way to deny the truth.

"That's just it," he said. "It doesn't look as if he ever left."

"What do you mean?"

"Some divers found his body locked inside an old metal footlocker. There were still some bits and pieces of his clothing in the locker...some leather that didn't rot...his wallet...shoes and the like. According to the old police report we had on what he was wearing when he disappeared, we're leaning toward the theory that he was still wearing the same clothes when he was put in the locker and dropped in the lake.''

Sarah's vision blurred. Her voice started to shake.

"What are you saying?"

"That your father was murdered...possibly by an accomplice who decided to keep the money for himself."

Sarah stood up slowly. She heard the words, but they were not making sense. All these years she'd assumed her daddy had been living it up in some faraway land on the money he'd stolen, when in truth he'd been rotting in a box at the bottom of a lake.

"No," she said.

Gallagher frowned, misunderstanding her response. "I'm sorry, Miss Whitman, but it *is* your father. We've made a positive ID from dental records."

"No," she repeated, "it's not that." Then she took a deep breath. "Twenty years ago the authorities said he stole that money and got away. Mother and I were treated as lepers in our own home. The law never quit blaming us. The innuendos were horrible…insinuations that we would soon leave and join him in spending his ill-gotten gains. My mother killed herself because of you people, and now you're telling me you were wrong about him getting away.'' Her voice grew louder as her convictions grew stronger. "So if you were wrong about that, then you could be wrong about everything else. What if he didn't take the money? What if he was nothing but the Judas goat for the real thief?''

"I know it's a possibility, but right now we're—''

"When can I get my father's remains?''

Her anger was obvious, and under the circumstances, he couldn't blame her.

"The coroner is backlogged, but as soon as he's able to start on the investigation, I'll—''

"Never mind,'' Sarah said sharply. "I'll be there as soon as I can get a flight.''

"But, Miss Whitman, there isn't—''

Sarah hung up in his ear.

Two

The Chicago windchill was below freezing as Tony DeMarco stepped out of the cab. Hunching his shoulders against the cold, he headed for the front doors of the bank. The renovations on his newest acquisition were almost finished, and he needed to move some money in his accounts to pay off the contractor.

Fifteen years ago he'd come to Chicago with a dream and little else. But determination, hard work and some backing from his uncle, Salvatore De-Marco, had soon set him on the path to making his fortune. It had taken eight years to build his reputation as a raconteur, but the time had been worth it. His first nightclub, Silk, was such a resounding success that he was about to open a counterpart downtown on Lakeshore Drive.

He strode into the bank with his head high and his shoulders back. His thick black hair was slightly windblown, his dark brown eyes focused on the man at the president's office across the room. He moved with the assurance of a man who was comfortable in his own skin, oblivious to the admiring female looks he was getting.

"Good morning, Charlotte. I need to talk to Dabney. Is he busy?"

A wide smile spread across the secretary's face as she looked up.

"Mr. DeMarco! How nice to see you."

"Silk! Come in! Come in!" the bank officer called.

Since his club had become so popular, many people called him by the nickname he'd had since he was in his teens. Now he answered to it as readily as he did to his own. He did as he was bidden, giving the secretary a quick smile as he passed her desk.

Within the hour, he had finished his business and was back in a cab on his way to his apartment overlooking Lake Michigan. Despite the years he'd lived in Chicago, there were times, like now, when he missed the deep woods of his home state. The view from his apartment was spectacular, but it had never come close to autumn in Maine. He missed the variegated colors of New England in the fall, and the walks he used to take through the woods as a child. Just thinking about the crunch of leaves underfoot and the scent of wood smoke from neigh-boring fireplaces made him homesick.

Five years ago he'd built a vacation home on the shores of Flagstaff Lake, near Marmet where he'd grown up, but since then, he had only been there twice. This year, however, he had promised himself some time away from the job. Even though Chicago had been largely responsible for the fortune he had amassed, it would be great to get out of the city, if only for a while.

A few minutes later the cab driver pulled up to the curb in front of his apartment. Silk handed the driver a twenty-dollar bill for a nine-dollar ride and got out of the cab without bothering to wait for change. His life was on such a smooth track that he felt generous. The cabby was still smiling as Tony disappeared into the building. A couple of minutes later he was unlocking the door to his pent-house apartment. After shrugging out of his coat, he hung it on the coatrack in the hall, paused to pick a stray bit of thread from the cashmere fabric and then moved toward the kitchen. After the chill outside, a cup of hot coffee sounded good.

In the midst of preparations, his phone rang. He reached for it without thinking to look at the caller ID, but smiled when he recognized the voice on the other end of the line.

"Hey, Silk…long time no see," the man said.

"Hey back at you, Web. It's been a while. What on earth are you up to?"

Webster Davidson signed his name on a contract his secretary shoved in front of him and then waved her away with a signal to hold all his calls.

"Staying busy…you know how it is."

"Still building houses?"

"Some, although my latest project is a mall."

"Better you than me," Tony said.

"That sounds suspiciously like negative thinking…something I never thought I'd hear from the infamous Anthony DeMarco."

"Oh…so I'm infamous, am I?"

"Well…maybe not so much anymore. Not since you went legit."

Tony laughed aloud. "Hell, Web. I was always legit. Just better looking than you."

Web chuckled. "No argument there," he said. "But talking about my beer gut and thinning hair is not why I called."

"So what's up?" Tony asked.

"Franklin Whitman."

Tony frowned. It had been years since he'd heard the name, but he remembered all too well the shock of what Franklin Whitman had done. Not only had he stolen a million dollars from the bank where he'd worked, he'd abandoned his family, as well. It was so unlike the man he'd known that, at the time, Tony had been stunned by the revelation.

"What about Whitman? Did they finally find him?"

"Oh yeah," Web said. "Or at least what was left of him."

The skin on the back of Tony's neck suddenly crawled.

"What do you mean...what's left of him?"

"A couple days ago a car went into Flagstaff Lake. Some divers from county search and rescue were searching the lake for a body when one of them found this metal trunk. When they opened it, they found what turned out to be Whitman's remains."

"Jesus." Then Tony remembered the little girl who used to watch him mow her daddy's yard. Only she wouldn't be so little anymore. "Whitman's daughter. Has she been notified?"

"That's what I heard. My sister's husband is a deputy with the Somerset County Sheriff's Department. Someone said she was coming in tomorrow to claim her father's remains."

"Alone?"

"Hell, Silk, I don't know. All I heard was that

she'd been living in New Orleans, and that when the sheriff called her she got mad...real mad.''

Tony sighed. ''Thanks for calling, Web. I appreciate it.''

''Yeah, no problem,'' Web said. ''I just thought you'd want to know. I remember you liked Whitman.''

''Yes, I liked him.''

''So...I guess I'd better get back to work. If you're ever up this way, give me a call.''

The line went dead. Tony hung up, then poured some of the coffee that had just brewed into a mug and carried it into the living room. He took a careful sip as he sank down into his favorite chair, then sighed and let his thoughts drift back into the past.

He thought of the child Sarah Whitman had been, remembering the last time he'd seen her—standing at her mother's grave with tears streaming down her little face. He'd been sixteen years old and uncertain how to comfort a ten-year-old kid, so he'd done nothing and, as a result, had never gotten over the guilt. Franklin Whitman had believed in Tony when no one else in the town of Marmet would give him a chance. His parents had both been drinkers— never holding a job for more than a few months at a time. Anthony DeMarco had run wild in the streets and more or less raised himself. By the time he was a teenager, he had a bad-boy reputation and the good looks to go with it. The nickname Silk had come from his male peers, who were envious of his sexual prowess and his smooth-as-silk manner with the opposite sex. But Silk DeMarco had been a boy on the verge of manhood and had known that being the high school stud wasn't going to get him out of the depressing lifestyle into which he'd been born. He wanted more for himself.

It was the summer of his sixteenth year when he strode into the bank where Franklin Whitman worked and asked him for a loan. He wanted to buy a lawn mower to start his own lawn service, knowing full well that even if he got the loan and bought the mower, there was a very good chance that the good people of Marmet might not trust him enough to hire him. To his surprise, Whitman had not only loaned him the money but became his first customer. Before the summer was over, Silk had acquired thirty regular customers and earned over three thousand dollars. It had been the first time he'd tasted success, and it had given him an appetite for more.

He took another sip of coffee, grunting with satisfaction that it had cooled enough to enjoy. Something splattered against the windows nearby, and he glanced up. It had started to rain. He frowned, wondering what Sarah Whitman looked like now, wondering if she was married. He remembered the way she and her mother had been treated after Whitman's disappearance. It had driven her mother crazy and ultimately caused her to take her own life. Web had said Sarah was going to Marmet to claim her father's remains. The thought of her facing that task alone made him sick. He'd let her down once, but not again.

He stood abruptly and headed for the phone. A few minutes later he was packing to go home.

Sarah held her breath as the plane touched down. Reluctantly she glanced out the window, imagining she could already smell the salt air, and then quickly looked away, dreading what lay ahead. Her aunt Lorett had offered to come with her, but Sarah had refused, asking her to oversee her restaurant, instead. It had been a feeble excuse, and they both knew it. Sarah had a very competent manager, and Lorett knew nothing about running a restaurant. Both of them knew Sarah needed to do this alone— she had to face the demons that had driven her away.

Her legs were shaking as she got off the plane. She made her way through the airport to baggage claim on auto pilot, and by the time she got to Rent-

A-Car to pick up the keys to the car she'd reserved, she was sick to her stomach.

Sarah pointed to a display rack behind the clerk. "I need a map of the state, please."

The clerk handed her one with the keys to the car.

"The lot is out this door and to your right," she said. "Your car should be at the far end of the lot, Row 8."

Sarah nodded, shouldered her purse to a more comfortable position, grabbed the handle of her suitcase and headed out the door. A short while later she was in the car and making her way out of the airport. As she steered the car into the traffic moving toward the city, she muttered a hasty prayer.

"God give me strength," she said, and melded into the long line of cars.

For a while she was too involved in making sure she took the right exit and got on the correct highway to think about where she was going. But after she cleared the city and was on the northbound highway, her anxiety returned. She'd only been ten when her world had imploded. There were nights when she still dreamed of waking up and finding her mother's dead body in the bedroom, lying in a congealing pool of blood. She had vague memories of wrapping her mother's bloody wrists with towels in a futile effort to stop the blood that had already ceased to flow. Then, because their phone service had been disconnected, she had run next door for help. The ensuing days were nothing but a blur. It wasn't until her aunt Lorett had come from New Orleans that she'd let herself cry, and then she'd been unable to stop.

The day after her mother's funeral, Lorett Boudreaux had helped her pack her clothes, given the authorities a copy of Catherine Whitman's will stating her wishes that Sarah would now live with her and left town without looking back. The townspeople were so glad to be rid of the duty of dealing with Frank Whitman's spawn that they'd made little to no fuss about a black woman claiming a white woman's child. That Lorett Boudreaux had papers signed by Catherine Whitman giving her sole custody of her daughter was enough for them. For the authorities in Marmet, it was a case of out of sight, out of mind.

Sarah had spent the next twenty years trying to do just that—put it out of her mind. She'd done a pretty good job of it, too, until she'd gotten the phone call from the Somerset County sheriff. Now everything she'd grown up believing had been turned upside down. If her father had been dead all those years, then that meant he hadn't abandoned them. On the contrary, he'd obviously been murdered, which led to the disintegration of another assumption under which she'd been living. There was every possibility that her father had been the scapegoat for the real thief. It hurt her heart to think she'd so easily believed his guilt. It didn't matter that she'd only been ten years old. She should have known that the gentle, loving man who'd always read her bedtime stories wouldn't have done the vile things of which he'd been accused. Now it was too late to tell him she was sorry, but it wasn't too late to clear his name.

She took a deep breath, telling herself to be calm. Yes, she was coming to reclaim what was left of the man she'd called Father, but she owed him more than a Christian burial. He deserved to rest in peace with his good name restored. It was the least she could do.

Sarah didn't think she'd remembered all that much about the first ten years of her life, but then she hit the city limits of Marmet. The neat Cape Cod houses and tree-lined streets were eerily familiar. She stared intently at each house she passed and at the people she saw on the streets, wondering if they would recognize her, wondering if they cared that they'd been so wrong about her father, wondering if they carried the guilt of her mother's death upon their souls. She blamed them. She blamed them all, just as she'd blamed her father. But she'd been wrong about him and was willing to admit it. It remained to be seen if they would be as generous.

A few minutes later she pulled up in front of the Sheriff's Department. For three long minutes she sat without moving, her fingers gripping the steering wheel like a lifeline. A police car pulled up and parked beside her. She watched the officer get out and wondered if he was someone she'd known before. Twenty years was a long time. People changed, but did they ever forget?

A few moments later the officer came back out, giving her a curious stare as he moved toward his car. Sarah looked away, unwilling to meet his gaze, and began gathering up her purse and keys. She got out as he drove away. When she walked into the station, the dispatcher behind the glass looked up.

"Can I help you, miss?" he asked.

"I need to talk to Sheriff Gallagher. He's expecting me."

"He's not in."

Sarah frowned. This wasn't going exactly as planned.

"When will he be back?"

"I can't say for sure. Leave your name and a number where you can be reached, and he can call you."

"I don't have a place to stay yet. Is there a hotel here?"

"No, miss, just a bed-and-breakfast on the outskirts of town, but Miss Hattie, who runs it, is in the hospital having her appendix out."

"Oh great," Sarah muttered, and looked around for a chair. "Maybe I'll just wait here until the sheriff comes back."

The dispatcher frowned. "No telling when that will be. He's still out at the lake."

Sarah turned abruptly. "Flagstaff Lake?"

The dispatcher nodded.

"Where they found Franklin Whitman's body?"

Suddenly the dispatcher realized he might be saying too much.

"Who are you? Are you with the press? If you are, you're wasting your time."

"My name is Sarah Whitman. Franklin Whitman was my father."

The frown deepened on the dispatcher's face. "I can't help you."

Sarah accepted the rejection. It was nothing she hadn't prepared herself for.

"I didn't expect help from anyone in this town," she said shortly, and headed for the door.

"Where are you going?" the dispatcher asked.

"None of your business," she muttered, letting the door slam behind her as she went.

By the time she got to the car, she was shaking with anger. She had vague memories of the lake but no idea how to get there. However, she hadn't come this far to be put off by a recalcitrant dispatcher. Making herself calm down, she unfolded the map of the state of Maine, then found the lake and the nearest highway. She was going to assume that once she was on the right road, there would be signs telling her where to go next.

Sheriff Ron Gallagher was just getting out of the motorboat when he saw an unfamiliar car drive up. He glanced at the bank of film crews a short distance away and figured one of the reporters had gotten impatient.

"If that's another journalist, get rid of him," he snapped.

"It's a woman," his deputy said.

"I don't care who it is, Red. If she's a reporter, I want her on the other side of the yellow tape with the rest of them."

"Yes, sir," the deputy said, and headed for the

woman who was approaching with purpose in her step.

"I'm sorry, miss, but this is a crime scene. You're going to have to leave."

Sarah stood her ground. "I need to talk to Sheriff Gallagher."

"The sheriff has already given a statement regarding the case. He has nothing more to say to the media."

"I'm not with the media," Sarah said. "I'm Sarah Whitman."

Red Miller knew he was gawking, but he couldn't stop. "I remember you," he said softly.

"I don't remember you," Sarah said, and lifted her chin, as if bracing herself for a verbal blow.

"My name is Steven Miller, but everyone calls me Red. I was four grades ahead of you in school."

Sarah looked for the child in the short, balding man, without success. "I'm sorry. I don't remember you."

Red ducked his head. "That's all right. It's been a long time." Then he looked up at her and added, "I'm real sorry about your father."

"Really?"

Red flushed. He'd been old enough to remember the treatment Sarah Whitman and her mother had received. He also remembered that her mother had committed suicide and that Sarah had been the one to find her. He couldn't imagine what that must have done to her and could hardly blame her for holding a grudge. Aware that there was little he could say that would make up for the past twenty years, he pointed at the sheriff.

"If you'll wait a minute, I'll tell Sheriff Gallagher you're here."

Sarah sighed, more than a little disgusted with herself as she watched him hurrying away. She'd been rude. It wasn't like her to behave this way. If she was going to find out what had really happened to her father, she was going to need some help from the authorities, and alienating the first person who'd been friendly wasn't going to help.

Then her gaze moved past the deputy to the massive body of water beyond. Despite the picturesque beauty of the autumnal offering from the trees surrounding the lake, she shivered. The water was motionless—a black mirror with a smooth surface that was deceptive, showing none of the horror that had been hidden beneath. She moved closer, pulled to the truth of what her father had endured, trying to envision what he'd gone through. Suddenly the pain of it made her breath catch. Her vision blurred as an onset of tears burned the back of her throat.

God. Oh, Daddy...who did this to you?

"Miss Whitman?"

Sarah shuddered as her concentration was broken. She turned, unaware that tears were rolling down her face.

"Sheriff Gallagher?"

It wasn't the first time in Ron Gallagher's life that he'd wished to be tall, dark and handsome, but right now he might have bartered away his soul for a chance to win this woman's heart. She was stunning, and it bothered him to see the weary, fragile look on her face. He wanted to slay dragons and find killers and make the tears go away. Instead, he offered her his hand.

"Miss Whitman. I'm very sorry to have had to give you this news."

Sarah shook his hand briefly, because it would have been rude to do otherwise, but truthfully, she was finding it more and more difficult to be cordial. There was a rage growing inside her that was beginning to hurt. Her family had been destroyed because of a murder and a lie, and someone needed to pay.

"Thank you," she said, and then clutched her hands against her stomach to keep them from shaking. "I've come for my father."

Ron sighed. *Well, hell.* The one thing she'd asked that he couldn't give.

"I'm sorry, Miss Whitman, but I can't release him...at least not just yet."

"What can you tell me that I want to hear?"

"At this point, not much...but it's early stages in the investigation, and you've got to understand that I'm working on a twenty-year-old case, with the crime scene under about eighty feet of water."

Sarah's fingers curled into fists as she looked past the sheriff at the surface of the lake. She swallowed twice before the words would come past her lips.

"I need to ask you something," she whispered.

She looked so hurt and so lost that Ron wanted to put his arms around her and pull her head onto his shoulder.

"Yes, ma'am?"

"Do they know if—" She shuddered, then took a deep breath, making herself focus on what she wanted to say instead of screaming aloud at the thought. "My daddy...do they know if he was alive when..."

She couldn't say the words, but Ron knew what she was trying to ask.

"I can't really comment on that."

"Oh God," Sarah muttered. Fresh tears spilled and rolled down her face.

Ron stifled a groan. What he was going to say

was against everything he'd been taught about law enforcement, but seeing her misery was too painful.

"Look...don't quote me on this, and if you say I said this, I'll deny every bit of it. However...if I was a betting man, I'd say your father was probably already dead before he was put in the trunk."

"Why do you say that?" Sarah asked.

"When we opened the trunk, the first thing I noticed was the crack in his skull. Whether he was still alive or not, I doubt he ever regained consciousness before he was dumped in the lake."

Sarah exhaled, then nodded slowly. "Thank you for that."

Gallagher shrugged. "Yes, ma'am... Well, as I said—"

Before he could finish what he'd been going to say, a van pulled up beside them and three people jumped out.

"Sarah Whitman? Sarah Whitman? What do you have to say about your father's body being found in Flagstaff Lake?"

Sarah recoiled as if she'd been slapped. It was a nightmare straight out of her past: watching as her mother had been confronted in just such a manner, standing helplessly by as the people she loved were dragged through disgrace.

Gallagher reacted with an angry curse.

"Get out now or I'll have you all arrested," he yelled, but it was to no avail. The reporter saw his chance and was too persistent to let the threat of an arrest stop what would be his big scoop.

"Tell us, Miss Whitman...do you believe your father was killed by his accomplices?"

Sarah spun and tried to make a break for her car, but they followed her, getting between her and her chance for escape.

"Leave me alone," she said, and tried to push through them, but the reporter shoved a microphone in her face while the other two had cameras turned on her, capturing her every reaction.

"Do you have any hard feelings toward the people of Marmet?" the reporter asked. "Is there anyone you blame for—"

Suddenly the sound of a powerful engine drowned out the rest of the reporter's question. She turned just as a black sports car came to a sliding halt beside her. She stared, too surprised to comment, when the passenger door opened. Someone inside yelled at her to get in. She reacted before she thought, and was in the seat and slamming the door shut just as the car began to move.

"Buckle up," the driver said.

Sarah reached for the seat belt without question. It was only after she'd buckled up and they were flying out of the area, leaving a tornado of autumn leaves flying in their wake, that she looked at her driver. For a moment she stared, trying to figure out why the profile was so familiar, and then he turned to her for a brief moment and smiled. At that point her heart skipped a beat. It had been twenty years since she'd seen that smile, but a girl never forgets her first crush.

"Silk?"

Tony grinned. "I go by Tony most of the time now, but…yes, Sarah Whitman, it's me."

Three

In the short space of time that Sarah had been in Tony DeMarco's car, she had come to the conclusion that it was as sleek and seductive as the man behind the wheel. While trying not to stare, she'd still noticed the expensive cut of his clothes, the Rolex watch on his left wrist, the diamond ring on his right hand and the go-to-hell glitter in his eyes. She was grateful that he'd come along when he had and rescued her from the reporters, but she couldn't wrap her mind around the reason he'd given for being here. He'd come all the way from Chicago for her? As much as she would have liked to believe him, it didn't ring true.

"Silk...I mean, Tony...may I ask you a personal question?"

He stifled a sigh as he steered the car around a sharp bend in the road. She didn't trust him. He'd seen it in her eyes. He understood it, but he was still surprised that it hurt his feelings.

"Yes, of course."

"Judging by your appearance, you've become a very successful man. What do you do for a living?"

He arched an eyebrow. "It's legal, I assure you."

Sarah blushed. "That's not what I—"

Tony laughed. "Ease up...I was just teasing. I own a nightclub in Chicago...actually two, although the second one is about a month away from the grand opening. The first one is called Silk."

Sarah looked at him fully then, judging the very cosmopolitan man against the boy she'd known. She knew firsthand that it cost a lot of money to start a business, especially one like that. She was still paying off the loan she'd taken for the renovations on her own restaurant. Silk's family had been poor—from time to time almost homeless. She thought of the million dollars her father had been accused of stealing and then looked at Silk De Marco anew. Could he have done something like that? Possibly. But the more pertinent question was, would he?

"How old were you when my father disappeared?"

"Sixteen," Tony said. "I'd just finished my junior year in high school."

"Too young," she murmured, more to herself than to him. She couldn't see a kid pulling off a million-dollar bank heist, then being smart enough to pick a scapegoat and make him disappear in order to point suspicion in another direction.

"Too young for what?" Tony asked.

Sarah blushed. She hadn't realized she'd spoken.

"Nothing," she said. "I was just thinking aloud."

Tony frowned as he turned off the main road and took a narrow one-lane road that led to his lakefront home. What could she possibly be...?

Then it hit him, and the shaft of anger that came with that understanding was quick and hard. He slammed on the brakes and then turned to her. Startled by his behavior, Sarah's first instinct was to reach for the door, but Tony grabbed her by the shoulder before she could bolt.

"My uncle Salvatore loaned me more than half my start-up money, then co-signed my first loan. I paid him back within two years of Silk's opening. I didn't steal the million dollars, and I didn't kill your father."

The anger in his voice made her flinch, but she wouldn't apologize for what she'd thought. Until she knew the truth about what had happened to her father, she trusted no one.

"I was ten years old when my world fell apart. Within three months of my father's disappearance,

I'd become an orphan. If it hadn't been for Aunt Lorett, I would have become a ward of the state, and there wasn't one person in the entire town of Marmet who would have been sorry it happened. I'm not going to apologize for what I asked you. You were the first one I questioned, but you won't be the last. I didn't come here just to claim my father's bones. I'm not leaving until I find the person who killed him.''

The determination on her face was matched by the fury in her eyes. Sarah Whitman had grown up, all right. She was no longer the helpless, innocent kid he'd last seen crying at her mother's grave. But what she was proposing was not only foolish, it was dangerous.

"You can't be serious," he said.

"Just watch me," she muttered.

"What do you do for a living?"

"What's that have to do with anything?"

"Just answer me," he said.

"I own and run my own restaurant."

He sighed. "What makes you think you can do something the police haven't been able to do?"

"For one thing, I'd be pursuing the evidence, which is something they never did."

Tony frowned. "You have no qualifications to solve a murder. Besides that, whatever evidence there might have been was underwater for the past twenty years."

"If I don't care, no one else will," she said shortly, then looked away, unwilling for him to see her tears.

Tony stared at her profile. Not only had she grown into a very beautiful woman, but she'd become tough. He guessed he could understand why. It was easier not to be hurt when you didn't let anyone get too close.

"It isn't that," Tony said gently and cupped the back of her head, forcing her to face him. "What if the killer is still here? What you're proposing could be dangerous."

She shrugged. "If you're afraid, all you have to do is take me back to my car."

He looked at her for a moment and then grinned. "Maybe I should have waited just a little bit longer before I came speeding to your rescue."

"Why?"

"Because I'm thinking that, despite your fragile appearance, you could have taken all three of them apart with one hand."

Sarah watched his face, seeing laughter and forgiveness in the quick grin he gave her.

"I'm sorry."

"For what?" Tony asked.

''For thinking you were no angel.''

This time his grin turned absolutely wicked. ''Oh, lady...don't apologize for that one because you were absolutely right. I'm no angel. Never have been. Never will be.'' Then he gave her hair a gentle tug. ''But I'm also not a crook. So can we call a truce?''

His hand slid from the back of her head to beneath her chin, and Sarah found herself shaking from the heat of his gaze.

''Yes,'' she said quickly, anxious that he get back to driving. At least then he had both hands on the wheel.

''Good,'' he said. ''Then it's a deal.''

He grabbed the steering wheel and pressed down on the accelerator again, taking them deeper into the maze of trees.

''Exactly where are we going?'' Sarah asked.

Tony began slowing down as he pointed.

''There.''

She looked up, more than a little startled by the opulence of what was obviously just a vacation home. If he could afford a place like this, he was even more of a success than she'd imagined.

''This is yours?''

He nodded.

''It's beautiful.''

He smiled as he turned onto a graveled driveway and stopped in front of the house. For a moment he let the car idle as he stared through the windshield at the scenic beauty of what was before them. The sprawling lake house blended into the trees as if it had sprouted and grown from where it was standing. It was a two-story structure of cedar and glass that reflected the scenery around it.

"Yes, it is, isn't it?" Tony said, and then jumped out of the car and ran around to her door. He bent down to help her out, then teased a smile from her when he added, "Come into my parlor, said the spider to the fly."

Sarah was still smiling as she got out of the car, but the smile quickly died when she realized that the dark waters of Flagstaff Lake were visible through the trees.

"You're really on the lake, aren't you?" she said.

Tony saw the look on her face and knew what she was thinking.

"There are no ghosts here, Sarah."

She gave him a doubtful look and then turned her attention to the house once more.

"All my things are in my car."

"I'll have someone get it and bring it here."

"I can't stay here indefinitely," she said.

"Why?"

She was a little startled by his intensity.

"Well...for starters, we don't really know each other, and I have an agenda of which you don't approve."

Tony cupped her face, and for a moment Sarah thought he would kiss her. Instead, he took his thumbs and smoothed the frown lines at the corners of her mouth.

"We knew each other once. We will know each other again. Besides, you forget what I told you about why I came. If making sure you have a place to stay while you're here is the only way I can repay my debt to your father, then so be it."

Then Tony slid his hand beneath Sarah's elbow, and she let him lead her into the house. The interior was warm and welcoming, and as they passed through the foyer she could smell the familiar scent of burning wood. As he led her into the living room, the scent intensified, because a great log was burning in a massive fireplace against the north wall. An oxblood leather sofa and two matching chairs were arranged in a casual semicircle in front of the hearth, while a bank of filled bookshelves on the opposite wall promised good reading on long, cold winter nights. Several paintings had been hung about the room, the choice of subjects eclectic.

There were two Native American paintings on either side of the fireplace, another that was similar in style to a Renoir, and two Wyeth-like landscapes, haunting in their simplicity. She moved closer, her eyes widening as she saw Andrew Wyeth's signature and realized they must be originals. She pivoted sharply, looking at Silk with distrust.

"Your nightclub must be very successful."

He saw the mistrust on her face and knew they were back to square one.

"I do all right," he said shortly, refusing to explain himself any further. "If you'll follow me, I'll give you the nickel tour of the house and then show you to your room."

Sarah followed him, making polite remarks about the homey feel and the style of decor.

"Thanks," Tony said. "There's no real rhyme or reason to it. It's just stuff I like."

Sarah looked up at him then as they paused in the hallway. "Well, you have very good taste."

"That I'll take as a compliment," he said.

Sarah sighed. "I've been rude."

He looked at the dark circles under her eyes and the slight trembling of her lower lip. The discovery of her father's body had obviously put her through hell. The least he could do was allow her the leeway to be pissed.

"Yeah, you have," he said softly, then lifted a stray lock of hair from the corner of her eye and pushed it back in place.

"I'm sorry."

"Don't apologize to me until you've tasted my cooking."

She laughed.

Tony stared at the transformation in her face. He'd thought she was beautiful before, but now...*hell*. Her laugh should be declared lethal. Ignoring the urge to pin her against the wall and kiss the smile right off her lips, he restrained himself by remembering to play host. He cupped her elbow.

"Your room is down here, last door on the left."

His grip was firm but gentle, and Sarah had to hurry to keep up with his long stride. Moments later he opened the door and then stepped aside.

"This will be your room for as long as you need. It has its own bath and sitting room. The phone is there on the table, in case you need to make any personal calls."

"Thanks, but I have my own cell phone."

"We don't always get a good signal up here, so if you need it, it's there."

She smiled tentatively as she glanced around the room. It looked as warm and inviting as the rest of the house. Finally she turned around. It was time to make peace.

"Silk... I mean, Tony—"

He interrupted. "You can call me Silk."

"But you said no one calls—"

"Some do," he said. "Besides, I like the sound of it on your tongue."

Her eyes narrowed thoughtfully. He was still smooth, maybe too smooth.

"Whatever," she said shortly.

He grinned, then pointed to the bed. "Why don't you rest while I make a few calls? I'll have your car and your clothes here within the hour and do a little damage control with the media."

Sarah looked startled. "What do you mean...damage control?"

"You think they're going to leave you alone now that they know you're here? No way, baby. Whether you like it or not, you're news...again."

"God," Sarah muttered, and dropped onto the bed with a thump.

"Don't worry, Sarah, you won't be bothered while you're in my home."

"But how—"

"Trust me," he said.

The tone of his voice was suddenly different. That sexy smile was gone. She could still see the angry young man he'd been, but with twenty more years of living to hone the passion and fury.

Before she could answer, he was gone, quietly closing the door behind him. Sarah sat for a moment without moving, wondering how a life as ordinary as hers had been could get screwed up so fast. The moment she thought it, she groaned. How could she be so self-absorbed as to feel sorry for the upheaval in her life? At least she was still alive, which was more than her father could say.

"Oh, Daddy...I'm so sorry for doubting you," she whispered, and then rolled over on her side and curled up in a little ball. "But I'll find out who did this to you. I promise."

Then she closed her eyes and sighed, intending to rest for just a moment. Within a minute, she was asleep.

Almost an hour had passed before Tony made his way back to Sarah's room. The door was slightly ajar as he started to knock, and then he looked past the door into the room and saw that she'd fallen asleep. Quietly he carried her bags into the room and set them down at the foot of the bed. He glanced up at her as he straightened, then frowned. He knew he should leave, but still he lingered, letting his gaze touch her in a way he dared not.

She was nothing like the shy ten-year-old he remembered, watching him mowing her daddy's yard when she thought he wasn't looking. She'd been all legs and arms, with long dark hair and braces. Rarely had she smiled, and looking back on it now, he supposed it was because of the braces on her teeth. But they were gone, and that skinny little girl had certainly filled out in all the right places. As he watched, her eyebrows suddenly knitted and her lower lip trembled. When a single tear slid out from beneath her eyelid, he looked away, knowing she would not appreciate him witnessing her weakness.

He took a deep breath and then shook off the guilt as he picked up a quilt from a nearby chair. Shaking it loose, he covered her, resisting the urge to tuck her in. As the cover settled over her, she shifted slightly, then subconsciously snuggled beneath its weight.

Sarah. Pretty Sarah Jane. He couldn't remember the last time he'd felt this uneasy, but her vow to find her father's killer had tied his gut in knots. This little trip that he'd made was turning into something far more involved than he'd expected. Yes, he could be the congenial host and stay long enough to make sure Sarah was familiar with his home and then leave her to her own defenses. But congeniality wasn't going to solve her problems, and he didn't have it in him to abandon her. Thanks to a streak of chivalry he hadn't known he possessed, he was already thinking about how to put himself between her and danger, but to do that, he had plans that needed to be changed.

The Coffee Cup was busier than normal. Most days Sophie Thomas's little shop was a gathering place for retirees and the occasional clerk on break from the supermarket across the street. But ever since they'd pulled Franklin Whitman's body from the lake, customers were wall to wall. Seating was at a premium, and many wound up leaning against the walls and standing in corners, unwilling to miss even a snippet of gossip regarding the ongoing investigation. The crush of customers was making it difficult for her to serve the seated customers promptly, but she was moving as fast as her short little legs would take her.

Sophie had moved to Marmet ten years earlier after a nasty divorce. She'd taken her settlement, purchased the building that now housed The Coffee Cup and promptly gained twenty-six pounds. Her ex liked his women slim, and since she'd dumped him, she was also getting rid of every manipulating thing he'd done to her. Now here she was, weaving her ample little butt between crowded tables, serving coffee and homemade muffins while the gossip flew fast and furious. Sophie had no preconceived opinions about the incident one way or the other. And while she was sorry that the boom in her business was because a man had been murdered, she wasn't one to look a gift horse in the mouth. She filled the tray with her last order and headed for the table in the corner, where four of Marmet society's finest had gathered to catch up on the latest news.

"Here you go, Moira," Sophie said, and served Moira Blake's double decaf latte, along with a sugar-free blueberry muffin.

"Smells wonderful...as usual," Moira said, and reached for a packet of artificial sweetener.

Annabeth Harold laid a napkin in her lap as Sophie set her soft drink and coffee cake in front of her. Not only was she the oldest of the four women, but since Moira's retirement a couple of years ago, she was the only one who still worked for a living.

Marcia Farrell had come a long way from the station of her birth. In high school she'd been known as the girl who was an easy lay; then she'd gone away to college and come back a young widow with a child who was now grown and living in Paris. Of course no one believed she'd ever been married, but she was accepted back into the community as if she'd never left. On her twenty-fourth birthday, she claimed to have inherited a great sum of money, and from that day on, she'd used it to assure herself a place in the upper echelons of Marmet society.

As Sophie served her, Marcia shifted her mink coat to the back of her chair and leaned away from Sophie's tray, as if unwilling to be touched by someone in such a menial position.

Tiny Bartlett sat directly across from her, perched on the edge of her chair as if readying for flight. Tiny's father owned one of the largest paper mills in the area and she'd never wanted for anything— except her father's approval. He'd wanted a son and had never forgiven her for being a girl. Out of spite and frustration, she'd married the son of the town drunk, who'd surprised them all by becoming an upstanding citizen and making her a mother three times over. But with her children away at college, Tiny always seemed to be at loose ends.

Tiny took a sip of her herbal tea and then leaned forward so that her voice did not carry to the next table, although the action was unnecessary. The noise level in the room was already close to a dull roar. She could barely hear what her friends were saying, never mind what was being said at the next table. Nevertheless, she dived right into the favorite topic of conversation, arching her painted-on eyebrows and pursing her lips.

"Did you hear the latest?" she asked.

"Hear what?" Marcia asked.

"She's back!"

"Who?" Moira asked.

"Sarah Whitman."

Moira's eyes widened as her expression softened. "Poor little Sarah. It's a shame that the children must suffer the sins of the father."

"But what if Franklin Whitman didn't commit the sins everyone said he committed?" Tiny asked.

Marcia frowned. "Of course he did. Don't be silly."

Moira shrugged. "He certainly didn't lock himself in that awful box, though."

Marcia yanked her napkin from the table and thrust it into her lap with an angry motion. Her daddy had been with the State Police twenty years ago and one of the investigating officers. Any rumor that her daddy had been wrong didn't go over well with her.

"He was probably betrayed by his cohorts, but that doesn't mean he was innocent."

Annabeth waved her hand across the table, as if to clear the air.

"Stop it right now," she demanded. "You're ruining our lunch with this ugly talk. I don't want to hear another word on such a distasteful subject."

Tiny pouted and then mumbled something beneath her breath as she picked up her fork and began crumbling her muffin.

"What did you say?" Annabeth asked.

Tiny was normally not one to make waves. "I said the subject is not nearly as ugly to us as it probably is to Sarah Whitman." When no one argued, she felt compelled to add, "It wasn't our fathers who were murdered. I just feel sorry for her is all."

Marcia sniffed. Annabeth frowned in disapproval. Moira smiled and patted Tiny's hand.

"You have a gentle heart, Tiny dear. It becomes you."

Tiny beamed.

"Pass the sugar," Marcia asked, and deftly changed the subject.

Sarah woke abruptly. Disoriented and a little bit frightened, she bolted from the bed and started for the door, then saw her bags on the floor. Immediately she remembered where she was and how she'd come to be there, then sat back down on the side of the bed with a groan. Tunneling her fingers through her hair, she massaged the ache at the back of her neck and then looked around for her shoes. She found them on the other side of the bed, where she'd kicked them off earlier, and put them back on. Remembering the look in Tony DeMarco's eyes made her nervous. He made her feel vulnerable in a way she hadn't felt in years.

She unpacked quickly and then ran a brush through her hair, thought about reapplying her makeup, and decided against it. The last thing she wanted was to give that man the idea that she was trying to impress him.

A short while later she made her way downstairs, only to find a note on the kitchen counter telling her to help herself to a snack and that they would go out to dinner when he got back. Torn between being peeved that he'd left her alone and glad not to have to face him just yet, she took him at his word and headed for the refrigerator. After choosing a bunch of grapes and a bottle of sparkling water, she went outside. Trying to ignore the obvious presence of the lake, she chose to admire the turning leaves, instead, and as she did, she noticed the roof of a very large house across the lake. It was partially concealed by distance and trees, but one thing about it was impossible to miss: it was red.

Wondering what sort of person would choose a

house with a red roof, she popped a grape into her mouth and had started to sit down when she saw an oversize swing hanging from a tree just beyond the deck. Intrigued, she picked a second grape, then left her food on a table as she headed for the swing.

A pair of squirrels scolded her from the branches above as she slid into the seat and pushed off with her toes. The immediate rush of air against the back of her head and then on her face brought back memories of her childhood. She closed her eyes as she swung to and fro, and for a time let go of the pain.

Four

Tony knew almost immediately when he came back into the house that Sarah was not inside. The solitude of his lake home, which had once been comforting, now just felt empty—even lonely. He went straight to the kitchen and then out to the deck, saw the grapes and bottle of water that she'd left on the table and frowned. Then he heard an odd and repetitive squeak. When he turned and saw her swinging, he relaxed.

He walked to the edge of the deck, his eyes narrowing against the glare of the setting sun, and watched the ebb and flow of her clothing as it was pulled by the breeze. The old swing had been hanging from that particular tree when he'd bought the property. He didn't know how many times, since he'd built this house, he had thought about removing it. Now he was glad he hadn't. Her eyes were closed, her head thrown back to the joy of childhood as the swing took her high in the air.

"Sarah," he said softly, trying out the sound of her name on his tongue and knowing that, with little effort, she could get very much under his skin.

"Hey you!" he called out.

At the sound of his voice, Sarah's solitary reverie ended with a jerk. Dragging her feet, she brought the swing to a stop and jumped off. The feel of solid ground beneath her shoes was more than a little disconcerting when only moments before she'd been flying.

"I didn't see you there," she said.

But I saw you. "No matter. I just arrived. Are you hungry?"

Sarah smiled. "Yes, actually, I am."

"Want to go out…or I could fire up the grill and put on a couple of steaks?"

"I vote for the steaks," Sarah said. "At this time, I'm not much in the mood for facing any more of the fine residents of Marmet."

"How do you like it cooked?"

"Medium rare."

He grinned his approval. "My kind of woman."

Sarah's eyes narrowed thoughtfully. "I would never have pictured you as so easy to please."

"I'm not," he said softly, and let his gaze rest on the curve of her mouth. When he saw her cheeks flush, he changed the mood of the moment by adding, "But since you're the culinary expert, why don't you oversee the rest of our meal? The fridge is full. Pick what sounds good to you." He cupped her elbow and led her into the house.

A short while later Sarah was at the kitchen sink, cleaning a stalk of broccoli and watching Tony through the window. He'd changed into a white sweatshirt and a pair of old, faded jeans, and was looking very domestic as he dodged the smoke from his gas grill.

"Domestic" was not a word she would ever have used in conjunction with Silk DeMarco, but as she watched him deftly adjust the height of the flame and absently wipe his hand on the leg of his jeans, she decided she might be wrong. He looked very competent—and oddly content. She thought of him building this house so far away from Chicago, where all his businesses were located, and wondered why, after he'd become successful, he would want anything to do with this place. The way she remembered it, his family had been considered little more than trash, and yet, when it had come to creating a hideaway from the rat race, he'd chosen the place where he'd grown up.

She stood for a moment, watching the play of muscles beneath his sweatshirt, and caught herself remembering that he had always mowed their yard without his shirt on, remembering how smooth and hard and brown he'd been. To her budding hormones, he'd been the epitome of sexy.

Suddenly she realized he was staring back at her through the window. She spun abruptly, embarrassed at being caught, and moved to the work island in the middle of the room. A bottle of merlot had already been decanted. She slid a pair of wineglasses from the rack above the island, picked up the bottle and joined him on the deck. Determined not to let him get under her skin, she decided to confront the demons of her libido by a simple, friendly gesture.

Tony was still trying to decipher the expression he'd seen on her face when she opened the patio door and came out on the deck.

"It's pretty chilly out here," he said.

"I brought something to warm us up," she said, then handed him a glass and filled it with wine.

He took it without removing his gaze from her face. The dying rays from the setting sun colored her dark hair with fiery tints and gave her complexion an exotic glow. He wanted to touch her hair, to see if it was as hot as it looked. Instead, he lifted his glass.

"To the sunset," he said softly, and touched his glass to hers.

The clear tinkle of fine crystal echoed between them. Sarah nodded.

"To the sunset," she repeated, and lifted the glass to her lips. "Mmm, good stuff."

"That's my motto...nothing but the best," he said, watching the sunset in the reflection in her eyes.

Ron Gallagher sat at his desk, looking at the plastic evidence bag that held the personal belongings they'd found on Franklin Whitman's body. There wasn't much left of the man's life—a body's worth of bones that now resided in the coroner's office, a water-damaged wallet, a ring of keys, a wedding ring, and a watch that had stopped at twenty minutes after one.

Most of the time Ron Gallagher liked being sheriff. In the entire twenty-three years of his career in law enforcement, he could count on one hand the number of times he'd wished he'd gone into another occupation. This was one of them. Just thinking about how cold the trail was on this crime made him sigh with frustration. It had taken his secretary a day and a half just to find the old file on the twenty-year-old bank robbery. To say it had been lacking in evidence would have been putting it mildly. The fact that Franklin Whitman had disappeared the same day as the money was the only fact the authorities had at the time to tie him to the theft. Obviously their theory had been sadly lacking.

Of course, Ron could afford to be generous in not criticizing the procedures of that day and time, because he had something they hadn't—namely, Whitman's body. He couldn't say for certain that Whitman had been completely innocent with regard to the theft, but it was obvious that even if he had been involved, there had been an accomplice, maybe two. Certainly someone had killed Franklin Whitman and locked him in the trunk. Unfortunately, the pitiful remnants in the evidence bag yielded nothing in telling him who that might be. Shoving aside a stack of files, he dumped the contents of the bag onto his desk.

Whitman's wallet was cracked and coming apart, although the leather had survived much better than the stitching that had held it together. The only things that had survived twenty years in the lake were plastic—an American Express credit card, his driver's license, and a card with Whitman's name and blood type. Whatever else had been in there had deteriorated and disappeared.

His gaze moved to the watch. The hands on the face had stopped at twenty minutes after one—indicating either the time of Whitman's death or, more likely, the time he was dumped into the lake. Until he got a report back from the coroner, they couldn't be entirely sure of the cause of death. It was possible that he had drowned, but there was that big crack in his skull. And in the long run, it didn't matter. The fact was that he'd been murdered, by whatever means.

There was only one useful item left that had been with the body—a set of keys on a ring with a red plastic fob with a "Number One Dad" logo. He sighed as he picked up the keys, thinking of the little girl Sarah Whitman had once been. How low her hero had fallen. Or had he? She seemed positive that her father had been a scapegoat for the real thief. Gallagher didn't know what to think except that, as an officer of the law, he had to keep an open mind. Despite public opinion, which was leaning toward the theory that Whitman had been double-crossed by his cronies, Gallagher knew he owed it to Sarah Whitman to be more thorough with the investigation this time around.

He fingered the keys, grimacing at the mud and rust that came away on his fingers. Two of the keys were obviously car keys, and, according to the records from the old file, one had to be a key to the bank. There were four more on the ring. One was most likely a key to his home, and he recognized a post office box key because he had one just like it on his own set of keys. There was another—long and flat, with a faint number on the head. Before he had time to pursue it further, his deputy knocked on his door and then stepped in.

"Sheriff...Mrs. Healey just called. She said Allen is trying to kick in her door again. Schuler is already on his way out there, but I thought you should know."

Gallagher dumped the evidence back in the bag and tossed it to his deputy. "Lock this in the evidence locker," he said. "And tell dispatch to let Schuler know I'm his backup."

The deputy hurried away to follow orders as Ron headed for his car. Allen Healey was a nice man, except when he drank. Unfortunately, he was drunk more often than not. The last time he'd come home in that condition, he'd broken his wife's collarbone and knocked out two of her teeth. Ron had been trying to keep Edith Healey alive long enough to convince her to file charges against the man and leave him, but so far, it hadn't happened.

He hit the lights and siren as he pulled away from the office. For now, the murder of Franklin Whitman had to take a back seat to the troubles of the living.

*   *   *

Paul Sorenson got up from the breakfast table and made his way to the sideboard, where he poured himself a second cup of coffee. He'd been born and raised in Maine and, before he'd gotten old, had never paid much attention to the weather. Now it was the focus of his days. For a man who'd once enjoyed all the sports that winter had to offer, he now hated the cold. It made his joints ache, sometimes unbearably. Today was no exception. The weatherman predicted a possibility of rain before the day was out, which meant if the temperature dropped below freezing, it might very well snow.

Leaving his dirty dishes on the table for the day helper to clean up, he took his coffee and the morning paper to the library to enjoy by the fire. As he sat down in the high wing chair, he sighed with relief, slightly disgusted that one of the main joys of his life nowadays was just getting off his feet.

A log in the fireplace snapped and popped, sending a shower of sparks against the fire screen and up the chimney. The familiar sound was comforting as he took a careful sip of the coffee, set it aside and opened the paper.

It wasn't much, as papers go, but reading it kept him up-to-date on who had died and who had gotten arrested. There wasn't much crime in a town the size of Marmet, but as president of the bank, Paul felt it necessary to know who the bad risks were when it came to lending money.

His gaze went straight to the headline, and as he read it, he frowned. It was just more of the same about finding Franklin Whitman's body in the lake.

Twenty years ago, when the robbery had occurred, he'd been a loan officer at the bank, well below Franklin Whitman in both rank and people skills. Paul had coveted Whitman's job with a passion and had spent many sleepless nights plotting ways to elevate himself in the boss's eyes. It hadn't taken long after Whitman disappeared. The bank's reputation had suffered, but he'd taken full advantage of Whitman's betrayal. During the reclamation process, he had worked diligently on his attitude with the public and it had paid off. For the past fifteen years he'd been president of Marmet National Bank, and he had no intention of letting bad memories ruin what he'd worked so hard to rebuild.

He scanned the article, frowning at the slant the journalist had taken on the crime. More and more people were starting to lean toward the theory that Franklin Whitman had been an innocent victim. He didn't like that. That meant the authorities would be digging up old bones, figuratively speaking, and that was the last thing he needed. He thought of

Whitman's daughter and wondered where she was, if she was even alive. Twenty years was a long time. Anything could happen, and he was sorry to admit it, but he hoped it had happened to her. She was the last person he ever wanted to see again.

Once, when he'd been in the break room at the bank, his lover had called. He'd been mildly displeased, since anonymity was of the utmost importance to their relationship, but it had also been a boon to his ego. The problem arose during the conversation, when he'd gotten caught up in their repartee and forgotten where he was. He'd laughed aloud, mentioning what he had planned for their next night together, some of which was decidedly risqué. Since he was single, no one would have thought anything about Paul's conversation other than that he was quite a stud. The only problem was, he'd called his lover by name. David.

No one in Marmet even suspected Paul's sexual persuasion. His entire life had been devoted to keeping it a secret. And he had, until that day in the break room when he'd gotten so careless, then looked up and seen Sarah Whitman standing in the door with a cookie in her hand.

"Who's David?" she'd asked, and he'd almost screamed at her to get out.

After that, he had lived in mortal fear that she

would reveal him for what he was. He considered it a blessing from God when Whitman had gone missing and, later, the kid had disappeared from the state.

Sarah was finishing a bowl of cereal when Tony came into the kitchen. His hair was still damp from his shower, and the blue jeans and sweatshirt he was wearing had seen better days, yet he still looked fashionable, even sexy.

The moment she thought it, she choked on her last bite.

"You okay?" Tony asked as he thumped her on the back.

"I'm fine," she said, and rose from the table to take her bowl to the sink, using it as an excuse to put some distance between them. She didn't want to think about Tony DeMarco and sex—at least, not in the same thought.

Tony saw the stiff set to her shoulders and frowned. She had accepted his invitation to stay at his house, but he was a long way from gaining her confidence. He opted for a change of subject.

"It's started to rain."

"Yes, I noticed," Sarah said, as she rinsed her dishes and put them in the dishwasher.

Tony tried another tack. "What are your plans?"

When Sarah turned abruptly and gave him a cool, judgmental stare, he felt obligated to add, "If you don't mind me asking."

"Why?"

He sighed. "I thought you might like some company."

"Are you offering?" she asked.

He almost smiled, but thought better of it.

"Yes."

She nodded. "Then thank you. I accept."

He had been prepared to argue his case and was surprised by her easy acquiescence.

"Where do you want to go?"

"Eventually, to the sheriff's office. However, there are a couple of places I want to stop at first."

"Like where?" he asked.

"I haven't been back to my mother's grave since I left Marmet."

"Where else?"

She glared.

When he realized she didn't like being questioned so closely, he changed the subject. "When do you want to go?"

"In about ten minutes...if that's all right with you. I have a phone call I need to make first."

"It's fine, Sarah, and please take your time. I'll be in the living room when you're ready." He added, "Dress warm. The rain could change to snow."

"I'm missing New Orleans already," she muttered.

As he watched her leave, he couldn't help but wonder if there were other reasons besides weather that made her long for New Orleans. And as he did, he decided he didn't like the thought of her with another man. It had been years since he'd experienced anything resembling jealousy, but he was feeling it now. He considered himself self-assured and confident, yet he felt more like a teenager wondering if he had a chance with the prom queen.

Upstairs, Sarah was curled up on her bed with the phone to her ear, counting the rings at Lorett Boudreaux's house. Just when she thought she was going to have to give up and try again later, her call was answered.

"Sarah Jane…it *is* you."

Sarah sighed, picturing the ebony features of her beloved Lorett wreathed in smiles.

"Don't pull that psychic stuff on me this early in the morning," Sarah said. "You have caller ID."

Lorett chuckled. "I still knew it was you."

Sarah laughed but didn't dispute her aunt's claims. There had been too many times when she'd seen her in action to doubt the gift she had. Just hearing Lorett's voice made her feel easier. She leaned back against the pillows on the bed and pulled her knees up to her chest, ready to unburden herself. She should have known it was unnecessary.

"Who is the man you are with?" Lorett asked.

Sarah rolled her eyes. Although there was no way Lorett could have known about Tony's unexpected appearance in her life, she'd never been able to hide anything from Aunt Lorett, so the question didn't really surprise her.

"A friend...I think. His name is Anthony DeMarco."

"That is not what he is called."

Sarah smiled. "As always, you're correct. Some people call him Silk."

There was a very pregnant silence, and then Lorett's whiskey-deep voice vibrated against Sarah's eardrum.

"He's a man with secrets, Sarah Jane."

Sarah glanced at the door, half expecting him to walk into the room. "Will they hurt me?" she asked.

"No."

"Everyone has secrets. His obviously don't concern me."

"Oh, but they do," Lorett said. "But that's for another time. How are you, *ma petite?*"

The tenderness in Lorett's voice brought a knot to Sarah's throat.

"I'm all right...or at least I will be when I can put Daddy to rest."

"He's been with the Lord for twenty years, Sarah Jane. It's you who must bury the past."

"I'm trying, Aunt Lorett, but I can't stop until I know who did this. He didn't just kill my father, he killed Mother, too. It wasn't only money he stole, he stole my life."

Lorett didn't like what she was hearing.

"Vengeance is dangerous."

"So is murder."

"It's not your place to seek justice. Leave that to the law."

"Just like we did before? I don't think so. Besides, I'm not a child anymore. This time they can't make me go away. Not until I'm ready."

"There are shadows in your future, Sarah Jane."

"Well, when you see who's hiding in them, let me know," she said, then looked at her watch. "I'll call you again in a day or so. Tony is waiting for me downstairs."

"You tell that man I said to keep you safe."

"Now, Aunt Lorett, if there's one thing you taught me, it's that I don't need a man to do anything for me. I'll keep myself safe."

"I did not raise you to hate men, Sarah Jane."

Sarah sighed. "No. Michael did that for me."

Lorett frowned, thinking back seven years to the man Sarah had been in love with, the man who'd given her a ring, the same man Sarah had caught in bed with her best friend only weeks before their wedding.

"Don't blame all men for one man's weaknesses."

"I know," Sarah said. "I didn't mean that to sound as bitter as it came out. I'm over Michael...really. It's just that all this has been so horrible and shocking. Each day I wake up, thinking it will all have been nothing more than a bad dream."

"You're a strong woman. You will do what has to be done."

"Yesterday I went to the lake."

Lorett said nothing, waiting for the rest of Sarah's pain to spill out, knowing it was the only way to cleanse the horror from her mind.

"It's different than I remembered. The surface of the water was like black glass." She shuddered. "I can see it from Tony's house."

"And this is a problem?"

"Just thinking about Daddy being down there for all that time gives me the creeps. Oh, Aunt Lorett, say prayers for me, will you?"

"You know I will. Now go to your man and remember what I said about shadows."

"Yes, all right," Sarah said, and then added before Lorett disconnected, "I love you, Aunt Lorett."

"*Oui, ma chère,* I love you, too."

It wasn't until Lorett disconnected that Sarah realized she had referred to Tony DeMarco as her man.

By the time they got to the cemetery, the rain had changed to a cold drizzle, leaving the air feeling thick, almost too thick to breathe. Moisture dripped from the harlequin-colored leaves, splattering onto the ground in intermittent patterns as they got out of the car.

Sarah looked out across the acres of tombstones and shuddered. Almost instantly, Tony was at her side. He slid a hand beneath the collar of her coat and gently squeezed the nape of her neck.

"Are you all right?"

She looked at him, seeing the concern and compassion in his eyes, and shrugged out of his grasp, unable to accept the tenderness for fear that she would cry.

"I haven't been all right for twenty years."

Tony ignored her quarrelsome attitude. Truth

was, he wasn't so damn sure that he wouldn't feel the same way—maybe worse.

"Do you know where your mother's grave is located?"

Sarah turned, her gaze shifting to the area on their left.

"Over there somewhere."

He held out his hand. "Come on. We'll find it together, then I promise to give you some space."

"You don't have to, you know."

He frowned. "Damn it, Sarah, I'm not the enemy. Let me help."

She hesitated before she shrugged. "Yes...all right. I—"

"Just a minute," Tony said, and went back to the car.

Sarah watched as he popped the trunk and leaned down.

When he stepped back, he was carrying a handful of amber chrysanthemums. She recognized them from the flower beds in front of his house.

"I thought you might want something to put on her grave," he said, and thrust them toward her.

His thoughtfulness shamed her as she took the bouquet and clutched it close to her chest.

"I don't know what to say." She lowered her head, inhaling the crisp scent of the blossoms.

" 'Thank you' will suffice."

She looked up. He was smiling. Tears filmed her vision and thickened her voice.

"You're not as tough as you would have people think, are you?" she asked.

"If you tell, I'll deny it," he said softly, and cupped her elbow. "Come on, honey. Let's go find your mother."

Sarah let him guide her, not because she felt incapable of dealing with the moment, but because he seemed so sincere in wanting to help.

"The day of the funeral, I remember standing next to a tombstone that was a praying angel."

"That should make it easier to find," he said, and started searching the horizon for something other than the traditional grave markers.

But before they'd gone far, a car pulled into the cemetery and parked behind Tony's car. Because they were intent on their search, the driver had gotten out of the car and was almost upon them before they realized they were no longer alone.

At first Sarah didn't recognize the woman, but then the woman smiled.

"Miss Blake?"

Moira Blake's smile widened as she enveloped Sarah in a hug.

"I wasn't sure if you'd remember me," Moira

said. Her smile softened. "It's wonderful to see you again, all grown-up."

Sarah was a little taken aback by the woman's friendly welcome. She barely remembered her as someone who'd worked in her father's bank.

"I was a little girl when you last saw me. I'm surprised you knew who I was."

Moira felt Sarah's reticence and realized she'd made a mistake in being so familiar. She shifted the flowers she was carrying to the crook of her arm and pulled the hood of her coat up over her hair.

"Nasty day, isn't it?" When Sarah didn't respond, she added, "Marmet is a small place, dear, and you're the only new face in town. Besides, I asked Sheriff Gallagher. He told me you were staying with Tony. When I saw him, I deduced who you might be. Makes me a good detective, right?"

Sarah looked from Tony to Moira. "You two seem to be on pretty good terms."

Tony shrugged. "I used to mow her yard, too," he said. "Besides, our homes are only a couple of miles apart."

"I'm very sorry about your father," Moira said.

Sarah gauged Moira's sincerity by the straightforward look in her eyes and decided she was telling the truth.

"Yes, well...thank you," Sarah said. "We're looking for my mother's grave."

"I was just on my way there. Follow me. I'll show you where it is."

"You go to my mother's grave?"

Moira shrugged. "Yes."

"Why?"

"Because I liked her."

Again Sarah caught herself judging Moira Blake's sincerity, but Moira's gaze never wavered. Finally she nodded.

"Thank you. I'd appreciate it."

Within minutes, Sarah found herself standing at the head of her mother's grave.

Anna Catherine Whitman. Born October 28, 1944. Died September 3, 1979.

Sarah stared at the words, waiting for a flood of emotion that never came.

"She was only thirty-four when she died. I don't think I remembered that," Sarah muttered, more to herself than to the others.

Tony leaned down. "I'll wait for you at the car," he said, and walked away.

Moira Blake stared at the expression on Sarah's face and followed Tony, pausing briefly to replace the clump of dead flowers on the single grave with the ones she'd been carrying.

Sarah stared at the bright red poinsettias against the brown earth, lifted her face to the sky and closed her eyes, feeling the drizzle fall soft against her skin. At that moment, she realized it had been raining the day of her mother's funeral, as well. She shuddered and looked down. Moisture was collecting rapidly on the petals of the flowers in her hands. She laid them down beside the poinsettias, then stepped back.

"I needed you, Mother. You shouldn't have left me." The lettering on the tombstone began to blur as Sarah drew a deep breath. "I'm not like you. I don't quit. I don't ever quit."

Then she lifted her head and walked away.

Five

"Where did Moira Blake go?" Sarah asked as she slid into the seat.

Tony could tell that the last thing Sarah cared about was the whereabouts of Moira Blake. However, he was willing to adhere to the change of subject to allow her time to regain her composure.

"She went home, but she did invite us to dinner one night this week. I told her we'd let her know."

Sarah leaned back against the seat and closed her eyes without commenting on the invitation.

She looked so vulnerable and so lost. He wanted to hold her but knew she would not welcome the familiarity.

"Where to next?" he asked.

"Into town, please."

"To the sheriff's office?"

"Eventually," Sarah said, and then looked at Tony. "Do you remember where I used to live?"

He nodded.

"Is it still there...the house, I mean?"

"Yes, but the last time I drove by, it wasn't in very good condition. In fact, I think it was empty and up for sale."

"Even better," Sarah muttered. "I want to go there next, please."

He started to ask why, then changed his mind and put the car in gear. He would find out soon enough.

Sarah rode into Marmet without further conversation, unaware that her fingers had curled into fists. The only things of which she was cognizant were the irregular thump of her heart and the constant fear that she was going to throw up.

If anyone had asked her a month ago how she felt about Marmet, Maine, she would have sworn she had few, if any, memories. But from the moment she'd gotten off the plane in Portland, dread had been growing. Now it had all but consumed her, and it wasn't just because she'd learned her father had been murdered. She was remembering the way she and her mother had been ostracized.

She took a deep breath and unconsciously lifted her chin. If they tried anything like that again, they were in for a big surprise. She wasn't a little girl anymore, and, unlike her mother, she wasn't the kind of woman to quit. She was a fighter, and she wouldn't be denied the chance to redeem her family's name.

"We're here," Tony said.

Sarah took a deep breath and turned her head. If he hadn't told her where they were, she wouldn't have recognized the house. The wide front porch she'd played on so often was gone. In its place was a small, wrought-iron stoop and a pair of rusting decorative lions. The concrete walk that led to the house was cracked and overgrown with weeds, and the big oak tree where her swing used to hang appeared to be dead.

"Are you sure this is it?" Sarah asked.

Tony pointed to the house number at the curb.

Sarah sighed. "Lord."

"You don't have to do this."

Sarah sat without moving, her gaze fixed on the house. Finally she sighed, as if in defeat.

"Yes. Yes, I do," she said. She had started to open the door when Tony grabbed her hand.

"You don't have to do all this by yourself."

The gentleness in his voice was almost her undoing.

"I know, and I appreciate all you're doing."

"Why do I feel like there's a 'but' in there?"

She managed a small smile. "I suppose because there is."

"So you're telling me you don't want any company?"

"I'll be fine. Besides, it's still drizzling. All you'll do is get wetter than you already are."

"And you won't?"

There was no need to comment on the obvious. Of course she was going to get wetter—and colder—but then, so had her father.

"I won't be long," Sarah said, and got out of the car before she could change her mind and beg him to come with her. It was getting harder and harder to face her ghosts alone.

The ankle-high grass in the yard was dead and brown, compliments of an early frost over a month ago. The ground was wet and spongy. Sarah dodged a couple of holes, seeing them just in time to keep from falling, and guessed that a neighborhood dog must have had a field day here, burying bones. She wouldn't let herself look at the house again. It was too sad and too depressing to see what time had done to it.

But when Aunt Lorett had taken her away all those years ago, she'd left something behind. Something that had, at the time, been very important to a ten-year-old. From the way things looked, there was every reason to believe it would no longer be here, but she'd come this far. There was no harm in looking.

She circled the house, shivering slightly as the wind hit her square in the face. Between the cold and the rain, she was all but asking to get sick, but coming to Marmet without doing this was impossible. She'd been thinking of her secret place and the little treasure chest she'd left behind ever since she'd boarded the plane in New Orleans. In a few minutes her questions would be answered. Either it was here or it wasn't. Suddenly anxious to be gone from this place, she hastened her steps.

The backyard looked smaller than she remembered, but she supposed that was normal, because she was bigger. It happened that way, all things being relative. The back porch was still there, although a bit decrepit. She ran to the east side of the steps and knelt, running her fingers along the old brick foundation. From the bottom step, she counted ten bricks to her right and then two bricks up. Now that she was here, she stopped and rocked back on her heels.

What am I doing…crawling around in the mud and the rain like a madwoman? Lord…Sarah Jane…don't you have enough to worry about without searching for a childhood pot of gold?

She stared at the brick, telling herself that if it

was gone, it wouldn't matter. But she knew, as she pushed her palm against the rough surface of the brick, that it *did* matter, more than she ever would have believed.

At first the brick didn't budge, and it occurred to her that someone could have reset it years ago. She pushed even harder. After this many years, it was bound to be somewhat stuck. Just while she was convincing herself it was hopeless, it suddenly gave.

She shot forward as her hand slipped through, taking no small amount of hide from the back of her arm when she fell. But the pain was soon forgotten as she began feeling around in the space behind, searching for the little bit of herself she'd left behind.

A couple of moments passed without any luck, and then suddenly she felt something small and solid and square. She leaned forward, resting her forehead against the side of the house, and tried not to cry.

"Thank you, Lord," she said softly, and pulled out a small plastic box, the box that held the treasures of a childhood.

It seemed to be intact, although it was covered in a thick layer of dirt. She set it down in front of her and took a tissue from her coat pocket, wiping the blood off the back of her arm before swiping it across the box. As she did, a small streak of green was revealed. Her heart skipped a beat, and she began scrubbing at the lid with frantic motions.

With each swipe, more and more of the true color of the small plastic box began to show through. Finally she tossed the tissues aside and pulled on the lid. Like the bricks behind which it had been hidden, it stuck. But Sarah kept pulling, and suddenly it came off in her hands, revealing an old photo. The image of her father's face was smiling up at her from the picture. Breath caught in the back of her throat as a quick film of tears blurred her vision. At the same moment, she realized that the contents of the box were going to get wet. In a panic, she slammed the lid back in place and jumped to her feet. Without looking back, she began to run, clutching the box to her breasts as if it were a baby.

Tony looked up just in time to see her come running from behind the house. The expression on her face was somewhere between shock and panic. Thinking that she was being chased, he jumped out of the car and ran toward her.

"What's wrong?"

"I need to get inside," she muttered, and bolted past him without further explanation.

He stood for a moment, half expecting to see someone behind her, but when no one appeared, he backtracked, following her to the car. He slid in behind the wheel, took one look at her wet hair and clothes, and then upped the heat a notch. He could see she was holding something in her lap, but it concerned him less than the blood running down the back of her hand.

"What the hell happened to your hand?"

Sarah jumped. The anger in his voice was startling. She looked down and shrugged.

"It's nothing. I just skinned my arm."

"You're bleeding. I'm taking you to the doctor."

"No," Sarah muttered, refusing to meet his gaze. "Just take me home."

"I thought you wanted to see the sheriff."

"Not today. Not today," she said softly, and curled her fingers around the small square box. "Just home." She looked at him then, putting everything she had into one word. "Please."

Tony cursed silently as he put the car in gear and spun away from the curb. Within minutes they were out of Marmet and speeding back toward the lake.

By the time they got to Tony's house, Sarah was shaking. When he pulled up beneath the carport and parked, it was all she could do to get out of the car on her own. Clutching the little green box against her chest, she let him lead her inside, then up the stairs to her room. The warmth of the house slowly seeped through her wet hair and clothing, leaving her in an even more weakened state. As they walked into her room, he turned to her.

"You need to get out of those wet clothes."

"I will, as soon as I—"

He gripped her shoulders, his nostrils flaring with anger.

"Either you strip now, or I'll do it for you."

There was a look in his eyes that Sarah had never seen before, a promise of something she didn't have the guts to pursue.

"I'll do it myself," she said. "But not until you're gone."

He nodded once, then headed for her bathroom.

"What are you doing?" she asked.

"Running a hot bath for you."

"Oh. Thank you," she added, but the sarcasm was lost on him.

She looked down at the box she was holding, then at the doorway through which he had disappeared. She heard water starting to flow and knew he was doing what he'd said he would do. She suspected he was capable of following through on the rest of his promises, too. The thought of his hands on her body, taking off her clothes piece by piece, made her weak in the knees. She stumbled to a chair and sat down with a plop, then set the little green box on the table beside her and began removing her shoes and coat. She was trying to unbuckle her belt when Tony came out of the bathroom, but her chilled fingers wouldn't cooperate.

''God, Sarah, I should have had my head examined for letting you out in this weather.''

''You're not my keeper. I make my own decisions and—''

''Then you needed to make some better ones than you did today,'' he said shortly, then moved her hands from the belt buckle and undid it for her.

Before she could argue, he popped the top snap of her jeans and pulled her shirt out of the waistband.

''Can you handle it from here?''

She clutched at the collar of her shirt, as if afraid he was going to reach for it next.

''Yes, I'm fine.''

''Yeah, right,'' he said, and walked out of the room.

He stomped downstairs, his hands doubled into fists. It wasn't until he reached the bottom that he began to question his anger. It made no sense to be angry with Sarah. She was going through a bad time. There wasn't a goddamned thing about this mess that could be considered positive. So what if she was reacting in negative ways.

He turned around and looked back up the stairs, imagining her stepping into the hot, steaming bath—picturing the water lapping at her knees, then her hips, then finally her breasts as she lowered herself into the heat. The picture in his mind was so vivid that a part of him wanted to go back just to see if his imagination was anywhere near correct. And as he stood there, it hit him why he'd been so angry with her. He'd come all this way to help her through this tragedy, but she wouldn't let him. She didn't trust him, and it hurt him in a way he would never have believed.

He turned away, his shoulders slumping in defeat as he headed for the kitchen to heat up some soup. It shouldn't matter whether she liked him or not. He owed the success he now enjoyed to Franklin Whitman. It shouldn't matter what his daughter thought of him.

A few minutes later he was emptying a couple of cans of soup into a pan when he finally admitted he was lying to himself. He'd reached the age of thirty-six without ever having had a serious emotional attachment. But he knew that Sarah Whitman could change all that. It mattered what she thought of him. He cared whether she trusted him or not. He wanted to help her, to know that she needed him, because he liked her. He admired her courage and her toughness. He liked the woman she'd become, but if that feeling was never returned, their relationship, such as it was, began and ended here. That was why he was angry. He didn't want it to be over.

Sarah sat in the tub until the water cooled and her fingertips were starting to pucker. Reluctantly she got out of the tub, then dried quickly and pulled a clean pair of jeans and a sweater from the dresser, along with a fresh set of lingerie. After dressing quickly, she ran her fingers through her hair in lieu of a comb and moved to the table where she'd left the little green box. When she picked it up, the box left a small residue of mud behind. Frowning, she went into the bathroom and cleaned it completely before taking it back to the table.

Her hands were shaking as she set the box down. Compared to the discovery of her father's body, this was a very insignificant thing, but the little girl in her needed to reclaim this part of her life. She said a small prayer, pulled the green box into her lap and lifted the lid.

The picture she'd glimpsed earlier was still on

top. She touched it with the tip of her finger, testing the fragility of the old paper, then carefully lifted it out. It was of her and her father, kneeling in the sand beside a half-built sand castle. She had a vague memory of the couple who'd stopped that day and taken the picture for them, and then the image blurred. Oh God, she wanted that back—the innocence and naiveté of believing she was safe and loved.

She looked again, remembering the photo had been taken on the day of her sixth birthday. Her mother had awakened with a sick headache, but rather than disappoint Sarah, her daddy had taken her to the shore by himself. They'd played in the surf, picking up seashells and making sand castles until the tide had come in and washed them away. Afterward, they'd eaten fish and chips wrapped in newspaper and then started the long journey home. Sarah remembered being overwhelmed with exhaustion as she curled up in the front seat, and the security of her father's hand upon her shoulder as she closed her eyes and slept.

She laid the picture aside and peered back into the box. She palmed a small, convoluted seashell, a keepsake of that day, and set it by the picture, then tilted the box into the light. The bluebird egg she'd found about a month before her father had disappeared had long since crumbled into bits, as had her lucky four-leaf clover. There was a small key that had belonged to a diary she'd never written in, and an ID bracelet with the name Sarah Jane engraved on the band. She fingered the chunk of iron pyrite that a friend of her father's had given her one day. He'd called it fool's gold and told her it was worthless, but the glittering spider veins running through the rock had looked real enough to her.

One by one, she removed the bits and pieces of what had once been her treasures until the little green box was empty. Then she set it aside and inhaled slowly, waiting for some kind of closure. It never came. Finally she got up, went into the bathroom and picked up her brush. Without really looking at herself, she brushed her hair and clipped the sides up and away from her face.

She was pulling on clean socks when Tony knocked on her door.

"Sarah?"

"Come in," she called, and reached for her loafers.

He opened the door but didn't come inside.

"I heated some soup."

"Sounds good. I'll be right there."

His gaze slid to the little green box and the odd assortment of items on the table beside it.

"Did you find what you were looking for?"

Sarah looked toward the table. "I found the box, but what I was looking for wasn't there."

The sadness was still on her face. Tony stuffed his hands in his pockets in frustration.

"Is there any way I can help?"

She stood, meeting his gaze full on.

"No, but thank you just the same."

"Are you sure?"

"You can't help. No one can."

"What is it you're looking for, Sarah?"

"It sounds stupid."

"Nothing is stupid if it matters to you."

Sarah sighed, and then moved to the table and traced the curve of the seashell.

"Sarah…?"

She pushed the shell aside and touched the shape of her father's face. When she looked up, she was crying.

"These were once the most important things in my life. When Aunt Lorett came and took me away, I forgot to take them with me. Now, it's too late."

Tony couldn't keep his distance any longer. He moved to her, then slid a hand across her back.

"As long as we live, it's never too late for change," he said.

"It's not about change," Sarah said. "It's just too late. I waited too long to come back, and now it's gone."

"What's gone, honey? What were you looking for?"

There was a catch in her breath, and then she answered.

"The love...but it isn't there. It'll never be there again. They killed it, I think, just like they killed my parents."

He couldn't bear to hear the hurt in her voice any longer.

"Come here," he said, and pulled her into his arms.

She resisted, but only briefly. Just for a moment, she needed to lean on someone else's strength. When his arms tightened around her, she started to cry, softly at first, then harder until her shoulders were shaking.

Tony winced as the sounds of her sobs tore through him, but he'd known the breakdown was inevitable. No one could harbor this much anger without eventually coming undone. He pulled her closer, holding her tighter as he laid his cheek against the crown of her head, and knew that this was what he'd been waiting to do since the day of her mother's funeral. She'd been white-faced and shaking as tears rolled down her cheeks, and he'd wanted, with everything there was in him, to have the guts to go to her. But he hadn't. Instead, he'd walked away, thinking there would be another day when he could express his sympathies. He hadn't known until days later that little Sarah Whitman had been taken away, and so he had carried that picture and the guilt in his mind all these years. Although she was finally here in his arms, he felt as helpless now as he had that day so long ago. He wanted to make her feel better and didn't have the faintest idea how to go about it.

Finally it was Sarah who began to pull away. Tony handed her his handkerchief and reluctantly gave her the space she needed to regain her composure.

"I can't believe I did that," she mumbled as she wiped at the tears on her face. "I'm so sorry."

"God, Sarah...do not, the hell, apologize, all right?"

She flinched, startled by the anger in Tony's voice. Then she saw the pain on his face and sighed. "Anthony James DeMarco..."

"Yeah?"

"I'm thinking it's way past time to thank you.

Thank you for caring enough to leave your home and work. Thank you for offering me your time and your home, and, most of all, thank you for loving my father.''

All the anger slid out of him as quickly as it had come. He touched the side of her face with the back of his hand and then let his hand fall back to his side.

''You're welcome.''

''About that soup…'' Sarah said.

She wanted to get past the awkwardness of the moment. He needed to put some space between them.

''Yeah, about that soup,'' he echoed, and grinned. ''Since you own your own restaurant, I'm sure you'll recognize quality food when you taste it. Come with me. You'll find out I'm damn good at opening cans.''

''I'm thinking you're damn good at a lot of things,'' Sarah said.

Before he could ask her to elaborate, she was out the door and on her way downstairs, following the scent of warm tomato soup and grilled cheese sandwiches.

Six

By late evening, the rain that had been falling all day began to turn to snow. Although Tony predicted it wouldn't stick, Sarah was still entranced by the sight. The flakes were huge and wet, melting almost as soon as they hit the ground.

Misreading her fascination for concern, Tony came up behind her as she stood at the window.

"Don't worry, it's not going to accumulate."

"Oh, I don't care about that," she said. "It's just that it's been years since I've seen snow."

"Really? Why?"

"Aunt Lorett doesn't like to leave New Orleans, and I didn't want to leave Aunt Lorett." Then she shrugged. "Probably a case of insecurity. She's all I have to call family."

When her emotions shut down, Tony knew there was something she wasn't saying. Then it dawned on him that, not once during their whole time together, had she mentioned a boyfriend or significant other. Part of that pleased him, because it meant there was no one standing between him and the chance to know her in a more personal way, but he was also curious. He reached for her, casually fingering the third finger on her left hand.

"I see you're not wearing a ring."

"Not now," Sarah said.

"You were married?"

"I came close," she said briefly.

"How close?"

"Close enough to find my fiancé in bed with another woman I thought was my friend."

"Ouch," Tony said softly. "That's tough to deal with. What did you do?"

"Well...I didn't kill him—or her, for that matter—but I cut my losses and never looked back. It's just as well. It left me free to put most of my energy into Ma Chère...that's the name of my restaurant. I suppose I have them to thank for my success."

"And there's been no one else?" Tony asked.

Sarah shook her head and then looked away, ignoring the thoughts that were swirling in her head. No, there had been no one else she'd even considered, until now.

It didn't seem particularly polite to be happy about someone's misfortune, but that was exactly the way he felt. And while he was glad she wasn't in a serious relationship, he didn't want her to get antsy and pull too far away from him before he had time to build up her trust, so he quickly changed the subject.

"It's a blessing you've had your aunt, then, isn't it? Sounds as if she was the answer to your prayers."

"Oh yes...more than that. She treated me as though I was her true daughter."

Something about the way she said that told him it hadn't all been clear sailing between them.

"But it wasn't the same, was it?"

Sarah frowned. "When everything happened and she came to get me, I barely remembered her from our few visits to New Orleans. Maybe if I hadn't ever known my real mother...maybe if I hadn't gone to Aunt Lorett under such a cloud of despair...but it took years for me to trust the fact that she would be there when I got home from school. Then it was a matter of being the outsider within her circle of family and friends." Sarah smiled briefly. "It wasn't easy being a white girl living within the black community in the South. There's been so much injustice and prejudice against them, even today. They didn't want me there, but they loved Lorett, so they tolerated me. It took quite a while for them to accept me."

"And now?" Tony asked.

"I'm still the white girl who Lorett Boudreaux took to raise, but they've come to know and like me, as I do them. It hasn't been easy for any of us." Then she added, "However, when I opened my restaurant, I raised myself up a notch in their estimation."

"Why's that?" he asked.

"Because I make damned good gumbo, and my jalapeño corn bread is nothing to ignore." Then she added, "And they know my aunt Lorett would hex them all if they were ever mean to me."

Tony laughed, but when Sarah didn't, he looked at her in disbelief.

"You were kidding about the hex stuff...right?"

"No way," Sarah said. "Back when Aunt Lorett was younger, she was into voodoo. She will swear that she's long since given up the practice, but still has the third eye."

"What's that?" Tony asked.

"In New Orleans, it's what some call psychic abilities."

Tony eyed her with new respect. "I'll bet it was hell keeping secrets from her."

"You have no idea." Then she shivered suddenly and wrapped her arms around herself. "Excuse me a minute, will you? I'm going to my room to get a sweater. I'm getting chilly.''

''Wait.'' Tony hurried to the entryway closet and took a cardigan from the shelf. ''Here, put this on, and I'll add a log to the fire.''

Sarah took the sweater gratefully, then followed him toward the fireplace. While she made herself comfortable in a large, overstuffed chair, he moved the fire screen aside and laid a new log on the fire. Sparks flew up the chimney as the new log displaced burning embers, and the popping and cracking sounds made Sarah think of popping corn. Tony stepped back and pulled the screen in place, then turned around.

''How about some hot chocolate?''

''Sounds good. I'll help,'' she said, and started to get up.

Tony shook his head. ''You stay here and get warm. I won't be long.'' Then he handed her a remote. ''Maybe you can find something interesting to watch on TV.''

Sarah took it, grateful not to have to move. ''Thanks, but I'm not used to being waited on.''

Tony brushed the top of her head, as he would have a child's, making sure there was no misunderstanding that it was done in friendship.

''So enjoy it. I won't always be around.''

Sarah watched him leave, reluctantly admiring his masculine swagger and toned body. Her head felt warm where he'd touched it, and, impulsively, she ran her fingers across the place where his hand had been, but it felt no different. She sighed, then leaned back and closed her eyes, but that didn't help. The scent of him was on the sweater, and she imagined him in it, holding her in an embrace.

At that point she shook off the mood. She was tired and overwrought, that was all. Just because a handsome man was being kind, it didn't mean anything. After all, he'd admitted he'd come to her aid because of a debt he felt he owed her father, not because of any personal connection to her.

A few minutes later he was back. When she heard his footsteps in the hallway, she reluctantly opened her eyes. He was carrying a tray with mugs of hot chocolate and a plateful of cookies, and still walking with the same sexy swagger. She wondered if he knew how appealing he was, and discarded the thought as foolish. Of course he knew. How could he not? She also wondered if he had a special woman back in Chicago but decided against asking. That was a question a woman might ask if she was interested in getting to know a man on a deeper level, but she wasn't interested in anything except finding out who had murdered her father and laying him to rest, which meant she was definitely, positively, not interested.

Tony set the tray down on the coffee table.

"I hope you like ginger snaps. They're all I had."

"Yes, actually, they're one of my favorites," she said.

He grinned. "Me, too. What are the odds of that?"

Sarah watched as he handed her a mug and a couple of cookies on a napkin. Friendly. He was just being friendly. She could handle that, as long as it didn't go any further.

That night, when Sarah finally went to bed, it was with a feeling of security. She'd come back to Marmet alone, but she didn't feel so alone anymore. Tony DeMarco had been the last person she would have expected to see, yet regardless of his reasons for being here, he was turning out to be a blessing.

She curled up on her side and pulled the covers over her shoulders, feeling thankful for the shelter and warmth of Tony's home. Outside, the snow flurries and wind still buffeted the house. Every now and then a branch would scrape against a window, but Sarah neither heard nor cared.

Just before dawn, she woke with a start, gasping

for air. She'd been dreaming that she was under-water and trying to get to the surface, yet no matter which way she swam, there was nothing but dark water. Just as she had started to give in to the in-evitable and take the first breath, which would mean death, she'd awakened.

"God," Sarah muttered, and flung back the covers.

The floor was cold beneath her bare feet, and she quickly pulled on a pair of woolly socks before go-ing to the bathroom. A few minutes later she emerged, looked longingly back at her bed and then shuddered. No way could she sleep anymore with that dream still so fresh in her mind. Instead, she reached for her robe and then went to the window, curious to see if there was any snow. Although it was still dark outside, she could see enough to know that Tony had been right. It was no longer snowing or raining, and the snow that had fallen had not accumulated. She couldn't see it right now, but the lake was out there in the darkness, ringed by trees and available to the public by a number of roads. She thought of all the years her father had lain in the trunk at the bottom of the lake while people had boated and played on his grave.

Just as she was about to turn away, something moved between the window and her line of vision.

Startled by the motion, she leaned closer to the glass, her gaze fixed on the place where movement had been, but she saw nothing.

Finally she convinced herself that it was nothing of consequence and turned away. After dressing quickly, she exited her bedroom, pausing in the hall to listen, but the house was silent. Satisfied that Tony was still asleep, she headed for the kitchen. If he had the fixings, she was going to make them a proper breakfast, New Orleans style.

Tony woke slowly, stretching his long body in lazy increments, just as a cat would wake. Then he pillowed his head on his hands and lay staring at the ceiling as the first light of morning slid through a part in the curtains. He closed his eyes momentarily, and as he did, his thoughts went straight to the woman who slept in the bed just down the hall.

Sarah Jane Whitman.

A plain and proper name for a New Englander, and yet there was nothing plain, prim or proper about her. She was lithe and sexy, with a go-to-hell look in her eyes. And the thick fall of dark hair that framed her face swayed in an enticing manner in direct opposition to the sway of her hips. It was a trick nature had unwittingly given her that kept causing him to lose focus around her. He never knew where to look first, at her face or her body, and either way, he kept getting lost in thoughts he couldn't pursue.

His body hardened and pulsed, eliciting a groan that drew him out of bed and sent him stumbling to the shower. Sometime later, he emerged from his room only to realize that he was not the first one up after all. The scent of cooking food wafted down the hall, and the faint but familiar sounds of lids banging on pans told him that breakfast was about to be served.

Sarah was taking a pan of biscuits from the oven when she realized she was no longer alone. She turned around. Tony was leaning against the doorway, with his arms folded across his chest.

"How long have you been standing there?" she asked.

Tony grinned. He was beginning to learn that Sarah Whitman did not like surprises.

"Good morning to you, too," he said, and sniffed the air appreciatively. "Something smells wonderful."

Sarah sighed and reached for a hand towel, then wiped her hands.

"Sorry, I didn't mean to sound like such a shrew, and I hope you don't mind that I cooked."

Tony's grin widened as he made a beeline for the pot of coffee.

"Mind that you cooked? Woman...have you gone crazy? There isn't a man standing who minds if someone's about to feed him."

Sarah laughed before she thought, and when she did, Tony turned abruptly, his gaze fixed hard and fast on her face. Breath caught in her throat as she watched his expression change from humor to something she couldn't name. But she knew what it meant. Her belly knotted as heat fired and spiraled downward. Stifling a groan, she looked away and began breaking eggs into a bowl while wondering what she would do if he decided to act on what he was thinking.

The moment she turned away, Tony realized she'd seen the wanting in his eyes. He frowned, frustrated with the situation in general. He wasn't used to denying himself a woman when the mood struck, but Sarah wasn't just any woman, and the circumstances under which they were sharing a roof were certainly less than conducive toward any kind of romantic moment.

But it had been that laugh. Unexpected. Exuberant, and so full of life. He wanted to hear it again, when she was in his arms with her head thrown back and her long, slender throat exposed to his mouth. In that moment, he realized that what he was feeling for her was not typical of him, nor was it going to go away.

"How hungry are you?" Sarah asked.

Hungry enough to eat you up. He didn't say what he was thinking. Instead, he made himself concentrate on the egg in her hands. "I'm thinking it's a three-egg morning."

She nodded and broke the other egg in the bowl, then started to beat them as she added, "You don't have any grits."

"Any what?"

"Grits."

"I don't have grits because I don't like grits," Tony said, and poured coffee into his cup.

"Breakfast isn't breakfast in New Orleans without grits."

He turned, looking at her from over the rim of his cup, and then murmured, "Yes, Dorothy, I understand, but you're not in Kansas anymore."

Sarah stifled another grin as she added cooked sausage and a variety of chopped fresh vegetables to the beaten eggs, then turned the whole mixture into a large skillet.

"What are you making?" Tony asked.

"It's a cross between an omelette and a frittata. You'll love it."

"Yes, I believe I will."

Sarah heard what he said but wouldn't look at him for fear there would be more in his expression than she was willing to face. Instead, she focused on serving the food and carrying it to the table.

"Breakfast is ready," she said. "As Aunt Lorett would say, come and get it before I feed it to the hogs."

Her humor was just the right note to set things straight between them again.

He grinned as he sat down.

"Did you and your aunt Lorett raise hogs?"

She arched an eyebrow. "Of course not."

"Sorry," he said, suitably chastened as she slid his plate before him.

"Only chickens—for that voodoo she wasn't supposed to practice."

He started to chuckle, then realized she wasn't laughing along with him.

"You're serious again, aren't you?"

"Eat your eggs," Sarah said, and reached for a biscuit as she sat down at the table across from him.

Despite yesterday's unruly weather, the day promised to be clear and sunny. Only a few clouds still lingered, stringing across the sky like wisps of cotton batting. The tension of not knowing what had happened to her father, along with the constant waiting, was getting to Sarah. She'd called the sheriff's office this morning, only to be told that he was out and wouldn't be in until later in the afternoon. Used to being her own boss and making things happen in the proper time, she was both frustrated and bored with the process.

After they'd eaten breakfast, Tony had excused himself and gone to the library to make some business calls. Thinking she would do the same, Sarah had called her restaurant. Upon learning that all was running smoothly without her, she didn't know whether to be grateful or miffed. Then she'd tried to call Lorett, but with no success. She'd hung up in frustration, not for the first time wishing her aunt could be persuaded to use an answering machine. Now Sarah was left with nothing to do but wait, and she'd never been good at waiting. She moved to the windows and parted the curtains, looking out toward the trees beyond the perimeter of the yard. The glorious colors of the leaves seemed a little dimmer than they had the day before, and she suspected it had more to do with her mood than the approaching winter. Beyond the trees, she could catch glimpses of the lake. This morning the sunshine on the surface of the water cast a glittering reflection, masking the somberness of the dark secrets that lay beneath. She stood for a few moments longer, then retrieved her coat from the closet, where Tony had hung it.

The air was brisk but inviting. She pulled the collar of her coat up around her neck and stuffed her hands in her pockets as she started to stroll about the grounds. She paused at a flower bed and bent down to pull out a handful of weeds. Tossing them aside, she brushed her hands on the legs of her jeans and continued her walk. There was a small wooden bench encircling one of the larger trees. Sarah made a mental note to sit there for a while after she'd finished her stroll.

Twice she paused and looked back at the house from different angles, appreciating the line and presence of the home that Tony had built. It fit perfectly within the available space, as much a part of the forest as the trees themselves. She thought of Tony again, and the fact that he'd chosen Marmet to create his hideaway, then wondered what else in him might surprise her.

As she was looking at the house, a bird suddenly flew across her line of vision, and she remembered what she'd seen from the window in the dark. Curious, she wondered if it might have been a bear or even a moose, and decided to see if she could find tracks. She started to walk, every now and then checking the ground, making a bet with herself as to what tracks she might see.

She was looking down when she saw them, and the moment she did, her heart skipped a beat. She stopped, staring at five perfect boot tracks that had been captured in the mud.

Immediately she spun and looked back at the house. As she did, she realized that from where she was standing, she had an almost perfect view of the windows to her room. She began to move away from the tracks, as if their mere presence alone posed a threat. She took a slow, shuddering breath, then turned her attention to the trees, telling herself the tracks probably meant nothing. It could have been a hunter out after dark, or a local used to passing through Tony's property, knowing that the house was rarely occupied. But the longer she stood, the more uneasy she felt. Suddenly she started back to the house. The closer she got, the faster she moved. By the time she reached the steps of the deck, she was running.

"Sarah...is anything wrong?"

Sarah gasped as Tony's fingers curled around her arms.

"Oh! You startled me!"

"You were running."

She glanced over her shoulder toward the place

where she'd seen the tracks, debating with herself about telling Tony, then decided against it. No need making herself out to be some helpless female, because it was the last thing she thought of herself as.

"Just getting my exercise," she said shortly, and pushed past him on the way into the house.

Tony frowned as she tore free of his grasp, then peered out beyond the deck where she'd been standing. He'd seen her from the windows and wondered what had been so interesting as she'd looked first at the house, then into the trees. He'd seen her pivot suddenly and move toward the house. When she'd started to run, he'd panicked. Now she was brushing him off as if it meant nothing, but Tony knew fear, and it had been on her face.

He glanced back toward the house, then stepped off the deck, moving in the direction of the place where she'd been. When he got there, he began searching the ground, on guard for something that would tell him what had set her off.

He examined the area for several minutes without any luck, and even after he saw the tracks, he almost missed their implication. It was the deep treads and larger size that finally alerted him to the fact that he wasn't looking at Sarah's footprints. He stood for a moment, staring down at them and wondering what it was about them that had alarmed her. Curious, he checked to see if she was out on the deck, but she was nowhere in sight. His gaze then slid from the deck upward, and as it did, he realized that, from where he was standing, he had a perfect view of her room.

The hair on the back of his neck suddenly rose. He spun toward the trees, certain he was being watched, but saw nothing that would cause him concern. He glanced up and then toward the lake, and as he did, remembered that she'd come back not just to claim her father's remains but to clear his name, as well. His gut clenched. It was the first time he'd thought of her as being in real danger, but if the killer was still in Marmet, then he would have every reason to want Sarah Whitman gone.

He stepped away from the tracks and headed for the house. If she was withholding information from him, she was going to tell him what it was. After that, he was calling the police.

Seven

"Sarah!"

Still rattled from the footprints, though she had no reason to believe the person who'd left them there had meant her any harm, she jumped at the sound of Tony's voice. Then he walked into the room, and she found herself back on the defensive.

"What aren't you telling me?" he snapped.

She recoiled as though he'd slapped her.

"I don't know what you—"

He stopped only inches from her face.

"Don't lie to me. Not to me, damn it! I'm not the bad guy, here, remember?"

Sarah's chin jutted as she met his gaze.

"You're standing in my space," she said shortly.

Tony relented, but only slightly, as he stepped back.

"I'm still waiting," he said.

She shrugged. "It's probably nothing, okay?"

"How about you let me decide if I think it's nothing, too?"

"Fine. I woke up really early this morning...before daylight...and wanted to see if it was still snowing. As I stood at the window, I saw something moving outside. I didn't think much of it and had actually forgotten it until I went out for a walk later."

She brushed her hands down the front of her sweater, as if smoothing out wrinkles, although none were there. She looked up at him then. His face was expressionless. She sighed, then made herself continue.

"It was later that I remembered and thought maybe if I located the place, I would find bear or moose tracks. It's been years since I've seen anything like that, and I was simply curious...you know?"

Tony's demeanor softened as he watched panic come and go on Sarah's face.

"But it wasn't animal tracks, was it, Sarah?"

"It doesn't have to mean anything, does it? I mean...surely this is hunting season of one sort or another? It was probably a hunter out early, or maybe just a local."

She waited for Tony to agree. Instead, he threw her assumption back in her face.

"Do you think it was a hunter?"

She hesitated, then shrugged. "I don't know."

"And neither do I," Tony said. "Is there anything else you're not telling me?"

"No."

"Then come with me."

"Where are we going?"

"To call the sheriff."

"He's not in."

"How do you know?" Tony asked.

"I already called his office this morning and was told he'd be out of town until sometime this afternoon."

"So he can come back early," Tony said. "This can't wait."

Sarah put her hand on Tony's arm, stopping him as he turned to leave.

"Tony?"

"What?"

"Do you think this is a bad sign?"

He didn't know what to say, so he hugged her.

"I don't know what to think, except that we're not taking chances," he said.

Sarah stiffened when his arms encircled her. "This isn't your problem, you know."

Tony stifled a sigh as he turned her loose. "Someone trespassed on my property, and that made it my business. Besides, we've been all through this before, and I don't want to hear it again.''

''Yes, okay, but don't feel bad if at any time you want me to—''

''When I want something more from you, you'll know it,'' he said, and headed for the phone.

Sarah watched him go, measuring his anger by the length of his stride, and knew that he was holding himself back, probably on her behalf. It wasn't until later that she thought of what he'd said and how he'd said it. Want something more from her? She didn't know whether to be interested or insulted.

Within the hour, Ron Gallagher was on Tony's doorstep.

The doorbell rang while Sarah was making a fresh pot of coffee. Her nerves tightened as she heard Tony greeting the sheriff. Moments later, they were coming her way.

''Sarah.''

She turned, recognizing the man she'd met at the lake the day she'd arrived.

''Sheriff Gallagher is here,'' Tony said.

Sarah nodded. ''We've met. Is there any news regarding my father's case?''

Regretfully Ron Gallagher shook his head. He would have liked nothing more than to put a smile on her face.

"I understand you had a bit of a scare this morning."

"I wasn't scared," she told the sheriff, and glared at Tony.

"Fine," Tony said briefly, then turned to the sheriff. "She wasn't scared. I was. The tracks are out back. Follow me."

Sarah stifled a grin as they left the kitchen. She'd just been dismissed, and quite thoroughly. She was beginning to understand that Tony DeMarco didn't play by any of the normal rules of society. Not once since he'd taken her into his house had he treated her disrespectfully, but he also, as Aunt Lorett might say, didn't take any crap. Curious as to what the sheriff would say about the tracks, she grabbed her coat and followed them out into the yard.

Gallagher had squatted down beside the tracks and was feeling the imprint with the tips of his fingers.

"When did it start raining here?" he asked.

Tony frowned, thinking back.

"It was before dark," Sarah said.

Both men turned.

Ignoring the knowing grin on Tony's face, she focused her attention on the sheriff.

"I remember because I was standing at the windows and watching the rain turn to snow. It's been years since I'd seen snow. It was still snowing when I went to bed last night, which was around eleven."

Gallagher nodded. "Tony tells me that you saw something from your window?"

She nodded. "Yes, early this morning, just before dawn. I woke early and was curious to see if it was still snowing, but of course it wasn't." She smiled slightly. "I have to admit, I was a bit disappointed not to see the ground covered in white. Anyway, as I was looking out into the darkness, I saw movement between the house and the trees. It was too dark to tell what it was, but I knew something was there. As I told Tony earlier, I'd forgotten all about it until I went for a walk. That's when I saw the tracks."

Gallagher nodded. "They probably don't mean anything. However, I'm going to look around a bit...see if I can pick up the tracks out in the woods. Why don't you two go back to the house? I'll let you know what I find before I leave."

"I'm going with you," Tony said, and Gallagher nodded an okay.

"I'm sure you're right about it being nothing,"

Sarah said. "They're just tracks. I have no reason to be concerned."

Both men turned to her then, but it was Gallagher who answered.

"Oh, you should definitely be concerned, Miss Whitman. There's an FBI agent in town who's asking questions about the day of the robbery. People were already dividing loyalties and taking sides on the issue...and then you arrived. You've stirred up quite a little hornet's nest by claiming that you're looking for your father's killer. And since I have no way of knowing who that is, or if he's still in the area, you shouldn't take your safety for granted."

Sarah felt sick. This was a nightmare in a downward spiral, but she refused to back down. She'd been reviled by this town once before, but never again.

"I take nothing for granted. The people in Marmet taught me that."

Her voice was shaking, but her gaze was steady. Tony reached for her, but she turned and walked away.

"She's got a lot of anger," Gallagher said. "It's a damned shame what happened to her. Guess I can't blame her."

Tony nodded, his gaze on the stiff set of Sarah's shoulders as she strode toward the house.

Gallagher glanced up at the sky and then down at his watch. "Well...we'd better get going. There's less than three hours of good light left today."

Tony watched until Sarah was in the house, then followed the sheriff into the woods.

The phone was ringing as Sarah entered the kitchen. Even as she was running to answer it, she thought about letting the answering machine pick up, because it wouldn't be for her. She was wrong.

"Sarah Jane, you need to come home."

"Aunt Lorett...is something wrong? Are you ill?"

"Yes, something is wrong. You are in the wrong place. You need to come back now."

The hair rose on the back of Sarah's arms. She'd heard that tone of voice too many times not to believe what Lorett was saying.

"I want to, Aunt Lorett. You have no idea how much, but if I leave now, it will be like before."

In her heart, Lorett had known Sarah would refuse, but she couldn't have lived with herself if she hadn't made the call.

"There are people who don't want you there," she said.

"I already knew that."

"They mean you harm."

Sarah's gut knotted. So the tracks weren't nothing after all. She thought about going after Tony and the sheriff and telling them she was really in danger, and then decided against it. She didn't want to have to explain that she was basing her information on a warning from a psychic, especially one with a background in voodoo.

"If I leave, it means they win again. Besides, they have yet to release my father's remains, and he's the reason I came back."

"Please, child. I could not bear to bury both of you," Lorett pleaded.

Sarah felt like crying. She could hear the fear in Lorett's voice, and it echoed that in her own heart.

"I love you, Aunt Lorett, and I promise I'll be careful."

Lorett sighed, accepting Sarah's decision as what must be.

"Then trust your man, Sarah Jane. He will take care of you."

"He's not my man, Aunt Lorett, and I can take care of myself."

"Not this time," Lorett said. "God be with you."

"I love you," Sarah said, but Lorett had already hung up.

Sarah replaced the receiver, then stood within the quiet of the house, absorbing what her aunt had said. So this wasn't going to be an easy trip after all. So what? She hadn't expected a vacation. Besides, forewarned was forearmed, and she had Aunt Lorett to thank for that.

Outside, Tony and Gallagher were coming to some serious conclusions of their own. The sheriff had found the place where someone had stood in the trees, obviously watching the house. From the set and depth of the prints, the watcher had been there during the rain and then the snow. They could tell because the tracks leading to the hiding place had been washed away, leaving them no way to tell where he'd come from. Only the tracks showing where he emerged from the woods and started toward the house were evident.

Tony had seen something on Gallagher's face that gave him cause for concern, but Gallagher had yet to voice what he was thinking. Tony's patience ended, as did the tracks on a bed of rocks and pine needles.

"It was deliberate, wasn't it?" Tony asked.

Gallagher hitched at the holster around his waist and then nodded.

"Best I can tell, I'd say yes. Someone was obviously watching your house, but it doesn't mean there was a threat, or that it was aimed at Miss Whitman."

"What do you mean?" Tony asked.

"Your house. It's quite a place for a vacation home. Got all the bells and whistles, too, you know? It could just as easily have been someone casing the location for a possible robbery, then realized the place was occupied, so he made a getaway before he was seen."

Tony shoved his hands into his pockets. From where they were standing, the roof of his house was just visible through the trees. Behind him was the lake, made ominous by the absence of sound. He liked it better in the summer, when there were boating and swimming going on. Now, every time he looked at it, he thought of Franklin Whitman lying at the bottom for the past twenty years. Stifling a shudder, he glanced at the sheriff.

"Robbery?" Tony asked.

"It's a possibility."

"I suppose.

"But what does your gut tell you?" Tony asked.

Gallagher shrugged. "Well...we haven't had a

robbery around here in two or three years. If I was betting, I'd be leaning toward Miss Whitman's presence being the trigger. However, it doesn't have to mean someone meant her any harm. People are a curious lot, and the locals around here are no different. She was a little girl when she left. She's come back as a woman on a mission.''

Tony glanced up at the sky. The North Star was already visible, although it had yet to get dark.

"I'm going to the house," he said. "She's been alone too long."

"I'll come with you. Pay my respects and then be on my way. If you have any other concerns, don't hesitate to call."

"Count on it," Tony said, and led the way through the trees.

Sarah was quiet all through dinner, answering only when spoken to and picking at her food. As much as Tony relished her presence, he didn't want her here like this. He would much rather have back the slightly belligerent woman she'd been. Finally he could stand it no longer. If he had to pick a fight with her to get a reaction, then so be it.

"Don't like my cooking?" he asked.

Sarah looked up, then down at her plate.

"Guess I'm not hungry," she said, and laid down her fork.

"Are you mad at me?" Tony asked.

"No! Of course not," she said. "You've been nothing but kind."

Kind? Tony sighed. He wanted her to think of him as more than that.

"Then what's wrong?"

"Aunt Lorett called."

"Is everything okay back home?"

Sarah frowned, wondering what he was going to think, then blurted it out, not caring what he thought.

"She told me to leave. She said I wasn't safe here."

Tony's stomach knotted. Last month he would have laughed at someone believing in psychics, but now he didn't know what he believed. All he knew was that he wanted Sarah to be safe.

"What did you tell her?" Tony asked.

Sarah looked up. "What do you think I told her?"

"That you weren't going anywhere."

Sarah arched an eyebrow and almost smiled. "Well...I'm thinking you know me better than I thought."

"But you're scared, aren't you, Sarah?"

She hesitated, then nodded. "A little. I know enough about Aunt Lorett not to doubt her, but I also know I won't tuck tail and run again. I can't." A muscle jerked in her jaw as she stared into Tony's face. "Do you understand?"

As much as he hated to agree with her, he nodded.

"Yes, I think I do."

Then Sarah grinned. "Besides, as long as I stick with you, I'll be fine. Aunt Lorett said so."

"Jesus," Tony muttered, while trying to absorb the fact that a psychic had pronounced him some sort of protector. "So what happens if I fail?"

Sarah's smile widened. "Oh...nothing much. She's fond of hexes...and there are always her favorite curses. But they rarely last past a generation or two. You might be screwed, but your descendants should be fine."

He glared. "You're loving this, aren't you?"

"For a smart man, you're pretty gullible about this voodoo stuff."

"Not really. My grandmother was Sicilian. There's a story in our family about her putting a curse on a man who cheated her husband out of a lot of money."

Sarah leaned forward, curious as to the climax of the story.

"So what happened to the man?"

"Well...the story goes that she cursed his manhood, saying he would never be able to, uh, how can I say this without offending propriety?"

"Just say it," Sarah urged.

Tony grinned. "Yeah, okay. The curse was that he would never 'get it up' again, and that his name would die with him."

"Wow! That's cold. Did it work?"

"Don't know. This was all before I was born. However, I do know that there were no people in the neighborhood with that last name when I was growing up."

Sarah smirked. "They probably moved. If I was a man who'd just had his balls cursed, I would have lit out for parts unknown."

Her bawdy answer surprised and then delighted him. God, but he liked her spirit. His grin widened.

"You're probably right. However, you can see why I grew up with a healthy respect for curses." Then he leaned across the table and covered her hand with his. "And I *will* take care of you, Sarah. Even if you don't need it, I need to do it, okay?"

She stared at him intently, acknowledging the concern on his face and wondering why it wasn't enough.

"Yes, sure, I understand. You're paying my father back, and I appreciate it."

His smile faded. "It's not just about your father anymore, and you know it, or you're not as smart as I thought you were," he said shortly, then got up from the table and began carrying the dirty dishes to the sink, leaving Sarah with a whole lot more to think about than an anonymous trespasser.

"Twenty years and you couldn't stay dead. Damn you, Frank Whitman, why couldn't you stay dead?"

The killer scrubbed at the mud tracks on the kitchen floor while stewing about the latest turn of events. It was bad enough that Whitman's body had been found, because that meant the case was reopened. But to have Whitman's daughter mouthing off to the world that she wouldn't rest until her father's killer was brought to justice just made everything worse. If she weren't here, the case would eventually fizzle from lack of evidence, but there was no telling what would happen now.

Finally the killer stood, giving the floor a judgmental glance, then pronounced it clean. It was a damn shame that Sarah Whitman wasn't as easy to get rid of as the mud, but living the past twenty years in a private purgatory had a way of hardening the kindest of hearts. Sarah Whitman still had a chance to save herself, even though she didn't know it. All she had to do was claim her father's bones and get the hell out of Marmet, and she would be fine. Then the killer's hands curled into fists.

But mess with me and you die.

Ron Gallagher turned his head sideways as he peered in the mirror, taking a last swipe at a streak of remaining lather from his morning shave, then washed and dried his face before splashing on aftershave. He was a particular man by nature, but this morning was different. Sarah Whitman would be coming into the office to view the articles they'd taken from her father's body. He had little hope of her being able to tell him anything new, but it had to be done just the same.

He neatly parted, then combed his hair carefully before giving it a light spritz of hair spray. If the men in the department knew he was going to so much trouble with his appearance, he would never hear the end of it, but Sarah Whitman got under his skin. He knew she would never see him as anything but a short, middle-aged man who'd been part of the hell of her past, but he couldn't help himself. He wanted her approval almost as much as he needed her forgiveness. Maybe then he could forgive himself for standing by and doing nothing while the good people of Marmet had crucified her and her mother.

Giving his thinning hair one last pat, he buckled on his gun belt, holstered his service revolver and left the house, grabbing his hat and coat as he went. No need giving himself a case of hat head until after Sarah Whitman's visit.

Sarah dressed carefully, choosing her clothes as if for a job interview instead of what was really going to happen. She had to be strong. Breaking down wasn't even a consideration. Not in front of the good citizens of Marmet. But it was going to be difficult to see her father's possessions—to touch that which had survived him and remember exactly what she'd lost.

She applied a thin coat of lipstick, then shook the hair away from her face and carefully eyed her appearance. Black slacks. Black turtleneck. Red-and-black plaid jacket. Neat but assertive. That was the look she was going for. She checked her shoes, then bent and rubbed at a scuff mark on one toe just as Tony knocked on her door.

''Coming,'' she called, and grabbed her coat and purse from the bed.

Tony's eyes widened appreciatively as Sarah opened the door.

"Nice," he said softly, and offered her an elbow.

"Do I look like I might kick some butt?" she asked.

He grinned. "Oh yes...at the very least some butt kicking."

"Maybe more?"

"Don't press your luck," he said. "Let's go. We don't want to keep the sheriff waiting."

Eight

Sarah's nerves were on edge as they drove into town. Her aunt's warnings were never far from her thoughts. Was she putting herself at needless risk by staying in a place she wasn't welcome? As they stopped at an intersection, waiting for the light to change, someone waved at them from a nearby yard.

"Who was that?" Sarah asked, eyeing the elderly woman, who had resumed her task of raking leaves.

"Mrs. Sheffield. She used to be the librarian, remember?"

Sarah stared, trying to put that face on the tall, stately redhead she remembered.

"But she's so old."

"Time did not stand still when you left," Tony said. "Everyone and everything is twenty years older now. Mrs. Sheffield's husband died several years back. One of her sisters came to live with her a couple of years ago because she was afraid to live alone.''

The light changed and Tony drove on past. Sarah leaned back in the seat. For several blocks more she said nothing. It wasn't until they were pulling up to the sheriff's department that she spoke.

''Tony?''

''Yes?''

''Am I tilting at windmills?''

Tony killed the engine and pocketed the keys as he turned to look at her. For the first time since her arrival, he saw defeat on her face.

''What do you mean?''

''Maybe I should be satisfied with the fact that my father was found. Maybe I should just bury him beside my mother and go home.''

''And not dwell on who killed him? Is that what you mean?''

She shrugged. ''I'll always dwell on that,'' she said softly. ''But what was I thinking when I said I wouldn't leave until his name was cleared? It's been twenty years, for God's sake. People have moved away. People have died. Whatever clues might have been left during the initial crime are certainly gone. Who's to say the real criminal is even still living?'' She slumped against the door and momentarily closed her eyes. "No matter how sincere my intentions, I can't fix this, can I?"

Tony reached across the seat and took her by the hand.

"Sarah."   .

She couldn't bear to see the sympathy in his eyes for fear that she would finally break down.

"Sarah...look at me."

She sighed, then lifted her head.

"Why did you really come to Marmet?"

"To claim my father's remains, of course."

"And...?"

For several moments, Sarah was silent. Tony waited, knowing that eventually she would find her own truth.

Sarah stared out the window, at the businesses and the streets. Some of them were familiar, as were the faces of people. The longer she looked, the more she understood what Tony was trying to get her to say. Finally she turned to him.

"They were wrong, you know."

"About what?" Tony asked.

"They shouldn't have treated us so badly."

Tony nodded. "You're right, honey. They shouldn't have done that."

"They made me feel guilty, like I'd done something wrong, too, but I didn't know how to make it right.'' She took a deep breath, unaware that her voice was starting to shake. ''No matter how successful I've become, there's a part of me that still keeps trying to overcome the stigma of being Franklin Whitman's daughter. Then I found out he wasn't the thief everyone made him out to be, and I felt a new kind of guilt that I'd believed, like everyone else in Marmet, that he was guilty. I thought if I cleared his name it would make me okay.''

''You're already okay,'' Tony said.

''On one level, I've always known that, but I need these people to look me in the face and admit that they were wrong. I know it won't bring my parents back, but it's the only thing I can do for them now.''

''So you want revenge?''

''No. Retribution. I want retribution.''

''Then what are you waiting for?''

For a moment all Sarah could do was stare at Tony's face. The expression in his beautiful dark eyes was urging her to trust him. The muscle jerking at the side of his jaw gave an intensity to his words.

''Nothing,'' she said.

''So let's go.''

Moments later they were out of the car and entering the sheriff's office. The woman behind the desk looked up as they entered.

"I'm Sarah Whitman. I have an appointment with the sheriff."

The woman smiled at Sarah as she stood and went to greet her.

"Sarah...it's good to see you again," she said.

Sarah frowned. "Do I know you?"

"I am...or rather, I *was* Margaret Thomason. I sat three desks in front of you in school. My name is Bishop now. Barney Bishop and I got married after I graduated high school."

Sarah smiled back, surprised by the genuineness of the woman's greeting. "Margaret! Yes, I remember you, and I remember Barney, too."

Margaret giggled. "He's changed for the better, trust me."

"So he's given up throwing spitballs, has he?"

"As I remember, that happened sometime around the sixth or seventh grade...when he started liking girls."

Tony grinned. "That'll do it every time."

Margaret eyed the tall, handsome man with Sarah Whitman. Silk DeMarco was something of a legend in Marmet. Talk about the town bad boy making good—he'd done that and more, and managed to stay single in the process. She knew women who once wouldn't have given him the time of day who would now give their last dollar to date him.

"Silk...it's been a while since you've been in Marmet," she said, and tried not to giggle again. It was hardly befitting a married woman and mother of three.

"Is the sheriff in?" Sarah asked.

Margaret suddenly remembered why they were there and pulled herself together.

"Yes. I'm sorry for going on about myself. He's expecting you. Follow me."

She paused at a doorway at the end of the hall, knocked once and then opened it.

"Ron, Sarah Whitman is here."

Ron Gallagher stood abruptly and circled the desk, urging them to come in.

Margaret put her hand on Sarah's arm and smiled shyly.

"It was nice to see you again."

A bit of the tension in Sarah's belly began to ease.

"Thank you, Margaret."

"For what?" the other woman asked.

"For making me feel welcome," Sarah said, then entered the office and took a seat beside Tony.

She cast a quick glance at his profile, absently eyeing the sensual cut of his lips and the strength in his jaw. Before she could look away, he caught her staring. A look passed between them that made Sarah's toes curl inside her shoes. Disgusted with herself for being so weak where this man was concerned, she tore her gaze away and fixed her attention on the sheriff.

Ron fiddled with a couple of paper clips as he rested his elbows on the surface of his desk, waiting for them to settle. He saw the exchange between DeMarco and Sarah and sighed, reminding himself that it was time to give up the daydreams. Not only was he too old and too short, Sarah Whitman was way out of his league.

"So, Miss Whitman, I trust you've recovered from your fright of yesterday."

Sarah fixed the sheriff with a cool, studied stare.

"As I told you yesterday, I wasn't scared, and considering the circumstances, I'm fine. I would like to see the items you found on my father's body now."

Ron unlocked a drawer in his desk and pulled out a large brown envelope. His hands felt all thumbs as he tried to undo the metal clasp. Finally it came open, and he slid the contents onto the surface of his desk.

"I'm afraid not much survived. Twenty years underwater does a lot of damage."

Sarah clenched her jaw to keep from saying something she might later regret and reached for the first thing she saw, which was her father's wallet.

"Easy," Gallagher cautioned. "The leather is pretty fragile and there's nothing that survived except his driver's license, which was laminated."

Sarah's fingers trembled as she unfolded the flap and, for the first time in twenty years, looked at her father's face.

"Oh God...oh, Daddy," Sarah whispered, and then touched the buckled plastic with the tip of her finger.

Tony leaned over and, without speaking, slid his arm around Sarah's shoulders. For a brief moment she rested against him, and then she straightened, eyed the faded picture of a sandy-haired smiling man one more time, and laid the wallet aside.

Gallagher pushed the ring of keys closer to her and, as he did, felt as if he was the outsider at a funeral home, intruding on a family viewing.

Breath caught at the back of Sarah's throat as she saw the key ring. "Number One Dad." She'd given it to him for Father's Day the same year he'd disappeared. She picked it up and turned to show Tony, only to find that no words would come.

"I see it, honey," he said softly. "Did you give it to your dad?"

She nodded.

"He was always real proud of you. Used to tell me how smart you were. Did you know that?"

"No."

It was a small, quiet word, but one that held a world of pain.

"Well, he did. Every time I mowed your yard, he had a new story to tell about you."

Sarah inhaled slowly, savoring the knowledge that she had mattered.

The sheriff was curious about some of the keys and wanted to ask Sarah about them.

"Miss Whitman, I was wondering if—"

"Please, call me Sarah," she said.

Gallagher nodded and smiled. "Sarah...about the keys on the ring. Can you identify any of them?"

As Sarah fingered the keys, a slight frown creased her forehead. She'd been so young, but maybe...

"This one opened the front door to our house. I remember because I had one just like it that I wore on a chain around my neck."

Gallagher marked the key with a piece of tape and made a note in a file he'd opened on his desk.

"What about these?" he asked.

"Car keys, I think," Sarah said. "They belong to a Ford, and we had a Ford. And these..." She fingered a pair of small, odd-shaped keys. "There were drawers in Daddy's desk that locked. I'm guessing these were the keys that went to those locks."

"What about that one?" Gallagher asked, pointing to the last one to be identified.

Sarah's frown deepened as she traced the shape of the long, flat key, trying to remember if she'd ever seen it before.

"Looks like a safety-deposit key to me," Tony said.

Gallagher's eyes widened at the thought. "You know, you might be right," he said.

Sarah laid the keys back on the desk. "I wouldn't know about that, although I'm sure my parents had one, and obviously it was at the bank where Daddy worked."

Gallagher picked up the keys. "I'll check it out, although if there was a safety-deposit box at the bank, I'm guessing that when the money went missing, it was probably opened."

"Maybe, maybe not. My mother didn't exactly cooperate with the investigation," Sarah said.

"They would have gotten a court order for a search," Gallagher said.

"I wouldn't know," Sarah said. "I was only ten." Then she picked up a coin from the small pile on the desk and turned it over. It was a 1973 dime.

"Old money," she said.

"Not then it wasn't," Tony said.

Sarah stared at the dime for a few moments and then laid it back down on the desk. Suddenly the idea of rehashing any more of her father's life with the sheriff seemed obscene. After all, he'd been part of the problem. How could she expect him to be part of the solution she now sought?

"Is this all of it?" Sarah asked.

Gallagher nodded.

"Do you have any more you can tell me about when my father's remains will be released?"

"They tell me about a week, maybe more. They're pretty backed up at the coroner's office, and this isn't—"

Gallagher stopped, but it was too late to undo the damage. Sarah's expression had already gone cold.

"What you started to say was, this isn't a case with a high priority, right? If there's nothing else you need from me, I will be leaving now."

Caught off guard by her abrupt dismissal, Gallagher stood abruptly, searching for something he could say that would make this all right. Nothing came to mind.

Tony didn't comment, but he'd seen the jut of her chin and knew she was serious. He reached for Ron's hand and shook it as he, too, stood along with Sarah, who was already putting on her coat.

"Ron, you know where to reach us if you have any other questions."

Ron nodded. "Miss Whitman, if there's anything further we can do for you, please let us know."

Sarah lifted her chin. "You want to help? Find the person who put my father at the bottom of Flagstaff Lake."

"I would like nothing better," Gallagher said.

"Why do I feel like there's a 'but' in there?" Sarah asked.

Unwilling to be cast as the uncaring monster in this mess, the sheriff pointed to the open file on his desk.

"This is everything I have on the case, and there's not one shred of evidence in there that leads us to anyone but your father. He was the last person in the bank the weekend the money went missing. It was Monday before it was discovered, and by then he was gone. Every employee showed up for work that day but him."

"And that's because he was already at the bottom of the lake,'' Sarah snapped, and took a deep breath, knowing she was on the verge of screaming. She leaned forward, putting the flats of both hands on his desk. "He didn't put himself there, did he, Sheriff?"

It was all Gallagher could manage to meet her gaze, but it was the least he could do.

"No, ma'am, he did not."

"So you people dropped the ball."

Gallagher frowned slightly. He didn't like to think that they'd been so wrong.

"Looks that way," he muttered.

"I need to know if you're going to do the right thing," Sarah asked.

This time Gallagher made no attempt to hide his displeasure.

"I always do the right thing, Miss Whitman. I don't always get the results I want, but I always do the right thing. I was just a rookie back then, but we pursued a theft in the best way we knew how and investigated the only suspect we had as thoroughly as possible."

"Tell me something," Sarah said.

"Anything I can."

"Did you ever look at anyone else as a suspect?"

Gallagher hesitated, then sighed. He couldn't lie. Not to her.

"Not to my knowledge."

"So what are you going to do about it?"

"I'm already doing something," he said.

"What?"

"I've reopened the investigation. If we uncover any new leads, you'll be the first to know."

Sarah made no move to hide her contempt.

"Another case of...don't call us, we'll call you. Right, Sheriff?"

Tony slid a hand beneath Sarah's elbow.

"Sarah."

"What?"

Tony cupped the back of her head. "He's trying."

At his touch, Sarah shuddered, then dropped her head. When she looked back up, her eyes were shimmering with unshed tears.

"I know," she said, then turned to Gallagher. "I'm sorry. It's just been so hard to—"

Ron put his hand on Sarah's arm. "You do not owe me an apology. In fact, it's more the reverse. Just give me time, Sarah. I'll do what it takes, even if it means pissing off every fine citizen in town."

The notion of that happening was too comical to ignore.

"If you do, I hope I'm around to see it happen,"

she said. "Now I'll get out of your hair and leave you to the business of stirring up ghosts."

"Yes, ma'am, that's what I'll be doing," Ron said, and closed the door to his office behind them as they left.

Sarah waved goodbye to Margaret, who was on the phone, and was reaching for the doorknob when she heard Tony curse beneath his breath. Surprised, she turned around to face him.

"What?" she asked.

"Out there," he said, pointing through the window to the street. "Looks like a news crew found you again."

Sarah flinched, and for a moment thought about trying to escape out the back; anger sparked.

"Good," she said. "I'm ready for them now."

"Are you sure?" Tony asked. "You can wait here while I tell Gallagher. We'll get rid of them for you."

"No. There are things that need to be said. Maybe then they'll leave me alone."

Tony's eyes narrowed, but he resisted the urge to argue and opened the door.

Almost immediately, the crew swarmed up to the door. Three cameras were aimed her way, while a half-dozen reporters thrust their mikes in her face.

"Miss Whitman! Miss Whitman! What can you

tell us about your father? Do you think he was killed by his accomplices? Are you bitter about—''

Tony stepped between Sarah and the crowd.

''Back off!'' he said sharply. ''Miss Whitman will not be answering any questions, but she has a statement to make.''

''Who are you?'' one of them asked. ''Are you her lawyer?''

He leveled his gaze toward the reporter. ''No. Now, do you want to hear what she has to say, or do I call the sheriff out here?''

They retreated but kept their cameras trained on Sarah's face as she stepped forward.

''As of today, the coroner has not released my father's remains, but I have been assured by the authorities that the case regarding the crime for which my father was blamed has been reopened. It's obvious to me that he was a scapegoat for the real thief, who not only got away with a million dollars but thinks he has gotten away with murder.'' Then she leaned forward, fixing her gaze on the bank of cameras. ''No matter where I am, I will not rest until my father's name is cleared and his murderer has been brought to justice. Twenty years ago, the good people of this town crucified me and my family. When the truth is revealed, I expect, at the least, an apology.''

They started shouting questions to Sarah, but once again Tony intervened.

"That's all. Now please excuse us," he said, and took Sarah by the arm and led her to his car. "Hurry and get in," he said, as he opened the door.

Sarah paused and looked up. "No, Tony. I'm not running. Not ever again."

He started to argue, then nodded. "You're calling the shots, kiddo," he said softly. "Is there anything else you want to do while we're in town?"

"Can we go to the supermarket? There are a few things I need to buy."

"Honey…today you can do any damn thing you want."

She smiled primly and settled herself in the seat as Tony circled the car and slid behind the wheel. Moments later they were pulling away from the curb and heading downtown to Marmet's one and only grocery store.

Half an hour later, they exited, each carrying a bag of groceries. Tony popped the trunk and was taking the bag from Sarah's arms to put inside when they realized someone was approaching them from behind.

Sarah turned around, half expecting more reporters, only to see a tall, elderly man with a small box in his arms.

"Sarah Jane…is that you?" he asked.

"Mr. Weatherly?"

Harmon Weatherly beamed. "You recognized me! It's been so long, I wasn't certain you would even remember me, my dear. How have you been?"

"I've been fine, Mr. Weatherly, and of course I would recognize you. You were the best teller in the bank. Daddy always said so."

The old man's smile tilted sideways, but only for a moment.

"I admired your father very much," he said. "He was always very fair. You don't often find that quality in men anymore."

"Thank you," Sarah said. "You don't know how much I appreciate you telling me this."

Harmon nodded, then glanced at Tony, as if trying to place him.

"Do I know you, sir?" he asked.

"Anthony DeMarco," Tony said, and held out his hand.

Harmon's eyebrows rose above his glasses as recognition dawned.

"I know you. You're Sylvester DeMarco's son, aren't you?"

Tony caught himself wanting to flinch. He had spent years trying to live down his upbringing, and now, in one sentence, this old man had put him right back in that hopeless niche.

"Yes, I am," Tony said.

"Knew him well," the old man said. "Your mother, too. Sorry to hear of their passing."

Tony managed to nod his thanks while concealing his shock. Not once in his entire life had his parents been mentioned without a derogatory comment. He didn't know whether to hug the old man or just keep quiet.

"Where do you live now?" Harmon asked.

"Chicago."

Harmon nodded. "Been there once. Didn't like it. It's too flat."

Tony grinned. "Yes, sir, compared to Maine, it certainly is."

"Well, then, it's been a pleasure to see you again," he said, then turned to Sarah and held out the box. "I tried to give this to your mother about a week after your father disappeared, but she wouldn't let me in the house. Now I suppose it belongs to you."

"What is it?" Sarah asked, as he set the box in her hands.

His white, bushy eyebrows met above his nose as he frowned.

"A day or so after your father disappeared, our loan officer, Sonny Romfield, was killed in a car accident just outside town. It was a terrible tragedy. Left a wife and two little kids behind. Anyway, I was given the job of cleaning out his desk, as well as your father's. I gave Mrs. Romfield the contents of Sonny's desk and tried to do the same for your mother, but she wouldn't answer the door. I thought I would give it to her later, after some of the hubbub died down, but then she...uh...passed away, too, and well...I just put it away. When I heard you'd come back to Marmet, I remembered the box. I can't say much about what's in it. I sealed it that day and haven't looked since, but it's yours, just the same."

Sarah's hands were shaking as she clutched the box to her chest.

"Thank you, Mr. Weatherly."

"You're welcome, child," he said, then dusted his hands down the front of his overcoat and nodded to Tony. "I'll be running along now. Take care, and I'm sure everything is going to work out. Truth, like cream, always rises to the top, you know."

Tony looked at Sarah, who seemed on the verge of tears again.

"Been a hell of a day, hasn't it, kid?"

She lifted her chin. "Better than I expected," she muttered. "I'm ready to go home if you are."

"You bet," Tony said.

Minutes later they were headed out of town. Sarah sat buckled in her seat belt, holding the box in her lap as if it were a bomb.

Nine

"I'll get the groceries. You go on in," Tony said as he unlocked the door.

Gratefully, Sarah hurried inside, carrying the box up the stairs and into her room. She dropped it on the bed and then stepped back, staring at the brown paper wrapping and the dusty string with which it was bound, wondering what other ghosts she would find inside. It had been excruciating to sit in front of the sheriff and go through the pitiful remnants that had been with her father's body. Would this be any easier? She didn't think so. There was no way of knowing what personal bits of his life he'd kept at work, but whatever they were, it was going to hurt to see them.

Instead of opening the box immediately, Sarah backed away and began taking off her coat. She hung it up, then headed to the bathroom and busied herself in there for almost five minutes before she ran out of things to do. When she came out, the box was still on her bed. It was a small box. Certainly not of a size to hold anything of much importance, and still she hesitated. The longer she stood, the weaker her knees became. She'd gone through life keeping her emotions to herself, but this, on top of everything else she'd endured during the past few days, was about to take her down.

Just as she was contemplating calling her aunt Lorett, Tony appeared in her doorway. She looked up at him, unaware that every emotion she was feeling was there on her face for him to see.

Whatever Tony had meant to say was forgotten. He'd stood by for days, watching Sarah suffering alone, staying at arm's length because that was what she wanted. But no more.

He moved. Within seconds, Sarah was in his arms. He bent his head, brushing the side of her cheek with his mouth. When she stiffened, he cupped her cheeks and tilted her chin, making her face him.

"Don't fight me, Sarah. Please, don't fight me now. You may not need this, but I damn sure do."

Sarah saw his mouth coming closer—felt the warmth of his breath on her face—and gave herself up to the inevitable.

Tony's lips were firm and warm, pressing gently, then insistently, against her mouth. His arms enfolded her, pulling her close against his body. She felt him shudder, heard him groan beneath his breath, and knew that she, too, was losing control. But instead of pushing him away, she slid her arms around his waist and clutched at the back of his sweater with both hands, trying to pull him closer.

Suddenly he tore his mouth away from her lips, lifted her off her feet and laid her down on the bed. Her soft cry of passion was lost in the shuffle of body against body.

Tony's heart was racing, his body yearning for a joining with the woman beneath him, and even so, he wouldn't take advantage of her vulnerability. Not this way. Not until she gave him the word. He paused in the act of undoing her blouse and kissed the hollow at the base of her throat before leaning back on one elbow for a perfect view of her face.

Her skin was flushed and damp, her eyelids fluttering softly as she teetered on the brink of promised ecstasy. He traced the shape of her lips, feeling the satiny softness of her skin. When she suddenly opened her mouth and drew the tip of his finger between her teeth, his eyes narrowed dangerously.

"Sarah...sweet God, woman, I'm not made of steel. If you want this to stop, you're going to have to say so now."

Sarah shivered beneath his dark, all-knowing

gaze, aware that with one move, he could take her to heaven, but then what?

"Silk...?"

He nuzzled the side of her neck. "What, baby? Say it and it's yours."

"I know what I want...but, God help me, I'm afraid."

"Of me?"

She winced. The shock on his face was her doing, but how to explain?

"Not *of* you, of what you'll do to my self-control. If I lose that, I don't think I'll be able to finish what I came to do."

He stopped, his hopes plummeting while his body still pulsed. As much as he wanted her, he understood.

"It's okay, Sarah...it's okay. We just went too fast."

Then he buried his face in the curve of her neck and stifled a groan. Whether she knew it or not, she'd said the magic word. He could bear anything but causing her fear.

"Lord help me," he muttered, levering himself up and away, then rolled off the bed and left her room without looking back.

Sarah had asked for this, and yet the moment Tony left her alone on the bed, she couldn't believe he was gone. She felt chilled and empty, yearning for a fulfillment that wasn't going to happen. When she rolled over on her stomach and looked up, she realized the box Harmon Weatherly had given her was still there, pushed up to the headboard and half-buried beneath a mound of pillows. Angry with herself and her cowardice, she grabbed the box and set it on the bedside table. Yesterday she hadn't even known it existed. It could damn well wait a while longer to be opened. Right now, she needed to make amends with Tony before it was too late.

She crawled off the bed and ran down the hall to his room, but the door was closed. Inside, she could hear the sound of running water and knew he was probably in the shower—and a cold one at that. Her shoulders slumped as she turned away.

"Well, so much for that big idea," she muttered, and took herself down the stairs before she did something completely foolish, like joining him.

Annabeth Harold was fussing with a doily beneath a bowl of nuts she'd just placed on the sideboard. It was Tuesday night and her turn to host their weekly card game, and she was pulling out all the stops. The doily was hand-crocheted—one of her great-grandmother's hand-me-downs that had gone into her hope chest when she was sixteen. It was a bit yellowed with age, but the workmanship was exquisite, and she liked to show it off. Tiny Bartlett always noticed such things, and Annabeth was just prideful enough to want it seen.

She dusted off the front of her dress, then inspected her manicure, although neither was in need of the attention. Next she glanced up into the mirror, making sure her hair was in place and her collar was lying flat. The girls would start arriving at any moment and she didn't want to be caught looking as if she had fussed. The key to proper fashion was to look good without appearing as if it had taken all day to get that way.

Just as she started to the kitchen, the doorbell rang. Pivoting sharply, she strode purposefully into the foyer, remembering to smile as she opened the door. It was Marcia Farrell, looking as elegant as always.

"Marcia, do come in from this awful chill."

Marcia shrugged out of her coat and hung it on the hall tree, as she'd done so many times before, then sniffed the air in appreciation.

"Mmm, Annabeth, something smells yummy. I do hope you've made some of your famous sausage cheese balls. I adore them."

Annabeth smiled primly. "Yes, actually, I did. I

was on my way into the kitchen to take them out of the oven.''

Marcia waved her away, smiling gaily. ''Then don't let me stop you. I'll make myself at home until the others arrive.''

''The television is on, although I haven't paid much attention to the programming. Have a seat near the fireplace, and I'll be back in a jiff.''

She started to leave, then paused. ''If the others arrive while I'm out in the kitchen, let them in, will you?''

''Sure thing,'' Marcia said, and headed for the living room in haste, anxious to claim the best chair nearest the fire.

A short while later, both Tiny Bartlett and Moira Blake had made their appearance and Annabeth was on her way into the living room with a tray of snacks when she heard the women gasp and then squeal. At the same time, Tiny yelled, ''Annabeth! Annabeth! Get in here fast!''

Annabeth dashed into the living room, only slightly disgruntled that her planned appearance had been dashed, and set the tray down on the sideboard.

''What's wrong?'' she asked. When Tiny waved her toward the TV, she hurried to where the trio had gathered around the television set.

"Look! It's that Whitman girl…she's on TV. Oh! That looks like Dewey Francis in that passing car," Tiny squealed. "My word! I do believe he's gone and traded that Cadillac off after all."

Marcia frowned. "Good grief, Tiny, Dewey's new car is not what's important!"

"Hush," Moira said. "Let's hear what Sarah Whitman is saying."

"It can't be anything good," Annabeth said. "She's very bitter, you know."

Moira's eyes saddened. "Can you blame her?"

No one wanted to admit that Sarah Whitman had any grounds for complaint, so they listened in silence, their focus centering on Sarah as she mentioned waiting for her father's remains to be released. Marcia shuddered and leaned back against her chair. She didn't like to think about dying. It was so…final.

But it wasn't until they heard Sarah say she would not give up until her father's killer was brought to justice that all four women gasped, then stared at each other with their mouths agape.

"Can you believe that?" Marcia asked. "What does she think she is…some hotshot detective? I can't believe they actually aired that. It makes it sound like we're harboring a murderer in our midst."

Moira sat silently, remembering Franklin Whitman. He'd been a nice man to work for and so crazy about his family. What had happened to that family was a shame. Conscience bade her at least speak up on his behalf, whether she agreed with Sarah Whitman's behavior or not.

"Well," Moira said, "Frank obviously did not put himself in that horrible trunk and throw himself into Flagstaff Lake."

There was a moment of shocked silence, and Annabeth's face reddened.

"That's beside the point!"

"Not to Franklin it wasn't," Moira muttered.

Annabeth pointed toward the television and Sarah's face, as if she could make herself heard through the TV.

"I don't like it! I don't like it at all. This will do nothing but dredge up things better left alone."

"It's too late," Tiny moaned. "Everything is going to be just awful again. I certainly hope that Sarah Whitman isn't crazy like her mother. I mean...killing herself and all. What was she thinking? Certainly not about her child."

Annabeth's nose wrinkled in disapproval. "She was always unstable. I remember when her daughter was born, she took to her bed for almost a month."

Considering the fact that Marcia's aunt had been a nurse at the hospital, she felt obliged to explain.

"Well, in all fairness, Catherine had a very rough delivery, as I recall. She was in labor for over twenty-four hours, and then they finally performed a C-section to deliver the baby, that's why she was so long in healing."

Annabeth frowned. She didn't like being corrected. "Still, she wasn't from here. Lord only knows what she was into before Franklin met her. She grew up down South in Louisiana, you know. And remember the black woman who came and took Sarah Whitman away? Land's sake, can you imagine giving your child to a woman like that to raise?"

"I didn't see anyone else offering," Moira said briefly, and then turned off the television, hoping to change the subject.

Tiny helped her by squealing, "Are those your famous sausage balls I smell?"

Annabeth smiled and moved toward the sideboard, where she'd set down the tray.

"Among other things," she said. "Please, help yourselves."

"Goody," Tiny said. "I'm starving."

"Take your plates to the card table," Annabeth

said. "There's plenty of room to snack while we play."

A few minutes later the four women were deep into a rousing game of poker while discussing the merits of sharp cheddar cheese as opposed to mild.

They laughed, and they played cards as always, but this time there was an underlying threat to their lives that had not been there before. The orderly existence that gave Marmet its charm had been disturbed in a mighty way. As the self-appointed pillars of Marmet society, they felt obliged to put it to rights, only not tonight. Tonight belonged to sausage balls, fellowship and drawing a good straight.

The Marmet matrons weren't the only residents who'd taken umbrage at Sarah Whitman's interview. Paul Sorenson had been enjoying a quiet evening at home before the fire, absently listening to the evening news while reading his mail. The day had been busier than usual, and he was heartily glad that it was nearly over. Today had been meeting day for the board of directors, and it had gone quite well; then he'd come home, had a nice dinner and settled down by the fire. But after hearing the Whitman interview, his good nature was gone.

He tossed the paper aside and got up from his chair with some discomfort, lightly cursing his latest attack of gout as he hobbled to the phone. Normally he didn't meddle in public affairs, limiting his concerns to money rather than politics, but this was different. Sheriff Gallagher was up for reelection next spring. It was time to remind him of that fact.

Ron Gallagher was still at the office when the dispatcher yelled at him from the other room.

"Hey, Sheriff, phone call for you on one."

"Okay, thanks," Ron called, and picked up the phone.

"Sheriff Gallagher."

"Ron...Paul Sorenson, here. Have you seen the evening news?"

"No. I just got back into the office. There was an accident on the logging road up north. Why?"

"That Whitman woman is making waves. What are you going to do about it?"

Ron frowned. "What do you mean?"

Sorenson was almost sputtering. "She's threatening the people of Marmet, that's what I mean. Her vow to find her father's killer makes it appear as if we've knowingly been harboring criminals. I want it stopped."

Ron's first instinct had been to tell Sorenson to

mind his own business. However, he took a deep breath, giving himself time to temper his words.

"Look, Paul, last time I checked, there was a clause in our national constitution that gives us freedom of speech, so unless she's slandering someone, she's perfectly free to say what she chooses. As for finding her father's killer, I intend to do just that. Someone did kill him. And someone's gotten away with it for more than twenty years. I'm thinking it's about time some justice is due that family."

Sorenson flushed. He didn't like to be thwarted.

"You make too many waves about this business and you'll find it damned hard to get yourself re-elected next spring."

Now Ron was really ticked. "Is that a threat?"

Sorenson blustered through what should have been an apology. "Of course not. Why would I feel the need to threaten you?"

"That's just what I was wondering," Ron said. "And since we're talking, I'll let you know ahead of time that I will be investigating anyone whose position has improved noticeably in the last twenty years."

Sorenson's heart skipped a beat. "What the hell do you mean?"

"I would think it's obvious," Ron said. "Since

it's quite clear that Frank Whitman didn't spend the missing million, someone else did.''

"You can't be accusing me?''

"I'm not accusing anyone...yet.''

Stunned that his phone call had backfired, Paul Sorenson hung up without another word. He stood at the desk, staring about the room and thinking of the elegance of his home and all that he had accumulated. His eyes narrowed angrily, giving his face a porcine appearance as he contemplated what he'd just been told. He hadn't sacrificed all these years just to have it taken away, and certainly not by some woman who didn't matter in the grand scheme of things. But she knew things about him that no one else did. Something had to give.

Tony picked up another chunk of wood and put it on the chopping block, then reached for the ax. The wood had been curing since last fall and was properly seasoned enough to burn in his fireplace, but he'd neglected to split it. Now he was glad he had something to do to get him out of the house.

The jarring thud of steel against solid wood ricocheted from his hands to his shoulders, then down to his toes. It had been months since he'd given himself such a vigorous workout, and it still might not be enough to make him forget how close he'd come to making love to Sarah. Not that he wanted to forget. But for Tony, when a woman said no, that was the end of that, no matter what he wanted.

He continued to chop, splitting the firewood and then stacking it aside, and made himself focus on the woodsy scent of newly split logs, thinking how great it would be to sit by a nice fire. Then his mind wandered. Maybe he would open a bottle of wine, get some cheese and crackers and…and Sarah? Where had she come from? She wasn't supposed to be in this fantasy. Not unless he wanted to spend the night in another cold shower.

"Hell's bells."

He gave the ax one last swing, splitting the wood on the block into halves, then stacking it with the rest. Once he was through, he carried the ax back to the small storage shed next to his house and hung it on the wall.

It wasn't until he came out of the shed that he realized how weary he was. But it was a good kind of tired. The satisfaction of knowing that what he'd done would provide heat for his home. Even though there was central heat and air in the house, there was something satisfyingly primal about man making fire to keep himself warm.

Pausing at the woodpile, he loaded himself down with an armload of split wood, then started toward the house. To his surprise, Sarah met him at the back door, holding it open for him as he shouldered his way inside.

"Thanks." He smiled. "I knew there was a reason I'd invited you here."

His teasing was the last thing she expected, but it alleviated the tension between them. She closed the door as he passed through, then turned in time to watch him exit the kitchen. As he did, she couldn't help but notice the corded muscles in his back and the sexy swagger of his hips. Granted, he was carrying an armload of firewood, which accounted for the play of muscles, but it did not account for his long legs and slim hips. And she had no one to blame but herself for the dull ache in the pit of her stomach. If she hadn't been such a coward, they would have had mad, passionate sex. And it would have been nothing but sex. She wasn't falling for him. She couldn't. She shouldn't. To fall in love with Silk DeMarco would be committing emotional suicide. He would be a marvelous lover, of that she had no doubt, but then what? There was too much going on in her life for her to open herself up to that kind of pain.

The solid clunk of wood on brick as Tony laid the logs near the fireplace broke her out of her reverie and sent her back to the stove to stir the pot of gumbo she had been cooking. The warm, familiar scents of shrimp, sausage and okra bubbling in the gumbo made her homesick for New Orleans. She turned the fire down under the pot and was in the act of setting the table when Tony came back in the room.

He stood in the doorway, drawn to the intensity of her expression. If she made love with as much passion as she cooked, she would be...

"Hell," he muttered.

Sarah spun. "I'm sorry. Did you say something to me?"

He sighed. "No. Just talking to myself." Then he made himself smile. "I never intended for you to play chef for us, but something certainly smells good."

Sarah shrugged. "I like to cook. It calms me."

He tugged playfully at a strand of hair that had fallen across her forehead, then gently smoothed it back in place.

"Do I have time to shower?"

"Again?" The moment she said it, she stifled a groan. "I mean..."

"It's okay, Sarah. Forget it." He pointed to the gumbo simmering on the stove. "I won't be long. Keep it hot." He winked, grinned and then left.

The moment he was gone, Sarah groaned. *Forget*

it? Not likely. Keep it hot? Good Lord…if I get any hotter I'll burst into flames.

Frustrated with herself and the situation in general, she resumed setting the table, then put some bread in the oven. Tony should be back by the time it was done. They would eat. They would chitchat. They would pretend they were nothing but old acquaintances. And for the short term of the lie, Sarah might be able to convince herself that she wasn't in over her head, both with the murder of her father and the man in whose house she was staying.

After that, it was up to her room to open the box. Harmon Weatherly had saved it all these years. It was past time to make some sort of peace with herself. Maybe the answers as to how to do that were inside.

Ten

"Do you have a pocketknife?" Sarah asked, as she crawled on the bed and pulled the box between her legs.

Tony thrust his hand into his pants pocket, pulled out a knife, then sat down on the edge of the bed.

"Look out," he warned before extending the knife toward her. With a flick of a button, the blade suddenly snapped open.

Sarah's eyes widened as she watched him slide it beneath the dusty string and lift. The string fell away like melting butter.

"That's impressive. Aren't switchblades illegal?"

He grinned. "A little holdover from my youth. I don't travel through airports with it, I assure you."

"That makes me feel so much better," she muttered, then focused on the package she was holding.

"Sarah."

"What?"

"It will be all right."

She sighed. "You must think I'm such a coward."

"On the contrary," he said gently. "You're one of the bravest women I've ever known. Now tear off that paper and let's get down to business. Who knows? There might be a clue as to what really happened to your father."

She frowned. "I hadn't thought of that. But surely the police would already have gone through his things in their attempts to find him and get back the money?"

"But they were looking for one thing. We're looking for another."

"You're right!" She ripped off the paper and cast it aside. "Here goes nothing," she said, and lifted the lid.

It was a jumble of things that had obviously been dropped into the box without rhyme or reason. A framed picture lay on top, the surface so dusty it was difficult to see the photo beneath.

"Here, let me," Tony said, and wiped the glass with his handkerchief before handing it back. "We can clean it better later. At least now you can see what it is."

Sarah nodded, then turned it faceup. Immediately

a knot formed in the back of her throat, but she willed herself not to cry.

"It's our family picture. We had it taken the Christmas before and sent it out with our Christmas cards." She touched the twenty-year-old image of her face, trying to remember what it felt like to be nine. "I loved that green dress. It was the first time I'd worn velvet. I felt so grown-up."

She put the picture aside and reached for the next item.

"Oh no," she whispered.

"What?" Tony asked.

She held up an oddly shaped dish. "It's an ashtray. I made it in Bible school one summer." Her voice was shaking as she set it aside, too. "Lord...Daddy didn't even smoke. What was I thinking?"

Tony touched the side of her cheek with the back of his hand.

"That you loved him?"

She looked up, her vision blurring with tears. "I did, didn't I?" Her jaw clenched as her mind jumped back twenty years. "Then why did I think my daddy was a thief? I should have known better."

"You were a kid, Sarah. You can't blame yourself for reacting to what was being said. Hell...I was six years older, and even though I had a hard time believing what everyone was saying, truth was, all the evidence pointed to him.''

"I guess you're right."

"Of course I am," Tony teased. "I'm a man."

She managed a small smile. "Thanks, I needed that."

"That's me...the original 'got what you need' man. How else do you think I came by the nickname?''

This time Sarah laughed. "You're impossible, aren't you?''

"No way, baby. I'm easy. Any time you want proof, just call for Silk and I'll be there."

Sarah rolled her eyes, aware that he was doing all he could to lighten the moment for her. Still, as she dug through the box, she couldn't let go of what he'd said. One of these days she just might take him up on the challenge.

She found another picture, a much smaller one in a little china frame, and realized it was a school picture.

"Fifth grade. The last one I had taken before everything was ruined," she said, and set it on top of the growing pile.

It was interesting and touching and sometimes downright sad to see the bits and pieces of what had mattered to her father, knowing that he'd cared so much for his little family that he'd taken mementos of them with him to his job.

The last thing in the box was an old-style Daily Glance desk calendar, one with a page for every day.

"Daddy's desk calendar," she said, as she set it between her legs.

She began to leaf through it, and as she did, she wondered why it hadn't been taken into evidence when he disappeared.

"Tony, look. This has a notation of every appointment and meeting Daddy had up until the day he disappeared. I wonder why the authorities didn't take this into evidence?"

"Who knows?" Tony said. "Looking back, I'd guess they immediately branded him the thief and were too busy trying to find out where he'd gone to worry about what he'd done before he left. Besides, this is such a small town, it would have been all but impossible to hide secrets for long. They may have looked at it and decided it meant nothing."

"But..." Then Sarah hushed. Tony was right. There was no use second-guessing what had been done before. It was what needed to be done now that mattered.

Curiously she thumbed through the pages, and as she did, she realized she'd known nothing about this part of her father's life. He'd just been Daddy to her. He lived with them, took care of them. He went to work at the bank every morning and came home every evening. Beyond that, she'd known nothing. It gave her an odd sense of loneliness, as if she'd only just now realized that her father had lived a life beyond that of being her daddy.

It wasn't until she was more than halfway through the calendar that she realized there was a common notation. Every other Wednesday at 1:00 p.m. there was a notation that simply said "Moose." Believing it had to do with meeting at the Moose Lodge to which he belonged, she thought nothing of it. Thumbing through the rest of the pages, she found nothing else that was even slightly notable and began to repack the box when she suddenly remembered that those meetings had always been at night.

"Tony, look at this," she said, and showed him the dates. "Every other Wednesday there's this note that says Moose—1:00 p.m. At first, I thought it was his lodge meetings, but I just remembered those were at night."

Tony thumbed through the pages, frowning as he

did. Then he handed the calendar back to Sarah without answering.

"So what do you think?" she asked.

"Do you really want to know?"

"Of course. It's past time to be worrying about any hidden skeletons in the family closet. I'm more concerned about the one they pulled out of the lake."

"Well, for starters, I think you need to show it to Gallagher. He seems to be serious about pursuing a new investigation, so it's only fair that he knows about this stuff, right?"

"You're right. I'll take it to him in the morning."

"What do you think about hiring a private investigator?"

Sarah's eyes widened, and she sat up straight. "I think it's a good idea." Then she frowned. "But I've never used one before. How do you find a reputable—"

"I have one on retainer," Tony said.

"You keep a P.I. on retainer? I thought you ran a nightclub?"

"I do."

"Do I want to know why you need a private investigator?"

He grinned. "I have other business interests, too."

She frowned. "Are they legal?"

He laughed, and then, before he thought, leaned over and kissed her lightly on the lips.

"Hell yes, Sarah Jane. They're legal, and so am I. I'm just careful, that's all."

She pulled back from the kiss, but not as quickly as she should have. Her lips were still warm and tingling when he stood up from the bed and took the box from her hands.

"Okay, we've looked at this stuff and the ghosts were nice to you. Nothing too threatening that can't be dealt with, right?"

Too bemused from the kiss to do more than nod, Sarah sat, waiting to see what happened next.

"So let's go toast the sunset from the deck with a glass of wine, what do you say?"

"The sun has already set."

Tony waved his hand in dismissal. "Details. Details. We can still drink the wine."

She sat for a moment, then started to grin. He was right. They could still drink the wine.

"If it's not too cool, we could watch the moon rise from the deck," she offered.

"Get your coat, kid. It's never too cold to watch the moon."

Sarah's heart felt lighter than it had in days as she followed him out of her room.

The killer stood in the dark beneath the trees, watching DeMarco's house. The light had gone out in Sarah Whitman's room, and her progress could be traced by the lights that came on as she and DeMarco moved through the house. When light appeared in the kitchen and she and DeMarco could be seen uncorking wine, it seemed that the long, cold wait would soon be over. The infrared scope on the nearby rifle allowed perfect sight in the dark. Perfect to kill by. Only not in haste. Never in haste. Patience was the killer's best quality, the past twenty years attested to that.

The patio door suddenly opened, and DeMarco and Sarah Whitman came out on the deck. The killer picked up the rifle and lifted it to face height, peering through the night-vision scope for a clearer view of the couple.

DeMarco was looking at Sarah as if he could eat her alive. The killer shifted the scope to Sarah's face. She looked nervous as she sipped at her wine, using a deck chair as a boundary between them. The killer had but a moment of regret. They would make quite a couple. However, playing cupid wasn't what mattered. It was all about protecting secrets.

The killer watched as Sarah turned around, giving a perfect view of her back. With trigger finger tightening, the killer took a deep breath—waiting—waiting—waiting....

Tony lifted his wineglass and then pointed upward.

"No moon. What are we going to toast?"

The outline of his features was blurred by the dark, so Sarah sensed more than saw the gleam in his eyes. She looked up at the sky and saw nothing, not even a few scattered stars. She raised her glass, then turned to him.

"To clouds...and old friends...and happy ever afters."

Tony touched his glass to hers. The clink of crystal to crystal was distinct.

"To clouds," he said softly, and took a small sip of wine. "And to old friends," he added, then took another small sip as Sarah followed suit. "And last, but never least...to happy ever afters."

He touched his glass to hers again. She sighed. So beautiful. He was so stunningly, devastatingly beautiful.

The light from the kitchen was weak, but it was

strong enough for Tony to see the wanting in her eyes. Instead of emptying his glass, he set it down and reached for her.

Sarah stepped forward.

The bullet sang past her head and plowed into the outside wall of the house at the same time that they heard the shot.

For a heartbeat they stood frozen, stunned by what they'd just heard, and then Sarah screamed as Tony propelled her downward, pressing her into the wooden deck with the weight of his body. His hands were gripping her hard as he kicked, then rolled, taking them both into the alcove formed by the wet bar next to the house.

Although they were not completely safe, the fact that the shooter could no longer see them gave Tony a brief moment of relief. Still lying on top of Sarah, he thrust a hand through her hair, praying he would not find blood.

"Tell me you're not hit," he muttered. "Please God, tell me you're not hit."

"I'm all right," she whispered, then she shuddered. "Did someone just try to shoot me?"

"No. Someone just tried to kill you. Be still. I need to get my phone out of my pocket."

"Oh God, oh God," Sarah said, then started to shake.

Tony made a quick call to the sheriff's office, giving the dispatcher a brief sketch of what had just happened, assuring him at the same time that there was no need for an ambulance, then held her as she started to cry.

A few minutes later the faint but reassuring sound of approaching sirens told them help was on the way.

Sarah couldn't quit shaking, and Tony wouldn't let her go. Even after the arrival of the deputy—and, soon afterward, Gallagher himself—she kept trembling. Tony had wrapped her in a thick blanket and set her before the fire. She'd had one cup of hot coffee and was sipping on a second one as she answered the sheriff's questions. A few minutes later, two of the deputies came back in the house through the kitchen.

"Sheriff, there's no one out there, but we found a fresh set of tracks just inside the tree line." He handed Gallagher a small plastic bag with a single spent shell and another with the slug they'd dug out of the house. "And this. We found this."

Gallagher lifted the plastic bags toward the light.

"Looks like a .30-30 caliber bullet, probably from a hunting rifle."

Sarah watched Tony and the sheriff, trying to

gauge the expressions on their faces against what they weren't saying.

"Are you trying to say it was a hunting accident? Who would be hunting at night...and so close to a house? I wouldn't think any game would come this close to where people live."

"That's just the problem," Ron said. "The animals have always been here. It's people who've intruded on their space. They come to the lake to drink at night. I suppose it's possible that someone could have been taking a shot at a deer or even a moose, although it's out of season. However, the footprints we found don't lend themselves too much to that theory. Hunters don't aim toward houses, and whoever shot this shell was aiming in this direction."

"It wasn't an accident," Tony said. "And if Sarah hadn't moved when she did, the shot would have hit her and not the house."

Ron nodded. "I tend to agree with you."

Then he looked at Sarah. Her face was pale and drawn, and there was a faint abrasion on her chin from where she'd fallen when Tony pulled her down. She'd been shaking when they'd pulled her off the deck and into the house, and she had yet to stop. Fighting a faceless, nameless enemy was a bit out of his league.

"What are you going to do?" Sarah asked.

Ron shoved his hat to the back of his head, absently scratching at a spot over one ear as he thought.

"There's not a lot I can do," he said. "Of course we'll come back in the morning when it's light, see if we can't follow the tracks. But if it's the same fellow as last time, I doubt we'll have much luck. He took pains not to be tracked."

"What am I going to do?" Sarah asked.

Ron hated the fear in her voice. He wanted nothing more than to be her hero, but right now, he was looking very inept.

"Don't go anywhere alone, and I wouldn't advise going outside until we know something definite." Then he added, "They're going to release your father's remains in a couple of days."

Sarah frowned. "Are you suggesting that I tuck tail and run after I bury him?"

"I'm not suggesting anything, Miss Whitman. I'm just telling you that I can't protect you very well until I know who it is I'm looking for."

Sarah wouldn't look at Tony. She didn't want to see disapproval on his face. But the sooner everyone understood where she was coming from, the better off they would all be.

"You need to know that I will not be driven

away from this town again,'' she said. ''I will leave here when I'm ready, and not a day sooner. My family's name was dragged through the dirt in every way possible, and I will not quit until it is cleared. Whoever killed my father is also indirectly responsible for my mother's death. They didn't just steal the bank's money, they stole my family and came close to destroying my life. Spread the word. The quicker everyone understands this, the less I will have to explain.''

Tony's heart sank. He admired her courage, but he was scared to death for her safety. As much as he wanted to be with her, he wished she would take herself back to New Orleans and out of the line of fire. However, there was something he could do until that day arrived.

''Gallagher, just so you know, there will be armed security on my property beginning tomorrow. Also, there will be two bodyguards inside my house at all times until this person is caught.''

Sarah's mouth dropped. ''Tony, you can't—''

He turned to her, his gaze fixed and cold. ''I can and I will, Sarah Jane, and you have nothing to say about it.''

Gallagher nodded in approval, while Sarah sank back against the chair in defeat. This was such a horrible mess. Everything was out of control. Then she remembered the calendar that had been in her father's things.

"Sheriff, there's something I intended to give you tomorrow, but since you're here, you may as well take it now."

"Are you talking about the calendar?" Tony asked.

She nodded.

"Sit still. I'll get it."

Sarah started to argue, then relented. Truth was, her legs were too weak to get up the stairs.

"What is it?" Ron asked, as Tony left the room.

"Earlier today, Harmon Weatherly gave me a box of things that had been cleared from my father's desk. He said he'd tried to give it to my mother back then, but she wouldn't let him in the house. He's kept it all this time. When we were going through the stuff, I found the calendar. There are some notations that don't make sense. I thought you should have it."

Ron's attention was piqued. "Good. Anything that would send us in a new direction would be great."

Tony came back just then and handed her the calendar. Quickly she leafed through the pages until she found one of the notations she didn't understand.

"This may not mean a thing," she said, as she showed him the notes. "At first I thought it was a reminder of the meetings Daddy used to attend at the Moose Lodge, but then I remembered those meetings were always at night. These are every other Wednesday, just after lunch."

"I see what you mean," Gallagher said. "I'll check it out. It might not mean a thing, but who knows? It could also be the break we needed."

"I'd like to have that returned when you're through with it," she said.

"I'll have the pages copied and send a deputy back with the original in the morning. How's that?"

Sarah nodded, for the first time managing a smile. "Thank you," she said, then looked at all the men, including Tony and the deputies. "I thank all of you, more than I can say. If there's nothing else you need of me, I'm going to my room. I've had all the fun I can stand for one night."

At that point, everyone stood.

"I'll see you men out," Tony said, eyeing Sarah's demeanor as she made her way from the room.

Ron Gallagher watched Sarah go, wishing he had something more concrete to tell her than the fact that he would try.

"I'll have one of my men swing by here every hour or so until morning," he said.

Tony shook Ron Gallagher's hand. "Thanks, Ron. I appreciate all you've done, and I know how frustrating this must be for your department."

Ron nodded. "It's hard to pick up the trail of a twenty-year-old crime, that's for sure."

The deputies were in their respective cars and driving away as Tony stopped Ron at the door.

"Just so you know, I'm putting a private investigator on this, and not because I think you can't do the job. I just wanted you to know, instead of learning about it after the fact."

"I'll take every bit of help I can get," the sheriff said. "Whatever he finds out, let me know, and I'll be sure to do the same. Just between you and me, the Feds think we're about as smart as rabbit pellets, which means they're not sharing everything they know. Frankly, I'm not counting on them for anything."

"Count on me," Tony said.

Ron grimaced.

"Damn shame what's happening to her. She's a real pretty woman who's had a hell of a lot of hard knocks. I'd hate to think I let anything else happen to her here."

"Whatever happens, it won't be because you're

letting it happen. It will be because someone is scared. And scared people are dangerous. I'm sure that when the divers found Whitman's body, it was not something the killer ever expected. After to-night, I'm equally sure that he will do what it takes to protect his identity and his secret.''

''Think you might be able to convince her to go home?'' Ron asked.

Tony shook his head. ''To paraphrase her words, the people in this town destroyed her family and threw her away. She's not going to let it happen again. So, no, she isn't the running kind.''

Gallagher sighed. ''I was afraid you'd say that.''

''Just find out who's doing this,'' Tony said. ''You've got a bullet and a bullet casing, which is more than you had this morning. Now all you have to do is find the gun from which it was fired and you've got your man, right?''

Ron smiled grimly. ''And we both know how difficult that's going to be in a place where nearly everyone owns at least one hunting rifle, if for no other reason than protection from bears or to scare away the odd moose.''

Tony looked around at the thickness of the trees surrounding his home. It was the first time he'd ever thought of the isolation of his house as anything but pleasurable.

"He's running scared, Ron. He'll make a mistake, and when he does, we'll get him."

Gallagher nodded. "Call me if you need anything."

"Drive safe," Tony said. "And keep us posted."

"You got it," Gallagher said, and walked away to his car.

Before his taillights had disappeared, Tony had locked the door and was on his way up to Sarah.

Eleven

Sarah was in the shower when she heard a knock on the bathroom door. She poked her head out from behind the curtain long enough to answer.

"Yes?"

"Just wanted you to know I'm up here," Tony said.

As soon as she heard Tony's voice, she began to relax.

"Okay...thank you," she added. "I'll be out in a minute."

She rinsed off quickly and turned off the water as she reached for a towel. The thick, heavy fabric cocooned her as she dried. When she had finished, she wrapped it around her body in lieu of the bathrobe she'd forgotten to bring in with her.

The moment she exited, Tony was at her side, handing her a nightgown, then turning his back as she slipped it over her head. "I'm decent now," she said.

He turned, his gaze searching her face and her body for signs of injury. The slight abrasion on her chin made him hurt, knowing he was the cause of it, but it was nothing to the thought that, but for the fact that he'd started to kiss her, she would already be dead.

"I know you're scared," he said.

She nodded.

"If it makes you feel any better, so am I."

"Am I being selfish by staying here? I'm putting you at risk just by being in your house. I think I should—"

"Don't think," he said, and took her in his arms. "Just be quiet and let me hold you. I'm still trying to get over the shock of thinking you were dead."

Sarah laid her cheek against his chest, feeling the softness of his brown cable-knit sweater against her skin and hearing the rhythmic thud of his heartbeat.

"Tony?"

"What?"

"You saved my life tonight."

At first he didn't answer, but Sarah felt his arms tightening around her. Then he rubbed his chin back and forth very gently at the crown of her hair and chuckled.

"So…does this mean that you owe me some

kind of mystical allegiance? That your life is mine to do with as I choose?"

"I was raised in Louisiana, not the Orient."

"Darn. I knew that sounded too good to be true."

"I will, however, grant you one wish," she said. "After that, my genie days are over."

This time he pulled back, eyeing her in disbelief.

"Anything I want?" he asked.

"Not exactly."

He rolled his eyes and pretended disgust.

"I knew there was a catch. There's always a catch."

"Hush," Sarah said. "Okay, here's the deal. I make three of the most decadent desserts you've ever tasted. One is a triple chocolate cheesecake with raspberry sauce, one is a pecan pie with a secret ingredient, and the last is called angel pie. It's a meringue shell slow-baked in the oven, served with fresh sliced strawberries and topped with whipped cream. You pick."

"Lord," he muttered, looking decidedly intrigued. "Are you serious?"

"Entirely."

"I'm a huge fan of chocolate and raspberries, but I've never had this angel pie concoction. And since I can't have you, I'll choose angel pie."

She smiled with satisfaction. "Good. It will give me something to do tomorrow besides wonder when the next shoe is going to fall."

Tony shook his head, marveling at her constant ability to bounce back.

"You know what? You're something."

"How so?" Sarah asked.

"No matter what happens to you, you seem to be able to land on your feet."

"Comes from having no expectations. That way I'm never disappointed."

Tony frowned. "I don't like the sound of that," he said. "Every woman should have expectations...of one sort or another."

"Are you offering?" she asked.

He grinned. "Hell no, honey girl, because if you knew what I was thinking right now, it would scare you half to death."

Intrigued, Sarah watched the mischief dancing in his eyes and grinned in spite of herself.

"Don't be too sure," she said. "The more I'm around you, the easier you are to take."

"Don't suppose I could talk you into a good-night kiss?" he asked.

She rolled her eyes. "Now he asks, when he knows I owe him my life."

Tony stood there, waiting for her to say no. When she didn't, he took it as a sign to proceed.

Sarah knew what was coming and thought she was braced for the contact. After all, it wasn't as if they hadn't done this. He'd kissed her senseless before, but she was ready for him now. She lifted her lips, half smiling as he lowered his head.

Contact came and, once again, good sense went.

Before she knew it, she had her arms around his neck and he was crushing her up against his chest. She heard him groan as her feet left the floor. Just as a series of mental fireworks were going off in her head, he turned her loose.

He was breathing heavily, his nostrils flaring as he struggled to pull air and sanity into his head. Knowing that there was nothing between him and her bare body but that damn gown was making him crazy.

"Well...now we know we can't do that again lightly. I'm going to make some phone calls. Is there anything I can get for you before you go to bed?"

"It's not even nine o'clock," Sarah said. "I don't want to go to bed."

Tony's fingers curled into fists, and then he jammed his hands into his pockets to keep from putting them back on her.

"Then do me a big favor and put on some more clothes," he muttered. "I'm tough, but I don't know how many more of these kisses I can take without finishing what I started."

"Aunt Lorett always says a person should never start more fires than he can put out."

His eyes narrowed in frustration. "Your aunt Lorett has too damn many sayings to suit me," he muttered. "I'll be in the library if you need me."

As he was leaving, the phone rang. He looked at the extension on the table, then at Sarah.

"You answer it," she said.

He picked it up, his greeting terse and brief.

"DeMarco."

"What has happened to my girl?"

Tony drew a deep breath. The soft melodic lilt to the woman's voice was a mixture of patois and English, and he knew immediately who it was.

"Lorett Boudreaux?"

There was a moment of silence and then a less than delicate snort.

"You play at being psychic?"

Tony grinned. "No, ma'am. I never mess with the real thing. But I'm not stupid, either, and the only other person who sounds remotely like you is standing in front of me. Being the reasonably intelligent man that I am, I'm saying to myself, this must be Sarah's aunt Lorett.''

He heard a chuckle in his ear and then a sigh.

''What happened to my baby?'' she asked.

''I'm going to pretend that I'm not surprised you already know and let her tell you the details. But I can assure you she's fine.''

''I will hear for myself,'' she said.

Tony handed Sarah the phone. ''It's your aunt Lorett. Put in a good word for me, will you? She's already on my case.''

He winked at Sarah and then left, giving her some privacy. He would make the calls he needed on his cell phone. He wanted security on the premises by morning.

''Baby girl…tell Aunt Lorett what has happened to you.''

The familiar voice and the concern in her words sent Sarah over the edge. She'd spent the evening making sure she stayed strong in front of the men, but now, hearing her surrogate mother's voice, she broke down.

''Someone shot at me tonight. If it hadn't been for Tony, I'd be dead.'' There was a catch in her voice, and she started to weep. ''Oh, Aunt Lorett, I can't do this by myself anymore. I need you. Can you come?''

"I will be there before the sun sets tomorrow. How will I find you?"

"Go to the Sheriff's Department in Marmet. They'll tell you how to get here. Or, better yet, when you get to Marmet, call and we'll come and get you."

"No. I come to you," she said. "Sleep well, *ma chère*, Tante Lorett will not let anyone hurt you."

Sarah hung up the phone and then dropped to the side of the bed. Relief swept through her in waves as she thought about having Lorett with her in this. Between her aunt and Tony, Sarah figured she just might survive this after all.

Tony was making a fresh pot of coffee when the doorbell rang. He noted the time and frowned. It was a quarter to nine. A little late for uninvited visitors. Still he hurried to the door, half expecting it to be one of the deputies or the sheriff. It was neither.

"Moira! What brings you out this late at night?" he asked.

Moira Blake hurried inside the house, her expression tense and anxious.

"I heard sirens," she said. "When I went out onto my back patio, I could see flashing lights here in front of your house. I know I should have called, but I was so worried. Is everything all right? Has someone taken ill?''

Tony took her coat and hung it on the hall tree as he escorted her into the living room.

''Come sit by the fire,'' he said. ''It's too cold to talk in the foyer.''

''Is Sarah ill?'' Moira asked. ''I know I should have followed up on my dinner invitation sooner, but I knew Sarah was dealing with a lot. I thought I'd give her some time.''

''I'm not ill, but thanks for asking,'' Sarah said.

They both turned. Tony was on his feet immediately and hurrying toward her.

''Come sit by the fire. You can fill Moira in on what's happened while I get us some coffee.''

Sarah smiled her thanks as she took a seat.

Moira leaned forward, clasping Sarah's hand with her own.

''Dear, what's happened? I saw lights and thought an ambulance had been called.''

''No, ma'am. It was the sheriff.''

Moira frowned. ''But why?''

''Someone tried to kill me.''

Moira gasped. ''No! Dear God, tell me you're not serious. Was it a prowler? Did you and Tony surprise a thief?''

''I wish,'' Sarah said, and then started to explain.

When she finished, Moira's face was a study in disbelief and Tony was handing her a cup of hot coffee.

"I just can't wrap my mind around this," the older woman said, then set the cup down on the table to keep from spilling it. "I can't tell you how sorry I am that this is happening to you."

"Thank you," Sarah said. "But you really don't need to apologize. It's not your fault someone wants me dead."

"I still don't understand," Moira said, looking to Tony for further explanation. "Why hurt Sarah?"

He glanced at Sarah, then shrugged. "Who knows? It's not as if killing her is going to stop the new investigation into who killed her father. I mean...that started before Sarah even knew his body had been found."

"Right," Moira said. "I guess that's why this makes no sense to me."

"My reappearance in Marmet stirred up a lot of muddy water," Sarah said. "But in my opinion, the man who killed my father is none too smart."

Moira frowned. "What do you mean?"

"If he'd been as smart as he thinks he is, he would have ignored my arrival and pretended shock along with everyone else when they pulled my daddy out of Flagstaff Lake. The authorities had no way of knowing if the real thief was even alive, or still lived in the area. By attacking me, he's given his existence away.''

Moira nodded thoughtfully. "You're right," she said. "Well, maybe he'll come to his senses and pull back."

"One can only hope," Sarah said.

"Anyway," Moira said, looking at both Tony and Sarah, "I'm so relieved to know you're both all right, and to celebrate, won't you please come to my house tomorrow night for dinner? Around eight? I've invited some other people who feel as sympathetic toward you as I do, so I promise no awkward moments for you."

"I don't know," Sarah said, looking at Tony as she thought how to answer. He had yet to know her aunt was coming.

"If you don't want to go, don't," Tony said. "My main purpose is to make this as easy for you as possible. The bodyguards will be here by then, so if you're worried about going out, don't be."

"Bodyguards!" Moira said.

"And security outside, as well. There won't be any more unnoticed trespassing on my property, I can assure you of that," Tony said.

Moira smiled. ''I can't blame you, and selfishly, I have to say that it makes me feel just that much safer, too. A woman living alone can never be too careful, and I don't live all that far away from you. So, can I expect you?''

Still Sarah hesitated. ''Tony, I haven't had time to tell you, but Aunt Lorett will be here sometime tomorrow.''

''Good. It's about time we met.''

Relieved that he'd taken the addition of another houseguest so well, Sarah began to relax. She looked back at Moira.

''I'd like to come, but only if you can handle another guest. There's no way I would go off and leave Aunt Lorett when she's just arrived.''

''Of course,'' Moira said. ''I'd be happy to have her. At my house, there's always room for one more at the table.''

''Then we'll say yes for now, and if she's delayed in some way, we'll call and let you know,'' Tony said.

''Perfect,'' Moira said.

She finished her coffee quickly and said her goodbyes, leaving Tony and Sarah alone.

''Are you upset with me for inviting my aunt without asking you first?''

''No. There's nothing you can do that will make

me upset with you, unless it's putting yourself at risk.''

''I won't do that,'' she promised.

''Good,'' Tony said. ''Because I need to know you're going to be in my life. Not just now, but after this is over, understand?''

Sarah nodded, but she didn't really understand and was too weary to ask. Was he talking about friendship, or something more?

''You know when you tried to get me to go to bed a while ago?'' she asked.

''Yes?''

''I think I'm ready.''

He grinned. ''Want me to tuck you in?''

''What I want and what's going to happen are two different things,'' Sarah said. ''So thank you again for saving my life and good night.''

''You're welcome, and good night to you, too,'' Tony said.

It wasn't until she was gone that what she'd said hit him. She hadn't said she didn't want him, she'd just said she wasn't going to give in to her desires—yet. Happier than he'd been in days, he grinned and tossed another log on the fire, then picked up the book he'd been trying to read for two days. It was about the power of positive thinking, but he figured he hadn't read far enough. If his thoughts had any power, he would be making love to Sarah.

* * *

The killer paced angrily, cursing bad aim and fate. Were it not for a kiss, Sarah would be dead and this mess would be over. Now the police were all over the place, and it would be next to impossible to get close to her again.

Well, fine. It would happen when it would happen. Fate wouldn't take everything away now—not when so many sacrifices had been made and so much loss had been suffered, of that the killer was certain.

If one thing had become clear over the years, it was that there was always a tomorrow to make things right.

Sarah went to sleep quickly, but her sleep wasn't sound. She kept hearing the rifle shot and then herself screaming as she fell downward beneath Tony's body. But instead of moving past the horror, it kept playing over and over in her mind, like a bad movie stuck on rewind. Tossing and turning, she became wrapped up in her covers, which exacerbated the nightmare. Finally, as the gunshot sounded yet again within her mind, she screamed, only this time she screamed aloud. The sound startled her, and she awoke with a fright and sat straight up in bed. Seconds later, Tony was in her room, half-naked and wild-eyed, brandishing the switchblade that had shocked Sarah before. He had the appearance of an overgrown teenager, ready to rumble.

"I'm sorry! I'm sorry!" she cried, and was out of the bed and running to him before she thought. "It was a dream, only a dream."

"God almighty!" Tony cried, and released the knife blade. It slid back into its sheath as he sagged against the doorjamb. "You scared the hell out of me."

Sarah stifled a grin. His thick, dark hair was mussed, and if she wasn't mistaken, his sweats were on backward.

"I know, and I'm sorry, really I am."

Tony looked at her and glared.

"Are you laughing?"

She bit the inside of her mouth and shook her head.

"You are, you little wretch," he muttered. "I'd like to know what's so damned funny about all this."

"Uh...well...your hair is sort of mussed, and you've got your pants on backward...and, I think, inside out."

He looked down at the tag on the front of his sweats. Damn. She was right.

"It's your fault," he muttered.

"I know," Sarah said, and then fell over on the bed backward, laughing as she'd never laughed before. In those moments, all the heartache and pain of the past few days fell away. She rolled onto her side, still laughing aloud, and saw the look on his face, which sent her into another fit of hysteria. Grabbing a pillow, she clamped it over her head, trying to stifle the sounds of her mirth.

"Sarah…"

The warning in his voice came through the stuffing of the pillow but did nothing to dampen her laughter.

"That's enough, damn it."

She bit her lip and peeked out from beneath the pillow, still chuckling. He looked like one of Aunt Lorett's roosters that had just had its tail feathers clipped. He didn't know whether to laugh along with her or make her sorry. Suddenly she knew that he'd opted for the latter.

"Think it's funny, do you?" he said, and stuck his thumbs in the waistband of his sweats and pushed downward. Not much, but just enough to taunt.

Sarah tossed the pillow aside and sat up in bed.

"Now, Tony, you can't blame me. It's not like—"

"Oh, I don't blame you at all, sweet thing. In fact, I want to thank you for calling this to my attention. Just give me a minute and I'll put them to rights."

He pushed his thumbs a little farther down, grinning as her eyes widened and her mouth dropped.

"Are you going to do what I think you're going to do?" Sarah muttered.

"What do you think I'm going to do?" he asked.

"Take off your pants."

"I was thinking along those lines," he said. "Want to help?"

She sat there for a moment, thinking about how close she'd come to dying tonight and how much she wanted this to happen. She got out of bed.

"Silk."

His heart skipped a beat. "Yeah?"

"Turn out the lights."

The room went dark. For a couple of moments no one moved. Then Sarah heard the snap of elastic and knew that Tony had shed his sweats. Shivering in anticipation, she crawled backward onto the bed.

"So, show me how you came by the name Silk."

"I thought you'd never ask."

Sarah held her breath as she felt the mattress give beneath his weight. Then his hands were on her body, lifting her nightgown over her head, then pressing her against the mattress.

"Oh...I—"

"Don't talk," he whispered. "Let me love you, Sarah. Just close your eyes and feel."

Just feel? She could do that.

Anthony DeMarco had earned his nickname honestly. The skill and speed with which he brought Sarah to the verge of insanity were frightening. One moment she was savoring the touch of his mouth on her body, and then she felt the tip of his tongue between her breasts. That was her last cognizant thought.

The next minutes of Sarah's life were lived in what could only be called heat. Her body was a tool, a part of the whole that would create the perfect pleasure, and Silk DeMarco knew how to turn it on. He brought her to the point of climax and then let her down three separate times before he included himself into the act.

Every muscle in Sarah's body was trembling when he levered himself above her and then eased himself in. The sigh that came out of her mouth was somewhere between joy and a groan of disbelief that the pleasure was soon to be over.

The tight warmth of Sarah's body was almost more than Tony could bear. He gritted his teeth as he started to move. When Sarah wrapped her arms and her legs around him and pulled him closer, he knew he was lost. This woman wasn't someone he could take and then walk away from later. He increased the tempo, and Sarah took it all and wanted more.

Muscle pounded upon muscle, hammering one

against the other in sweat-slicked ecstasy until the passion had wound so tightly between them that an explosion was imminent.

Suddenly Sarah stiffened and then started to moan. Tony felt her body tightening around him, pulling at his willpower until he started to break. Just as he was afraid he would not outlast her after all, she suddenly shattered, crying out his name as the climax racked her body.

At that point Tony buried his face against the curve of her neck and followed her down. It was, for him, both life-affirming and frightening. Making love to Sarah Whitman had proved one thing to him that he wasn't sure she could face.

He was falling in love, but he was pretty sure that, for her, it was just mind-blowing sex. He rolled over, taking her with him so that his weight was no longer on her body, then held her close. It was terrifying, knowing that, for the first time in his life, he was falling in love with a woman who might never love him back.

Twelve

Sarah lay in Tony's arms, listening to the even breathing of his sleep and wondering where she went from here. Years ago, she'd promised herself never to be vulnerable to a man again, and yet, in the middle of a life-threatening experience, she'd done just that. What the hell was she thinking? Then she sighed. That was just the problem. It hadn't been thought that had gotten Silk DeMarco in bed with her, it had been reaction. Trouble was, she couldn't find it in herself to be sorry. The intensity of making love with him had been frightening, but she would do it again in a heartbeat, just to feel the tenderness and the power.

"Ah, Silk," she said softly. "What have I done?"

He didn't hear her, and it was just as well, because there was nothing he could have said to change what had already happened.

Sometime close to daybreak, she slipped out of

his arms and into the shower, letting the warm fingers of the water wash away any lingering regrets. She'd made love to Silk DeMarco. So be it. She might even do it again, but it still wouldn't change what she'd come to do.

When Tony woke up alone, he knew what Sarah had done. Last night had been magic, but in the light of day, she was already pulling back from the intimacy. Instead of letting it get him down, he shrugged off the disappointment. No way was this going to be the end of anything between them. If he had his way, it was only the beginning.

He got out of bed and went across the hall to his room, quickly showering and dressing with care. Today was going to be, as his daddy used to say, an ass-kicker. The private investigator would be arriving around two. The armed security guards and the bodyguards would be there late afternoon, and Sarah's aunt sometime after that. Also, there was the dinner party at Moira Blake's house tonight, and while there was a part of him that wanted to keep Sarah completely under wraps until this mess was cleaned up, he knew it would be good for her to get out and mingle with some nice, ordinary people, instead of looking for guilt in every face that she saw.

The doorbell was ringing as he came downstairs, but Sarah was already at the door before he could stop her. Luckily it was the deputy, returning the desk calendar and not some gunman waiting to finish off what he'd failed to accomplish last night.

"Miss Whitman, Sheriff Gallagher asked me to give this to you," the deputy said.

Sarah smiled as the deputy tipped his hat.

"Thank you. Would you care for a cup of coffee?"

He hesitated, then nodded quickly. "That would be great, but I'll need to take it to go, if you don't mind. I've got a cup in the cruiser."

"Sure," Sarah said. "When you find it, I'll be in the kitchen. I'm sure you remember the way from last night."

He headed for the car as Sarah closed the door on the chill. When she turned around, Tony was standing at the foot of the stairs.

"Let me answer the door from now on, okay?"

It hadn't occurred to her that something as simple as answering a door could be dangerous. Then she thought of last night and how close she'd come to dying.

"You're right. I just didn't think. The deputy is coming back. Will you bring him to the kitchen? I have some muffins I need to take out of the oven."

Tony held out his arms. "Yes, I'll do that, but not before I get a morning hug."

Sarah hesitated, then let him hold her, but she didn't return the embrace.

"You can play cold with me, woman," he said softly. "But I know what lies beneath, so don't think I buy the act."

"I'm not playing games. I just don't want the muffins to burn."

"Say it for yourself, Sarah, but not for me. I don't believe you." Before she could argue further, he turned her toward the kitchen and gave her a gentle push. "So, Betty Crocker, go tend your muffins, but I'll bet they won't be as tasty as you."

She felt herself flush and made a dash for the kitchen, retrieving the muffins before they burned, all the while mumbling beneath her breath about smart-ass men who were too good-looking for their own welfare.

Tiny Bartlett waved one hand in the air to dry her nails as she dialed the phone with the other. Moira's dinner party was tonight, and she was looking forward to the event, especially after she'd learned that Moira had invited both Tony DeMarco and Sarah Whitman. The fact that Lorett Boudreaux was coming was just icing on the cake.

Annabeth Harold was at work when the phone rang on her desk. She hit Save on the keyboard of her computer and picked up the phone.

"Hello. Dewey, Dewey and Cline, how may I help you?"

"Annabeth, it's me, Tiny. Are you busy?"

Annabeth smiled. Tiny Bartlett had no concept of what it meant to work.

"I'm always busy when I'm at work, but I can talk a moment. What's up?"

"What are you wearing to Moira's dinner party tonight?"

Annabeth rolled her eyes, resisting the urge to snort. It was such an unladylike gesture, although it would pretty much express how she felt. Wear? Why did it matter what she wore?

"Oh, I don't know. Why?"

"Girl…you want to look your best. Silk De-Marco is going to be there."

"Tiny, I try not to think about such things often, but I am, at the least, fifteen years older than he is, maybe more. It can't possibly matter what he thinks about me."

Tiny gasped. "It always matters, Annabeth. Why don't you wear the burgandy pantsuit? You know, the one you wore last month when we went to dinner in Portland?"

Annabeth frowned, trying to remember if it was even clean.

"Maybe…if it's not at the cleaners."

"Goody," Tiny said. "So, have you talked to Marcia?"

"No, I was out last night," she said.

"Out? Where did you go?"

Annabeth's frown deepened. "Nowhere special. I was just out running errands and the like."

"Oh, well, I would have thought you'd done all that before dark."

"I don't see how," Annabeth said dryly. "I work until five, and at this time of year, it's already getting dark by the time I leave." Then she chuckled. "I swear, Tiny, you have no idea how the real world operates, do you?"

Tiny's lower lip slid forward, but luckily Annabeth couldn't see. Tiny hated being reminded that she was privileged. She so desperately needed to be "one of the girls."

"I'm sorry," she said. "I didn't think. Of course, you're right. I'll be glad when spring comes, won't you?"

"Well, we have yet to have winter, but yes, I do prefer the warmer days. Now I need to get back to work, so I'll see you tonight, all right?"

Tiny beamed. "Yes. Tonight. We'll see you to-night."

She hung up the phone and ran into the library, where her husband, Charles, was at the computer.

"Charlie, don't forget we're having dinner at Moira's tonight."

"I won't," he muttered, without looking up.

Tiny stared at him for a bit, trying to find the daredevil boy she'd married, but for the life of her, she couldn't see him a bit. Then Charles looked up and caught the wistful expression on Tiny's face, and he grinned.

At that point Tiny sighed. There he was, lurking behind all the responsibilities. She didn't want to think that she'd wasted her one act of defiance by marrying a man like her father.

"I'm going to get my hair done," she said.

Charlie checked out her appearance. It was perfect, as always.

"You already look good," he said.

Tiny beamed and threw her arms around Charles Bartlett's neck.

"I do love you, Charlie Bartlett."

He pulled her down on his lap and kissed her thoroughly, just to remind himself that there was more to life than business.

Tiny was giggling as she left him to his work,

unaware that Charles Bartlett's expression had turned into a frown. He didn't want to go to Moira Blake's, but turning her down was not an option. She and Tiny were best friends, so that was that. However, sitting down to dinner with Silk DeMarco was the last thing he wanted to do. They'd come from the same side of town, and while they'd both done well for themselves, Charles did not like to be reminded of his past. There were too many skeletons in that closet for him to ever want them disturbed.

It was two minutes past two when the doorbell rang again, and Tony was already moving toward it. He'd seen the old car coming up the driveway and recognized it from before.

"Maury, you made good time," Tony said, as the tiny, stoop-shouldered man walked into the foyer.

"Drove all night," Maury said, eyeing the house and the furnishings; then he looked at Tony and grinned. "Nice digs, Silk."

At that point Sarah came into the room. Maury looked past Tony to the woman and added, "Nice view, too."

"Ease up, Maury, she's not only off-limits, she's out of your league."

Sarah resisted the urge to shudder. The man wasn't at all what she'd expected. His manner was almost disrespectful, and his appearance was absolutely disgusting.

Tony saw the look on Sarah's face and knew what she was thinking. Truthfully, he'd thought the same thing the first time they'd been introduced, but Maury Overstreet was a genius at what he did, and because of that trait alone, Tony used him and nobody else.

Maury grinned at Sarah, then shrugged. "Can't blame a man for trying, now can you, doll?"

Sarah's eyebrows arched halfway to her hairline.

"Doll? Doll?" She looked at Tony. "Where did you find him? *The Twilight Zone?*"

Maury slapped his leg and laughed out loud.

"Damn, Silk...I'm thinking this one might be more than you can handle."

"You let me worry about that," Tony said. "Just be nice, you hear? She's had a week of hell and doesn't deserve any more grief."

Almost immediately, the too-familiar leer on the little man's face disappeared.

"I'm real sorry, lady," he said. "Didn't mean no disrespect."

"None taken," Sarah said, and then looked to Tony. "There's fresh coffee. Do you want—"

"Thank you, Sarah, but you do not wait on me, understand?"

"I've got to do something or go nuts," Sarah said. "Understand? So do you want coffee or not?"

Tony grinned. "Absolutely, and while you're at it, bring a couple of those apple cinnamon muffins you made this morning. Maury has a sweet tooth."

Maury's beady eyes narrowed thoughtfully as he looked from Sarah to Tony. He started grinning at Tony as Sarah left the room.

"She's cooking for you an' everything, huh?"

Tony pointed a finger in Maury's face. "Don't start with me, Maury. Hang your coat on the hall tree and then follow me. I'll give you everything we know."

Suddenly Maury was all business. He took off his coat and began fidgeting with the collar of his business suit, which was almost thirty years old and a midnight-blue polyester, as he followed Tony into the library.

By the time Sarah came in with a tray of coffee and muffins, the little man was in his shirtsleeves and taking notes as efficiently as the most proficient secretary.

"Have a seat," Tony said, and then handed Sarah's cup of coffee to her. "Maury has some questions he needs to ask."

Sarah nodded.

"I know you were a kid when this all went down," Maury said. "Still, kids always know more than they think, okay?"

"Okay," Sarah said.

"First…I need to know that you didn't bring none of this with you. You got any baggage back in New Orleans that you ain't mentioned?"

Sarah stared at the man as if he'd just lost his mind.

"Excuse me?"

Tony resisted the urge to laugh. "He's just covering all the bases, honey. What he means is, did you have trouble in New Orleans previous to coming here? Was someone hassling you there?"

"Absolutely not," Sarah said, indignation rich in her voice. "I'm a responsible person, Mr. Overstreet. I own a successful business. I pay my taxes and go to church every Sunday."

"Yeah…so did John Gotti…didn't mean he was no saint," Maury said.

Sarah hid a smile. She was beginning to see what Tony saw in the fellow. He was as persistent as a bulldog, even if his delivery left something to be desired.

"Okay, point taken," she said. "And I'm sorry.

Ask anything. I will answer as truthfully and honestly as I know how.''

Maury took a bite of one of the muffins as he made a couple of notes, then looked up at Sarah, swallowed and groaned.

"Man alive, lady, you sure can cook. You say you run a restaurant?"

"Yes."

Maury looked at Tony. "Don't let this one get away, Silk. Even if she loses her looks and figure, you'll always have the food to make up for it."

Sarah's mouth dropped. For a moment she didn't know what to say—until she looked at Tony. He appeared to be alternating between the urge to throttle Maury and laugh. Enjoying his discomfort, she couldn't help adding, "Yeah, Silk...even if I go to hell physically, I'll make sure you always get fed real good."

Tony glared at them both as his cheeks turned bright red.

"Shut up. Both of you."

Sarah grinned. Maury took another bite of muffin and rolled his eyes in ecstasy.

"Ask the damn question," Tony said.

Maury dusted the cinnamon sugar from his fingers and picked up his pen.

"Yeah, right. Okay...uh...so we're assuming the

trouble started when your old man's bones was found in the lake?''

Sarah flinched. It was the truth, no matter how crudely put.

''Yes, that and the fact that I said I wasn't leaving until the person who killed my father was found.''

Maury's eyes widened with new appreciation.

''Damn, Silk...she's more like you than I—''

''Maury, so help me God...if you don't stuff the commentary, you're going to find yourself working this blind.''

Maury nodded quickly. He hated working a cold case worse than anything, and Tony knew.

''Didn't mean nothing by it,'' he said, and polished off the muffin, washing it down with a big gulp of coffee, then rechecked his notes.

''So, you were ten when the money disappeared from the bank, right?''

Sarah nodded.

''Your mother...what did she say to you about it? What did she do when your old man didn't come home?''

Sarah stiffened noticeably. This was no longer fun.

''She said Daddy was innocent, then, about two

months later, she cut her wrists, crawled into bed and bled to death.''

Tony flinched at the cold, expressionless tone in her voice. Even Maury was affected as he tried to imagine a ten-year-old kid finding something like that. He made a couple of notes and quickly moved on without comment.

''About this calendar,'' he said, and picked up the calendar the deputy had returned that morning. ''What can you tell me about your father's whereabouts during this time?''

''Nothing,'' she said. ''I was ten. He was my daddy. He went to work at the bank. He came home around five. My world was home and school and the block where I lived. I was unaware of any meetings he might or might not have had during the day. However, I do know that his meetings at the Moose Lodge were always at night, so the references to Moose at 1:00 p.m. make no sense to me.''

''No prob,'' he said. ''I'll find out what it means.''

Sarah stared at him. ''Just like that? Twenty years and no earthly idea as to where to start first, and you think you can find out?''

Maury shrugged. ''It's what I do.''

''Now you see why he works for me,'' Tony said.

Maury nodded, while eyeing the last muffin. "Anybody gonna eat that last muffin?"

"Help yourself," Tony said.

And the interview proceeded.

About an hour later, Maury left, but not before he'd tried making one last pass at Sarah. Maury was out the door and heading down the driveway before Sarah found her voice.

"My God, Tony! Where did you find him?"

"Jail."

She stared at him for a moment, then held up her hands.

"Information overload," she muttered.

"You asked."

"Sorry. Next time, remind me to curb my curiosity."

"And when I do, remember it was at your request."

Sarah grinned, then punched Tony on the arm. He grabbed her before she could move, swung her off her feet and kissed her soundly.

"Remember that, too," Tony said, then put her down. "I know this is exhausting for you, baby, but let me help. Don't shut me out."

Sarah stood for a moment, trying to find the right words. Finally she just blurted out what she was thinking.

"We've done this all so fast," she said.

"Are you sorry?"

She hesitated briefly. "No. How could I be sorry for the most beautiful, passionate night of my life?"

"It wasn't about sex," Tony said. "Not for me."

"That's just it," Sarah said. "How could it be anything else? No one falls in love in less than a week."

"Who said?" Tony asked. "Besides, I think I've been falling in love with you forever. You were quite a knockout at ten, remember?"

She grinned. "You are so full of it. I remember looking in the mirror and thinking that my eyes were too big, and my hair was too straight."

"I've always been partial to owls."

She laughed aloud and wrapped her arms around his neck.

"Lord help me, how can I resist such a sweet-talking man?"

"Don't try," Tony said. "And don't think about how long we've been together. Think about how many years we have left."

Sarah shook her head. "I'm going to pretend I didn't hear that, and trust me, when this is all over, you'll thank me, scurry back to Chicago and forget you ever knew me."

The smile died in Tony's eyes. "That's never going to happen."

Before she could respond, the phone rang. Tony brushed the back of his hand against her cheek and went to answer it, leaving her with both the touch and the taste of him on her skin.

Moments later, he was calling her name,

"Sarah, it's your aunt for you."

Sarah raced to the phone. "Aunt Lorett! Where are you? Are you already here?"

"No, *ma chère,* I will not be coming until tomorrow."

Sarah tried not to let the disappointment show in her voice, but it was hard.

"Is everything all right?" she asked.

"No. Michelle was in a car accident. She was bruised only slightly, but she's very shaken. I am with her until Francois arrives."

"Oh no! I am so sorry," Sarah said. "Please give her my love and tell her I'll pray for her swift recovery."

"*Oui,* I will tell her that," Lorett said. She added, "You are okay?"

"Oh yes, I'm fine, Aunt Lorett. Don't worry about me. Tony has hired bodyguards and extra security for the grounds, as well as put a private investigator on the case. Actually, I'm sorry I asked you to come. You should stay there and be with your daughter.''

"You, too, are my daughter, Sarah Jane. I will be there tomorrow. Know that.''

Sarah's eyes filled, but with joy, not sadness.

"Thank you, Aunt Lorett. You are so precious to me.''

"As precious as that pretty man who stands beside you?''

Sarah blinked. Even though she was used to her aunt's unusual skills, she was still surprised from time to time.

"How do you know what he looks like?''

Lorett laughed abruptly. "I looked him up on the Internet. There was an article on him and his nightclub in some fancy magazine. I suspect the picture did not do him justice.''

Sarah laughed. "You are such a wretch.''

"I have been called worse. Now stay beside that man and do not venture out alone.''

"Yes, ma'am.''

"I will see you tomorrow.''

"Yes, ma'am.''

"Do not mock me, Sarah Jane. You are never too old to scold.''

Sarah smiled. "I would never mock you, Aunt Lorett. You might turn me into a toad.''

Lorett Boudreaux's laugh came through the phone line loud and clear, and then she hung up.

"Something wrong?" Tony asked.

"Aunt Lorett's youngest daughter, Michelle, was in an accident. She's not hurt seriously, but pretty shaken up. Aunt Lorett is staying with Michelle until her husband, Francois returns."

"Where is he?"

"Probably on a plane somewhere between New York and Los Angeles."

"What does he do?"

"Plays professional football for the New Orleans Saints. But he's supposed to be home sometime today. As soon as he gets there, Aunt Lorett will leave to come here."

"Are you disappointed?"

Sarah was a little surprised by his perception.

"I thought I was going to be, until she told me why she couldn't come. Tragedy always puts everything into perspective." Then she added, "Besides, Aunt Lorett says to stay close to you."

Interest spread quickly across his face. "What else did she say about me?"

"Well...she called you a pretty boy."

He almost blushed. "Damn. Can she tell what someone looks like just from listening to their voice?"

"No. She did a little investigating on her own. Looked you up on the Internet."

"The hell you say," Tony muttered. "I didn't even know I was there."

"Something about some article on you and your nightclub."

"I'll be damned," Tony said, and grinned. "She's a pistol, isn't she?"

"Oh, you have no idea...but you're going to find out."

"Should I be worried?"

Sarah looked up at him, studying the face that was coming to mean so much to her.

"I don't know. Should you?"

Tony touched her face, then her hair. "As long as she doesn't get between me and what I feel for you, we'll get along fine."

Even as Sarah was lifting her face for his kiss, she knew she should be keeping an emotional distance, at least until the drama of her life settled down. She'd been taught from an early age to say no to drugs and smoking, to drinking and driving. But no one had ever taught her how to say no to a man like Silk.

Thirteen

The bodyguards and the men who would be in charge of security on the property arrived around four. Sarah got a quick introduction to two very large, beefy bodyguards with big chests and no necks who went by the names of Dunn and Farley. Privately she thought their names sounded like a law office and realized that, unlike Maury Overstreet, they saw her as nothing but a job to be done. The security guards spoke briefly to Tony and then disappeared into the woods as Tony showed Dunn and Farley to a room downstairs. It had a sitting area, a television that they probably wouldn't be watching, and a couple of beds. From the way they settled in, Sarah suspected they'd done this countless times before. She also found out that nothing was expected of her except to go about her business as if they were invisible. It seemed an impossible task, considering the fact that they weighed a good five hundred pounds plus between them, but she was willing to give it a try.

When Tony and Sarah started over to Moira Blake's for dinner that night, she got the giggles, picturing the expressions on the guests' faces when they arrived with Frick and Frack in tow.

Tony let her joke about the men behind them in a second car, because he would rather she see the humor in the situation than the danger that really existed.

"I can't imagine what she's going to say," Sarah said, as they pulled up in front of Moira's house.

"Probably nothing. She's quite a lady. I'd expect her to welcome them in without a hitch, although I'd give a lot to know what she's thinking as she does."

Sarah smiled. "Yes, imagine trying to fill up two men their size."

"They're on duty. They won't be eating," Tony said.

"That seems mean," Sarah said.

"Trust me. They probably wouldn't eat what she's serving, anyway."

"Why?"

"Because except for the steroids I'm pretty sure they're on, they're both health-food fanatics."

"Really?" Sarah said, intrigued in spite of herself, as Dunn opened the car door for her, while Farley stood watch, searching the tree line beyond the Blake yard.

When they turned around, Moira was in the doorway. Although she was a bit taken aback by the presence of two human behemoths, she welcomed them graciously.

"I'm sorry your aunt was delayed. However, I'm so glad you could come. As you can tell by the array of vehicles outside, everyone else is here, anxiously awaiting your arrival."

"These gentlemen will not be dining with us," Tony said, and stifled a grin when a very relieved expression spread across Moira's face.

"I hope we're not late," Sarah said, as Dunn and Farley made themselves scarce. "You did say eight?"

Moira put her arm around Sarah's shoulders as she led her to the living room, where the guests were having cocktails.

"You're right on time," she said. "The others are regulars at my dinner parties, and I secretly suspect they like my appetizers better than my entrées."

Sarah rolled her eyes in appreciation. "I can't wait to taste."

"Sarah owns her own restaurant," Tony added. "So be prepared for some serious judging."

"Tony, stop it," Sarah said. "I've promised him a special dessert, but if he doesn't behave, I'm reneging."

"I'll be good," Tony said. "Just don't stop feeding me."

Moira looked at Sarah. "You must be quite skilled as a cook."

"Why?" Sarah asked.

"Because at Tony's level in Chicago society, the good life is taken for granted. If he says your cooking is good, it must be outstanding."

"She's an amazing chef," he said. "As for me living the good life, any way besides the way I grew up would be an improvement."

"You're just being modest," Moira said. "I remember you when you were just a young man."

"Yes, so do I," Sarah said, and smiled at Tony, who gave her a wink.

Moira saw the looks and the wink that passed between them and sighed. Oh, to be young again. As soon as they entered the living room, introductions began.

"Tony, I think you know everyone here. Everyone, this is our own little Sarah Whitman, all grown-up. Sarah...Tony...these are some of my dearest friends. Tiny Bartlett and her husband, Charles. He's a very successful C.P.A. Marcia Farrell is the redhead on the sofa. She's one of our most prominent citizens, active in all sorts of charity works. The gentleman beside her is Paul Sorenson, president of Marmet National Bank. Annabeth Harold is by the fireplace. She works for a law firm, and the man to her left is Harmon Weatherly, retired from the bank.''

Sarah's gaze went straight to Harmon Weatherly. She smiled warmly.

''Mr. Weatherly and I have already met.''

''Really?'' Moira said.

Harmon volunteered the information. ''I met Sarah yesterday outside the supermarket.''

Sarah added. ''He's being modest,'' she said. ''He actually came seeking me out. It seems he'd been saving some of my father's memorabilia all these years, and he made a point of giving them to me.'' Then she glanced over the chair where Harmon was sitting and pointed to a picture on the wall. ''There was one just like that in Daddy's things.''

Moira nodded sadly. ''Everyone in the picture received a copy. It was taken, I believe, for the bank's seventy-fifth anniversary. I remember being the one designated to serve punch to the customers that day, and Emma Toller's miniature poodle jumped out of her arms and into the bowl.''

Everyone laughed at the story, including Moira's footnote about the fact that it took months for the red color of the punch to wash out of the dog's white fur.

Marcia Farrell moved closer to the picture, then pointed to a young, fair-haired man standing to the right of a much younger Harmon Weatherly.

"Look, there's poor Sonny Romfield. I haven't thought of him in years."

"What happened to him?" Sarah asked.

"He was killed in a car accident only days after your father's…uh…disappearance."

"It was a sad time for the bank," Harmon said.

"He had a wife and two young children," Tiny said. "I wonder what ever happened to them?"

"They moved right after the funeral," Moira said.

"Rather quick, don't you think?" Annabeth noted.

"They were in the midst of getting a divorce," Moira added.

"I didn't know that!" Tiny squealed. "You never told us!"

Moira frowned, then shrugged. "Goodness me,

it was so long ago. Why would I even think about the Romfields one way or the other?''

Sarah listened intently, although she couldn't help noticing that Paul Sorenson had not contributed to the conversation at all. Curious, she turned, fixing him with a pointed stare.

''Are you in this picture?'' she asked.

Sorenson pointed. ''That's me to the right of your father.''

''That's when you still had all your hair,'' Annabeth said, and patted his nearly bald pate affectionately.

Sorenson scowled as the others chuckled.

''There are worse things than losing your hair,'' Sarah said.

The laughter trickled to a few nervous giggles. It seemed that no matter what Sarah said, they all took it as judgment against their belief in Franklin Whitman's guilt.

Sorenson's heart felt as if it would leap out of his chest. Every time Sarah Whitman looked at him, he feared she would denounce him for the fraud that he was. God, after all this time, to be afraid for someone to find out he was nothing but an aging queen. He'd heard the rumors that she harbored great hate. If that was so, he was a prime target for her venom, even though his secret had nothing to do with her father's death.

Tony offered Sarah a canapé. When she opened her mouth, he obligingly popped it in, then pointedly licked his own fingers. Again, the intimacy was not lost on the guests.

When Sarah turned around, she surprised herself, as well as Harmon, when she hugged him.

"Mr. Weatherly, I can't tell you how much I treasure the contents of that box. I don't know why you decided to hold on to them all this time, but I'm profoundly glad you did."

"It's nothing," Harmon said, but his smile was proof of his pleasure.

Tiny Bartlett fidgeted in the chair where she was seated and, when there was a break in the conversation, quickly piped up. "How nice for you to have some keepsakes."

Judging from her expression, Sarah obviously wanted the topic to change, so Tony took it upon himself to do so.

"Among other things," he said cryptically, and then picked up a second canapé from a tray on the sideboard, put it on a napkin and offered it to Sarah. "May I pour you a glass of wine?"

She took the canapé and nodded. "Whatever you're having is fine with me."

"What other things are you talking about?" Annabeth asked.

For the first time Sarah really looked at the people around her, separating them from the whole that she'd taken in upon her arrival. She remembered Annabeth Harold. She'd been holding her mother's hand when Annabeth had asked her to resign as chairman of the Fall Festival.

"I remember you," Sarah said.

Annabeth smiled.

"You fired my mother as chairman of the Fall Festival after Daddy disappeared." Then she looked at Moira. "This canapé is delicious. What is it?"

Tony stifled a grin. Good for Sarah. She'd agreed to dine with these people, but she didn't have to be polite.

"Uh...I believe that one is smoked salmon on a rusk of rye, with a bit of dilled yogurt on top."

"It's very good," Sarah announced. "I can't wait to try your entrée."

"Sarah owns and runs her own restaurant in New Orleans," Moira said, desperately searching for a new topic of conversation.

"Indeed?" Paul Sorenson asked.

Sarah looked at the aging man over the rim of her wineglass and nodded. "Indeed."

He flushed. She remembered! He could tell by the way she was looking. He wondered how rude it would appear if he pretended to take ill and just up and left. The moment he thought it, he discarded the thought. What if she talked about him after he left? He would have no way of knowing that he'd been outed until the gossip began to spread. Before he could make a decision, the doorbell rang.

"That would be the last guest," Moira said. "Excuse me for a moment."

"Who else has she invited?" Marcia asked. "I thought we were all here. Now we'll be uneven."

"We can always get Dunn or Farley to sit in to even things up," Sarah said, and then chuckled at her own wit when the others looked properly horrified.

"Oh, do hush all the fussing," Sorenson said. "We'll find out soon enough."

Within seconds, Moira was back with a tall, elegant woman of indeterminate age at her side. The woman was dressed in black silk to match her obviously dyed hair, and the glitter at her neck appeared to Sarah to be real diamonds.

"Everyone, you know Laura." Then she turned to Tony and Sarah. "This is Laura Hilliard. Sarah, you might remember her as Laura King."

The woman ignored Sarah and extended an elegant, manicured hand toward Tony, smiling seductively.

"Silk, darling, it's been a while."

Tony smiled. "Laura, I didn't know you'd moved back to Marmet."

"Oh yes...I have a house just across the lake. In fact, I can see the lights of your house from my bedroom. Surely you've noticed my place?"

Sarah stared. "The house with the red roof."

Laura turned, eyeing Sarah slowly, then nodded and smiled.

"Yes. I see you're quite an observant woman."

"Never doubt it," Sarah said. "I'm sorry, but I don't remember you at all."

"It's not surprising," Laura drawled. "I used to work out of town."

Tony offered to pour Laura a glass of wine. Someone across the room muttered the word *hooker,* but it was said so softly, Sarah couldn't tell who'd said it. She stifled a grin. It seemed Moira Blake had invited quite an eclectic mix of guests for her dinner party.

"Who brought the two bookends standing guard outside?" Laura asked.

"They're with me," Tony said.

Laura eyed him curiously; her glance slid to Sarah.

"I see," she said, and took a sip of her wine, then lifted her glass to Sarah. "I heard about your troubles. Please accept my condolences."

Sarah eyed her coolly. The sympathy didn't sound sincere, and she wasn't in the mood to pretend.

"Dinner is ready," Moira said. "Please follow me."

"Sarah, you'll be sitting between Paul and Tiny," Moira announced.

Tony slipped a hand beneath Sarah's elbow.

"No, she's sitting with me. Paul won't mind trading places, I'm sure." Then he shrugged an apology. "It's either that, or the bookends will be sitting at the table with Sarah."

"Really!" Laura drawled, as she gave Sarah a more serious look. "She must mean more to you than I thought."

"Someone tried to kill her," Tony said. "I take no chances with people I care for."

There was a communal gasp among the guests and then a twitter of indistinguishable words that all amounted to the fact that they'd already heard, but were just now finding a way to express their dismay. After that, there was a moment of pregnant silence, and then Moira giggled nervously.

"Of course you must sit beside Sarah. Do whatever makes you comfortable. After all, you *are* the guest of honor,'' she said, and gave Sarah's arm a quick pat. "This way, please.''

The group followed Moira toward an array of enticing scents, and so the evening went.

It wasn't until they were waiting for the dessert to be served that Charles Bartlett became anything more than the man on Tiny Bartlett's left.

"So, Silk...I hear you're building a second club. How is it progressing?'' he asked.

Tony looked at Charles and nodded.

"Yes, actually, it's almost finished. It will open before Christmas, but I'll have the grand opening on New Year's Eve.''

Bartlett barely managed to stifle a sneer. "Always chasing the almighty buck. When will you have enough?''

There was an embarrassed lull in the conversation as everyone looked uncomfortably from Tony to Charles and then back again. But it was Sarah who took the burden of answering away from Tony.

"Charles...I'm curious as to what you consider enough. You have a most charming and attractive wife, and from the conversation, I gather you're quite successful. You've come a long way over the past twenty years yourself. Are you not happy with your life?''

Charles was pinned, and he knew it. He lifted his glass to Sarah and grinned wryly before covering Tiny's hand with his own.

"On the contrary, I am extremely happy. With a woman like my Tiny, who could ask for anything more?"

"Exactly," Sarah said, and then impulsively lifted her glass and made an impromptu toast to Tiny.

"To happy marriages," she said softly.

"To happy marriages," everyone echoed.

"What did I miss?" Moira cried, as she came back into the room with a towering chocolate cake dripping with fresh raspberry sauce.

"Just a toast," Annabeth said, and tried not to feel left out of the fact that she had no husband—ex, deceased, or otherwise—to toast.

"Who wants dessert?" Moira asked.

All hands went up except Laura's. "I never indulge," she said, and ran her hands down her svelte figure.

Sarah didn't like Laura Hilliard. It had taken less than five minutes for her to come to that decision, and she was honest enough with herself to realize that part of it was because she suspected Tony and Laura had some kind of a history. While she wasn't one to be jealous, she was also aware that she could match Laura curve for curve with a good twenty years of youth on her side. Besides that, she was sick of her snide remarks.

Smiling sweetly, she let her glance linger just a bit longer than proper on Tony's face before answering.

"I'll have some. I always indulge," she said, and then pretended great interest in the cake Moira was cutting.

Anger surged, but Laura hid it admirably. Being reminded of her fading youth by some insignificant woman from the South did nothing to make her fate any less inevitable.

"You'll pay for it one day, trust me," she said.

Remembering Maury Overstreet's warning to Tony, Sarah started to laugh.

"Oh…I've already been warned, and by someone much more daunting than you. But I've got a hole card, you see."

"Really," Laura asked. "If it's not a big secret, I'm sure we'd all love to know what it is."

Now it was Tony's turn to save Sarah from answering. He was already chuckling when he put an arm around her shoulders and gave her a quick hug.

"Oh, I can tell you that," he said. "She was recently told by an expert in the field that when she loses her face and figure, she'll never lose her man, right, honey?''

Sarah grinned.

''And why not?'' Laura asked.

''Because she can cook like an angel, and when it's all said and done, we know that the way to a man's heart is truly through his stomach.''

Laura smirked. ''Unless of course you have the money to pay for fine gourmet chefs. Then you could have it all,'' she told Tony.

''That brings up an interesting question,'' Sarah said.

Tony held his breath. The moment Laura had mentioned money, he'd known what was coming, and for a moment, he almost felt sorry for her.

''And that question would be?'' Laura drawled.

''You said you used to be a working girl?''

Laura flushed angrily. ''I said I used to work out of town.''

''Oh. Right. Sorry,'' Sarah said, but she wasn't. ''About that money...exactly where did you get yours?''

A slight gasp rose around the table. In fine circles, it was extremely rude to speak of money, although Charles had skirted the issue briefly already.

''I can't see as how it could possibly be any of your business,'' Laura said.

Sarah leaned forward, her gaze raking the guests at Moira's table.

"There's a million dollars still missing from the bank where my father worked, and we all know he damn sure didn't take it or spend it. So...I am extremely interested in anyone in Marmet whose circumstances have improved since that time."

Tiny gasped. "And you suspect one of us?"

"In my eyes, no one is innocent until Sheriff Gallagher finds the person responsible for what happened to my family."

"I heard you were on some quest for revenge," Sorenson said.

"It's not about revenge, Mr. Sorenson. It's about justice."

Then she smiled at Moira, who had just served her a piece of cake. "It looks marvelous," she said. "I can't wait to taste."

Moira managed a smile and then sighed. It served her right. She should have known better than to try to bring peace to people when the continuity of their lives had been broken by a murder and a lie.

"I thought that went well," Sarah said, as Tony took the last curve in the road toward his home.

He rolled his eyes. "Now I know what the straight man feels like," he said.

Sarah grinned. "Why? Did you feel as if I was ignoring you? You were my dinner partner, and I'm sorry if I was rude to you in my efforts to cause strife and concern to all assembled."

He laughed aloud. "God, Sarah, remind me never to make an enemy of you."

"I can't think why you would even say something like that to me," she said primly.

"You're incorrigible, and you know it, so don't play innocent."

She looked at him, her face lit by nothing but the dashboard light, and still he could see the wanting in her eyes.

"I'm not an innocent," she said. "I haven't been for a long, long time."

"Is that an invitation?" he asked, his voice suddenly husky.

"Take it any way you like."

"Oh, trust me, sweet thing, I most definitely will."

The promise of what was to come was there on his face for her to see. She shuddered suddenly, but from longing, not fear. She'd spent the day with Tony, but when it got dark, she wanted Silk in her bed.

"As soon as you put Frick and Frack to bed, you know where I'll be," she said.

"They don't sleep," he said.

"Vampires?"

He rolled his eyes.

She grinned. "Okay, I was just teasing."

"I should have qualified that statement by add-ing...at least not at the same time."

"Just keep them off the second floor, okay?"

"Why?" Tony asked.

"Just because."

"Good enough for me," Tony said, and took the turn into his driveway in a skid.

Fourteen

Tony was sprawled out on the bed behind Sarah, spent from the passion of their lovemaking, but she hadn't been able to sleep. The stimulus of the dinner party earlier in the evening had kept her mind too active to relax. Reluctantly she'd crawled out of her warm bed and Tony's arms and gone to the windows.

As usual, the security lights on the property cast a glow in the back, but only to a certain distance. Beyond that was total darkness. Once she'd seen the shadow of an intruder from these windows. Another time she'd stood on Tony's deck and come close to losing her life. Now the fears she might have had were stilled, thanks to the men she knew were on guard. They did not sleep so that she and Tony could.

She looked back at Tony and sighed. If only she could sleep. She wanted nothing more than to lie down and forget, even if it was just for the night.

As she stood at the windows, a cloud that had been covering the sliver of moon began to pass, and as it did, for the first time, she could see the lake. The perfection of the view was slightly marred by the presence of trees, but there was enough space between the limbs for her to see the glitter of moonlight on the water.

She would never be able to see that lake and not think of it as anything but a place of concealment and horror. Swimming in it would be like playing on her father's grave. She was thankful that Marmet was no longer her home. It was a place of too many secrets. She'd seen that for herself tonight at Moira Blake's. All the money and fine trappings in the world would not have been able to hide the undercurrents of jealousy and old sins that had been present at the table.

Charles Bartlett was a strange man. He seemed to have it made, yet his envy of Tony was obvious. And then there was Paul Sorenson. She felt certain he resented her—maybe even hated her—and she had no idea why. Harmon Weatherly was a nice, gentle man. She'd sensed that from their meeting in town. Tonight, at the dinner table, he'd done his best to keep the conversation light and congenial.

She shivered, wishing for the bright lights and vivacity of New Orleans to take away this damp, clinging chill, and thought of the pretty women who worked the streets of New Orleans like the pros that they were. Sometimes, a couple of them would come into her restaurant for a cup of coffee and a beignet, other times they would be with a "date." She'd never judged them. But for the grace of God and Lorett Boudreaux, she might have wound up the same way.

As for the women who'd been at Moira's, they were an odd collection, to say the least. Tiny Bartlett was pretty, but she tried too hard. Tony had mentioned earlier that he and Charles Bartlett had grown up on the same side of town. Apparently Tiny had married beneath her, but it seemed to have paid off. Her husband's business acumen had been obvious, and he worked hard to maintain an image with which he had not been born. His nails were manicured, his haircut perfection. He wore the finest of suits and shoes. But the veneer between his public persona and the street kid he'd been was thin at best.

Annabeth Harold had seemed, to Sarah, the odd person out. She still worked at a job, had never been married, and was much lower on the financial scale than the others. More than once during the night, Sarah had caught a look that might have been envy on the older woman's face, but it had been so fleeting that she'd passed it off as her imagination. She understood why Annabeth might feel that way, but these people were her friends. They accepted her as she was. Why, then, didn't she accept herself?

Marcia Farrell was a widow, or so she'd been told, but she'd overheard enough chitchat between Tiny and Annabeth to realize that when Marcia had left Marmet years ago, she'd been an ordinary woman, trained in simple secretarial skills. She'd come back to Marmet a few years later claiming widowhood, but with a child in tow. Soon after, she had inherited a great deal of money, making her a very wealthy widow. Tiny had mentioned the sadness of the husband's passing without even knowing his name. She said Marcia never liked to talk about him, so they honored her tender feelings.

And then there was Laura Hilliard. Besides the fact that she'd been all over Tony, Sarah flat out didn't like her. She was too smooth, too cold, and too sure of herself—basically, an emotionless bitch.

Correction. Rich bitch.

According to Tony, she had more money than she would ever be able to spend in one lifetime. A million dollars would have been the perfect seed money in acquiring such a fortune.

And then there was Moira. Poor Moira. She'd

tried so hard to make everything nice. Sarah sighed. Part of it was her own fault for baiting the guests. But she'd never been able to bear condescension, and the room had been full of it. All Sarah knew about Moira was the little Tony had mentioned. She had been widowed a few years back, was recently retired from the bank where her father had worked, and she'd lived in the same house for ages. Nothing remarkable. Nothing new. But she did make good chocolate cake.

Tony shifted on the bed behind her, and Sarah turned, eyeing his long body beneath the covers and remembering how quickly he could bring her to joy. He was an amazing man who, with the help of a well-to-do uncle, had made something of himself. She felt just the least bit of guilt in thinking that she'd never checked into his story of how he'd made good and then shrugged away the thought. He'd been too young to pull off a bank heist and a murder, never mind the fact that he wasn't that kind of man. And before she could chide herself for being swayed by the fact that he was damned good in bed, she reminded herself that she considered herself a good judge of character. No way could she be falling in love with the man who had heartlessly stuffed her father's body into a trunk and dropped it into Flagstaff Lake.

No way.

Then what she'd thought hit her, and she leaned against the windowsill to steady herself. Falling in love? Was that what this was? This heart-wrenching, blood-thundering, weak-kneed feeling of helplessness, coupled with the adrenaline rush that came from something as simple as his smile?

Oh, fine. She'd waited all these years to fall in love again and she had to do it now—when all hell seemed to be breaking loose in her life?

She shuddered once, then turned back to the window. And as she did, she caught a brief glimpse of motion on the water. From this distance, it appeared as little more than a small, round object, and then it was gone. More than likely it was a loon, or even a piece of deadwood from the many trees surrounding the lake.

Tony murmured in his sleep. Suddenly weary and tired of being afraid, she crawled back into bed and into his arms. Within minutes, she was asleep.

The storm broke around three. A large clap of thunder pulled Sarah out of her sleep, leaving her momentarily disoriented. But the flash of lightning that followed told her there was a storm, and the brief illumination it shed across the room confirmed the fact that she was alone in her bed. She got up and turned on the light before looking out in the hall for Tony. There was a light on downstairs, and she remembered the bodyguards. He was probably with them.

Thinking little of it, she looked around the room for her robe, saw it on the chair and quickly put it on. Moments later she was running down the stairs, calling Tony's name as she went. Just as her foot hit the bottom step, the power went out and the house went dark. Power went off all the time during storms, so she was only mildly irritated.

"Tony! I hope you have a flashlight or some candles," she called.

To her surprise, no one answered. No one came.

She moved toward the front door, and as she did, a gust of wind swung it inward, bringing a wash of blowing rain. She gasped and ran to close it, and as she did, she tried to imagine a reason why Tony and the bodyguards would be outside. She ran to the front windows, peering through the darkness and intermittent flashes of lightning, trying to see where they'd gone, but she saw only blowing leaves and rain.

A faint sound from somewhere behind her sent her spinning around.

"Tony! Is that you?"

Again no one answered. Again no one came.

Now her nerves were definitely on edge. Where the hell were those bodyguards who were supposed to be so great? Why wasn't one of them in here waving a flashlight in her face?

"Dunn! Farley! Where is everyone?"

She heard a board creak overhead and stifled a gasp. Someone was upstairs moving around in the dark. If it was someone who belonged here, they would have answered her calls. A second board squeaked, then a third, and she knew that whoever it was, they were coming down the hall. Suddenly she was very, very scared.

"Oh God, oh God."

Without thinking, she started to run.

Thanks to the racket from the storm, her bare feet were soundless as she ran across the polished pine floors. Almost immediately, she remembered a small cubby of a closet beneath the stairs and bolted for it. It wasn't all that large, but there was enough space for her to hide in, and that was all she could think to do.

The doorknob turned silently beneath her grasp, and the hinges were equally silent when she pulled the door open. Quickly she moved inside and closed the door just as the intruder started down the stairs. He was moving quickly now, taking the stairs two at a time. She grasped the doorknob with both hands and held her breath, afraid to inhale for fear she would be heard. Now he was at the bottom of the steps. A cold sweat suddenly covered her body, and, instinctively, she started to pray, silently begging God to save her.

The intruder was hurrying now as he moved down the hall past where she was hiding. Just when she thought she was going to be safe, she heard the footsteps stop.

No, no, no.

Sarah was shaking so hard she could barely stand. Slowly, slowly, the sound of footsteps came closer, until she actually felt the intruder's energy on the other side of the door.

Sweet Jesus, save me. Don't let me die.

The doorknob turned slightly beneath her hands, and just when she thought it was over, the lights flickered twice and the power returned. The thin thread of light beneath the door was, to Sarah, a most welcome and beautiful sight. Following that, she felt the intruder's shock as vividly as if they'd been face-to-face.

Immediately, the pressure on the doorknob ceased, and Sarah heard a muffled curse, then running footsteps. Before it occurred to her to look and see who was running away, it was silent. She started to open the door and then stopped, wondering if she was being conned, if the intruder would be waiting for her on the other side, ready to finish her off. She waited a moment, and then took a deep breath before pushing the door wide.

The hall was empty; the only thing visible were a few wet tracks on the polished floor. She turned slowly, looking behind her, and as she turned, she noticed a darker shadow inside the closet in which she'd been hiding. She stepped back and turned, then started to scream. It was Tony, unconscious and bleeding from the head. She ran to the front door, screaming for help as she went. Within minutes the house was crawling with security, and Sarah was hustled to one side under armed guard, while the others took over.

She had blurred images of finding Dunn and Farley unconscious in their room, and the flashing lights of ambulances and sirens as both they and Tony were taken away. Sarah begged and cried to go with Tony, but the head of the security team Tony had hired wouldn't let her out of his sight. Sobbing hysterically, with nowhere to turn, she was oddly consoled by the appearance of Sheriff Gallagher and two of his men.

"Sarah! Tell me what happened?" Gallagher said, as he took her into the living room.

"I woke up when the storm hit. I couldn't find

Tony or either one of the bodyguards, and then the power went off. I kept calling for them, but they never answered. Then I heard someone moving around upstairs and knew that whoever it was, they didn't belong there. If it had been Tony or the guards, they would have answered me.''

Ron nodded. He'd already heard most of this from some of the men on the security team, but he let Sarah talk because it was calming her down.

"What did you do next?" he asked.

"I heard the footsteps coming along the upstairs hall so I ran and hid in the closet beneath the stairs.'' Her chin quivered, her eyes filling with tears as she looked up at Ron. "Tony was in there all that time and I didn't know.'' She shuddered. "God...just like Daddy. All those years people swam and boated on that lake...they were playing while he was down there in that trunk.''

"Don't think like that," Ron said, and pointed at one of his deputies. "Get her a drink of whiskey, neat, from the bar.''

"I don't want anything to drink," Sarah said. "I want to see Tony. I need to know if he's going to be all right." Then she started to sob. "This is all my fault. He got involved because of me, and if he doesn't...if he—''

"He's going to be okay," Ron said, even though he didn't know that for a fact.

The deputy handed a shot of whiskey to Ron, who handed it to Sarah. "Drink this."

She took it like medicine, shuddering as it went all the way down.

"Good girl," Ron said. "Now tell me what you did after you hid."

Sarah closed her eyes briefly, remembering the horror and the fear.

"It was still dark, and I hid in the closet with my hands on the doorknob because there was no lock. I heard the intruder running down the stairs and then past the closet where I was hiding. And then the footsteps stopped and began coming back. I was so scared. I just knew I was going to be found. Just as he was about to open the door, the power came back. I could tell it startled him. He turned and ran. When I came out, I was alone, and then I turned and saw Tony and…" She covered her face with her hands.

Ron touched the crown of her hair briefly, absently noting that it was as soft and silky as it looked, then turned to the man who was in charge of the security team.

"Did your men see anything?"

"Not a damn thing," he said. "We weren't

aware of any problem inside the house until we heard Miss Whitman scream." Then he added, as if absolving them of any blame, "We were assigned to the exterior of the property. We had no way of knowing that the security team inside had been immobilized."

"It's okay," Sarah said. "No one's blaming you. I just thank God you were there."

The man looked at Sarah for a moment and then made some sort of decision. "I'll have men posted directly outside the house, as well as on the property, until Mr. DeMarco orders otherwise. No one will enter the house without our permission." Then he walked away, giving orders as he went.

Sarah stood abruptly, gathering her robe around her.

"Where are you going?" Gallagher asked.

"To get dressed. I'm going to the hospital to see Tony."

Ron sighed. "Go ahead and get dressed," he said. "I'll take you myself."

"I have a car," she said. "It's not that far into Marmet."

"They've taken Tony to Portland," he said.

Sarah groaned. "That far?"

"Like I said, I'll get you there, but you're going to have to put up with a bodyguard."

"Better than the other two, I hope," she muttered.

"I heard one of the paramedics say they thought the men had been drugged."

Sarah frowned. "That makes no sense. How could they have been drugged? Tony said they're into health food. I think they even prepare their own meals."

"I don't know. That's just what I heard. They'll know more after they run tests on everyone concerned. Now, if you don't mind, I'll accompany you upstairs and we can see if anything is missing."

Sarah flinched as if she'd been slapped. That was something she hadn't even considered.

"I just assumed the intruder was looking for me."

"Probably," Ron said. "But we'll check to make sure."

They started up the stairs with Sarah sandwiched between the sheriff and an armed security guard carrying a semiautomatic. If she hadn't been so scared, she would have laughed. This was like something out of a bad B movie. Girl running for her life in a dark house, then finding her lover unconscious and bleeding. Enter the police, and pitiful heroine is reduced to having total strangers guarding her as she dresses.

"Have mercy," Sarah muttered.

"You say something, miss?"

"What? Oh. No," she said, and made a mental note to keep her thoughts to herself.

It wasn't until she was dressed and looking for her shoes that Sarah realized what was missing. She turned abruptly, looking at the table where the box with her father's things had been sitting.

"The box! It's gone!" she cried.

Ron had already inspected her room and was across the hall in Tony's room, trying to see if anything had been disturbed, when Sarah cried out. He came running back, his weapon drawn, although the security guard was still outside her door.

"What's wrong?" he asked, as he ran into the room.

She pointed to the table. "I didn't notice it before, when we were looking through the room, but the box with the things from my father's desk was on that table. Now it's gone."

"You're sure you didn't put it somewhere else and then forget?"

"Positive," Sarah said, and sat down on the bed with a thump. "Why would anyone want to steal a box of silly little keepsakes?"

"Maybe there was more in there than you thought," Ron said.

"The only thing that might have been useful was that calendar," Sarah said. "Thank goodness you have a copy of the pages."

Ron frowned. "How many people know that?" he asked.

She shrugged. "I didn't tell anyone, so no one except me, Tony, you and your staff. Oh...and Maury Overstreet."

"Who's Maury Overstreet," Ron asked.

"The private investigator Tony put on the case."

"Oh yeah, right. For now, let's just keep it that way," he said.

Sarah nodded and then remembered her shoes. "I can't find my shoes," she said.

The sheriff turned around, searching the room, then pointed at the closet.

"Have you looked in the closet?" he asked.

She grimaced. "I know this sounds silly, but I never put my shoes in the closet, at least, not the ones I wear every day."

Ron went to the door and opened it. "Are these the ones?" he asked, pointing to a pair of black loafers.

The skin crawled on Sarah's back. "I didn't put them in there."

"Maybe Tony did."

"They were by that chair when I went looking for him."

"How can you be sure?"

"Because I saw them there when I turned on the light to get my robe."

Ron frowned and looked at the shoes again. "Are you saying that the intruder put your shoes away?"

She couldn't quit shuddering, imagining the man going through her personal belongings. She felt violated, as if she'd been raped.

"He was the only other person up here besides me."

Ron spun immediately and ran to the door, then yelled down the stairs.

"Evans! Bring me a large evidence bag!"

A minute or so later, one of his deputies came running and handed the sheriff a large plastic bag. Ron knelt, lifting Sarah's shoes with the tip of a ballpoint pen and dropping them into the bag.

"Hope you've got another pair," he said.

Sarah shrugged. "Tennis shoes and slippers."

"I'd recommend the former," he drawled. "May I?" He pointed back into the closet where a pair of white tennis shoes with blue trim were sitting.

"Please," Sarah said. When he handed them to her, she put them on quickly and stood, her coat and purse in hand. "Now will you take me to Tony?"

"Yes."

By the time Gallagher drove into Portland, day-break was on the horizon. The drive had been quiet. Only a couple of times had Sarah even bothered to start up a conversation. The last time she had, she'd asked Ron to watch out for her aunt and to see that she reached Tony's house safely. He'd promised her that and would have promised her more, but she needed nothing from him but his badge. However, over the past few days, he'd had a revelation about the woman on the seat beside him. It wasn't that he dreamed of having a relationship with her. Not in reality.

What he really wanted—and needed—was absolution. He'd been part of the past that had destroyed her family, and it was something he would always regret. But solving this twenty-year-old crime, knowing that he'd been as instrumental in clearing her family name as he had been in ruining it, was all he would ask.

"There will be an armed guard posted at the hospital," he said. "They're guarding Tony in case anyone comes after him again. And I'm going to insist one of them stays with you at all times."

The look in Sarah's eyes was haunted. "Will this ever be over?"

"Yes, Sarah. I give you my word."

Her shoulders slumped as he took a turn into the parking lot of a large hospital, but she managed a faint smile.

"I would like to be one of the survivors, when all's said and done."

"You already are," Gallagher said. "Just remember that and you'll be fine."

Sarah thought about his words all the way up to Tony's room. Ron got her past the head nurse on the floor, then past the policeman standing guard outside Tony's room, but once inside, she was on her own. He left her at the doorway with a promise to return the moment he was needed.

Impulsively Sarah hugged him and then went to Tony.

Ron Gallagher flinched only once when her arms encircled his neck, and then he patted her gently, as he would have a child, and left in haste. There was a lot to do before the day got any older.

Fifteen

Sarah raced to Tony's side. He was asleep or unconscious, she wasn't sure which, but the monitor hooked to his heart showed a steady, even pulse, so she willed herself to relax. Except for a small white bandage on the side of his head just above his right eye, he appeared to be sleeping.

She leaned over and brushed his cheek with her lips. His skin was warm and supple. Cautiously she pulled a chair up beside his bed. For a moment she sat and watched his face; then, gently, she threaded her fingers through his, laid her head on the side of the bed and closed her eyes. She fell asleep with the memory of her own screams replaying in her mind.

Tony flinched as he opened his eyes, then wondered why it hurt to move. Groaning softly, he reached toward his head and saw he'd been hooked up to an IV.

"What the—" Suddenly he remembered. Sarah. Dear God, what had happened to—

"Tony, darling, don't move."

Her voice—her sweet, bossy voice—was next to his ear. All he could think was, *Thank you, God.*

"Sarah?"

She cupped his cheek, then patted his hand, easing his arm back onto the bed before he could disturb the IV.

"I'm here."

"He was in the house."

"I know, sweetheart. Please don't move. Just rest. We'll talk about it later."

But Tony wanted to talk about it now.

"What time is it?" he asked.

"Almost noon."

"Is it still today?"

"Technically, yes. The attack happened after midnight."

"I heard something downstairs and thought it was Dunn. He was on duty first. When I didn't find him, I went to his room. Dunn was lying on the floor. Farley was on the bed. I reached down to check on him, and someone hit me from behind. I turned my head just as I sensed their presence, but was too late to see anything but some black pants and black shoes."

"Gallagher said he heard the paramedics talking. They were guessing that both men had been drugged, and I've been trying to think when it might have happened. Now I think I know."

"But how?" Tony asked. "They were with us all the time."

"Right," Sarah said. "At Moira's party."

"You think someone slipped something to them there?"

"Where else?" she said. "I know they had a thermos of coffee with them. I saw Farley set it on the table in the foyer when Moira let us in."

"Did you tell Ron?"

She nodded. "I mentioned it on the way into Portland, but I had no idea who could have done it. During the evening, it could have been any one of the guests. We were all over the house, remember? Moira dragged us into the library to see her late husband's paintings, then back into the living room for an after-dinner brandy. I know I saw four different people talking to the bodyguards at one time or another, and everyone there was talking about them."

"But that means it was one of the guests."

"Not necessarily," Sarah said. "Someone could have come in and done it when we were all elsewhere in the house."

"Damn," Tony said. "For a minute I thought we had narrowed the field."

"I haven't done anything but cause you trouble," Sarah said. "And just so you know, I'm thinking seriously of leaving as soon as my father's remains are released."

He grabbed her hand. "No. You can't leave, Sarah. How will I know you're safe?"

"I don't know. I'll manage. But if I leave, at least I'll know you're out of harm's way." Then her voice broke. "When I saw you...just for a moment, I thought—"

Tony groaned softly, then pulled her close to him.

"Don't, baby. Don't cry. I knew what I was getting into. I was just careless, that's all."

"You don't owe me this kind of loyalty," she said. "Don't you understand? Whatever debt you feel you owed my father has long since been paid. Please, Tony. For your sake and my sanity, let me do this my way."

His chin jutted angrily. "No."

Sarah sighed. "You're crazy, you know that?"

"Crazy for you."

"Ah, Silk...there you go talking pretty."

"It's in my nature, baby. I can't give you up, so don't ask."

A long look passed between them, and finally she lowered her head in subjugation.

"I want to go home," Tony said.

Sarah grinned wryly.

"What's so funny?" he asked.

"The doctor...he was here earlier. I told him you'd say that."

Tony's smile was a bit wan, but the cockiness was still there.

"So what's holding up the process?"

"You," she said. "You wouldn't wake up."

"I'm awake now. Go find the man. I want out of here."

"He'll be back in a—"

"Either you find him or I will," Tony said. "There's nothing wrong with me but a bump on the head."

"Lord," Sarah muttered. "Give me a few minutes, okay?"

She had started toward the door when it occurred to Tony that he didn't want to let her out of his sight.

"Wait!"

"What now?" she asked.

"I don't want you wandering around the hospital by yourself. That nut might have followed you here."

"Oh, don't worry," she said. "Gallagher has a guard on your door and one outside assigned to me."

He relaxed, but only slightly. "Okay, then, but hurry back."

Sarah put her hands on her hips in a gesture of frustration.

"Either I find the doctor or I stay here, but I can't promise to hurry when I don't know where he is."

He grinned. "I like it when you get ticked."

She smiled back. "Oh...you have yet to see me really mad."

His eyes widened. "Am I going to like it?"

"Depends how much bloodshed you can stand."

He was laughing and holding his head when she left the room.

The ride home from the hospital would have been long and uncomfortable for Tony unless he'd gone in an ambulance, which he refused to do. So, being the take-charge man that he was, he'd chartered a helicopter. Sarah was still coming to terms with the ride when the pilot began circling the area over Flagstaff Lake near Tony's property. Tony had assured the pilot that there was ample space behind his house, but because of the slope of the land, the pilot had opted for the front area instead. That made a phone call necessary, and moments later they watched from the air as people spilled out of the house to move vehicles. Sarah counted two police cruisers, two vans belonging to the security team, the car in which Dunn and Farley had arrived, and another she didn't recognize. When an armed man came out of the house and moved it, Sarah suddenly remembered her aunt's imminent arrival and guessed it might be hers.

As for poor Dunn and Farley, they were no worse for wear once the sedatives they'd ingested had worn off, but they hadn't been any help in figuring out what had happened. Whatever they'd been given had not only knocked them out but had rendered their short-term memories blank. Their images had been tarnished, and the ride home in the chopper dashed what was left. Dunn had used the only airsick bag on the plane, so Farley had to use his hat. Both gruesome little mementos were tossed out of the chopper over a river, and Sarah had grinned as she'd watched the objects falling, hoping there were no unsuspecting fishermen below who were about to get a rather nasty surprise.

A minute or so later, the area in front of Tony's house was completely devoid of vehicles. The pilot gave Tony a nod of approval and down they went. Sarah heard Dunn burping behind her, and Farley made a slight gagging sound. Tony turned around and gave them a look, after which there was silence.

Moments later the chopper was on the ground. As soon as the doors opened, security spilled from behind every tree and out of the house until it looked as if the president of the United States himself must have landed. Sarah stifled a giggle of disbelief. She wanted to ask if all this firepower was necessary, but she knew that were it not for Tony's influence and interference in her life, she would already be dead.

"Wait," Tony mouthed, motioning for Sarah to stay inside, when she started to dismount.

She sat with the wind currents from the circulating rotors whipping her hair about her face and in her eyes until she thought she would go blind. It wasn't until a good half-dozen armed men stood before her that she was allowed to get out. Then they encircled her quickly. Before she could look to see where Tony had gone, she felt a guard on either side of her slide an arm around her waist. Her feet left the ground as they started to run. They carried her the entire one-hundred-plus yards from the chopper to the front door before they put her down. She was too taken aback to do more than mutter a quick thanks before they shoved her inside the house and shut the door.

She spun immediately, looking for Tony. He was, after all, the one who needed to be in bed, but he was nowhere in sight. She had started to backtrack, when someone called her name. She turned.

"Quite an entrance, baby girl," Lorett Boudreaux drawled.

"Aunt Lorett! Thank God you're here."

Sarah fell into her arms and just held her. She was safe. Now she was safe. Then she remembered Lorett's youngest daughter.

"Michelle…is she all right?"

Lorett smiled as she brushed her hands across Sarah's windswept hair.

"She is fine, *chère*. Don't you worry none about Michelle. Francois arrived. She has no more need for her mama."

"I have need of you," Sarah said, and then her eyes filled with tears. "Oh, Aunt Lorett. Terrible things are going on."

"I know, baby, I know. Some I knew before I came. Your sheriff, he has told me the rest."

"I don't know what to do," Sarah said. "I've put Tony in terrible danger by being in his home."

"He made his choices," she said. "I think he is man enough to stand by them."

At that point the front door opened and Tony walked in. He took one look at the woman beside

Sarah and knew that Aunt Lorett had finally arrived. She was looking at him, then almost through him, and in that moment he knew Sarah had not exaggerated Lorett's talents. He grinned.

Lorett's nostrils flared slightly as she looked at the man who had stolen her baby's heart. And she knew it was so, whether they did or not. His clothes were expensive—she could tell by the way they fit his body—and his olive-colored skin was pleasing to her eyes, as were his thick black hair and dark eyes. His body was muscular but lean, and his legs were long and strong. The small white bandage on his forehead was, to Lorett, a badge of his courage. He'd been hurt protecting her child.

"Come here to me," she said softly.

Tony found himself following her orders. When he stood before her, he held out his hand.

"Welcome to my home, Ms. Boudreaux."

"Lorett," she said softly, and hugged him.

Tony was surprised by the gesture, but pleased. It never hurt to be on the good side of one's in-laws-to-be, even though he had yet to inform Miss Whitman of his intentions. Then, to his further surprise, Lorett put her hand on his forehead and closed her eyes. Almost immediately, he felt heat.

Startled, he began to move back, but she gripped his arm, holding him fast.

"It's okay," Sarah said. "Trust me."

He stood still. Moments later, Lorett released him and stepped away.

"You were injured protecting my baby girl. I thank you."

Tony nodded, a little embarrassed in spite of himself, and quickly changed the subject.

"Have you found a room yet?" he asked. "There's one next door to Sarah."

She looked at Sarah and then Tony. Her lips twitched, but she didn't smile.

"I chose one downstairs," she said. "It is close enough."

Sarah blushed. Good Lord. Was she never to have a secret from this woman? Aunt Lorett knew that she and Tony were lovers. How embarrassing was that?

Tony grinned again, and this time he was the one who gave Lorett a hug.

"I knew I was going to like you," he said, and kissed her soundly on the cheek.

Lorett's laugh broke the tension between them, and she turned to Sarah.

"This man…he is something, Sarah Jane. You do not let him get away."

Sarah didn't know whether to say, "Yes,

ma'am,'' or tell her aunt to shut up. She opted for cautioning Tony instead.

"You need to be in bed," she said shortly.

A very devilish smile spread slowly across his face. "Why, Sarah, can't you at least wait until dark?"

Her eyes widened, and her jaw dropped. "Anthony DeMarco! Have you no shame?"

"No."

Lorett laughed again, only gentler, as she took Sarah into her arms.

"Never be ashamed of what is natural," she said. "This has been a long time in coming. It is no more than you deserve."

"Good lord," Sarah muttered. "I feel like I'm getting that sex talk all over again, only this time in front of an audience."

"If she leaves out any of the good parts, I'll be glad to fill you in," Tony offered.

Lorett threw back her head and laughed aloud.

"This man, he will fit into the family, you know. Let him be, Sarah Jane. It is part of why you love him." Then she gathered herself mentally and returned to the business at hand. "I am in the kitchen preparing food. When you feel hungry, you will come." With that, she swept out of the room with majesty in every step.

"She's the most amazing, stunning, intriguing woman I've met in quite a while—except for you, of course," Tony said.

Sarah laughed and shrugged. "No, it's okay. You can say it. After all it's the truth. Lorett is a kingdom unto herself. I'm just thankful she's on my side."

Tony nodded thoughtfully. "Yes, I think she would make a formidable enemy."

Sarah took him by the hand. "Are you hungry just yet?"

"Not really. I think I *will* go lie down, although to be truthful, my head feels fine."

"Of course," Sarah said. "She laid hands on you."

Tony frowned. "Yes, I know she touched the—" Then he frowned as he fingered the bandage. "Are you saying that she healed me...just by touching my head?"

"You said it no longer hurt. I think you've answered your own question. Now come to bed," she urged.

"Only if you come, too."

"For a minute, but only to tuck you in," Sarah said.

He grinned. "Did you say—?"

"Tuck. I said tuck, not—oh, never mind. Behave, or I'll have Dunn and Bradstreet put you to bed.''

''Dunn and Farley,'' he corrected.

''Whatever,'' she muttered. ''Now up!'' And she pointed toward the stairs.

It was just past two in the afternoon when Tony came downstairs. He had showered and changed into dark red sweats and was wearing thick woolly socks instead of shoes. His hair was still damp and sticking together in clumps, as if he'd used his fingers in lieu of a comb. He'd discarded the bandage on his forehead, leaving the wound open to the air. Except for a slight bump, some early bruising and four stitches, he looked as if nothing had happened.

''I feel great,'' he said, as he entered the kitchen. ''What smells so good?''

Sarah looked up from the table where she'd been thumbing through a cookbook.

''Soup. Want some?''

''Yes, please,'' he said, then followed her to the stove and watched her serve some into a bowl.

''Wow! What kind of soup is that?'' he asked.

''Aunt Lorett's cure-all soup.''

''Do I dare ask?''

''She always made it at home when any of us were sick or feeling sad.''

He carried it to the table and took the first bite, rolling his eyes in near ecstasy.

"Oh, man…this stuff could make her rich. Have you ever talked her into giving you the recipe?"

"I know the recipe," Sarah said. "I serve it at the restaurant from time to time."

"Smart woman," Tony said, and buttered a slice of warm French bread that Sarah set before him. "Have you had some?"

"Yes. I ate a couple of hours ago. Don't worry about me. Besides, I need to just sit here and watch you."

He happily swallowed a mouthful, then asked why.

"Last night, I thought I'd lost you."

Tony put down his spoon and reached for her hand.

"No," Sarah said. "I need to say this. Do you know what I was thinking all the way to Portland?"

He shook his head.

"That I'd waited too long to tell you the truth."

"What truth is that, Sarah Jane?"

"When I think about it, none of this makes much sense. I mean…we've hardly known each other for a week."

"No," Tony said. "I've known you all my life."

She smiled. "I know, but not as adults. You know what I mean."

He shrugged. "History is a great equalizer, honey girl, and we have a lot of history between us. I mean...you knew me when I had nothing, and you still didn't hate my guts."

She grinned shyly. "Oh, I had a monster crush on you then, and you know it."

He beamed. "See! All we've done is confirm the fact that you had the hots for me."

She laughed. "If I had the hots at the age of ten, I wasn't sure what it meant. But I will say that I used to hide behind the shrubbery when you came to mow and all but held my breath until you got hot enough that you finally took off your shirt."

Tony grinned and winked. "Like I said...the hots."

"Okay, okay, but let me finish."

He nodded and took another spoonful of soup.

"I owe you much more than my life. In this short space of time, you've made me believe in love again, and I would have sworn that wasn't possible."

"It's easy, baby, because you're easy to love."

"Am I, Silk? Am I really?"

Tony stopped, leaned across the table and kissed her hard and swift.

"I want you to promise me something," he said.

"Anything."

His eyes darkened as his gaze raked her face. "Be careful. I may ask something of you that you don't want to give."

"Never."

"Would you leave New Orleans?" he asked.

"What do you mean?"

"Would you live somewhere else?"

"Depends on where and with whom."

He kissed her again. This time softer. This time longer.

"Remember that," he whispered, then pulled back and tilted her chin, making her look him straight in the eyes. "About that promise."

She waited.

"Promise that you'll never doubt me or yourself again."

She exhaled softly. "I can do that. Now eat your soup before you say something you might regret."

"Never."

She held the thought to her heart as he finished his food. *If* only this mess were over. *If* only they could really focus on a relationship instead of just staying alive. *If* only. Then she thought of her aunt's favorite saying.

If never got anything done. Maybe it was done.

As Tony was carrying his dish to the sink, the doorbell rang. Sarah turned, then stopped, knowing that she was no longer allowed to answer the door. Moments later, Lorett came into the kitchen with a scowl on her face.

"There is a woman at the door who wants to talk to your man."

"Who is it?" Tony asked.

"I didn't ask her name."

"Why not?" Sarah asked.

"Because there's an evil in her heart," Lorett said, and left the room.

Sixteen

Laura Hilliard was in the foyer, being detained by one of the armed guards, when Tony entered the hall. She saw the wound on his head, threw her hands up in dismay and started toward him.

"Tony! Dear God! Then the gossip is true."

The guard stepped in front of her, barring her way.

"It's okay," Tony said. "Let her by."

Laura pushed past the guard, her indignation showing, and threw herself into Tony's arms. Sarah arrived just as Laura was wailing over the wound on his head.

Laura looked over Tony's shoulder, and the expression on her face took Sarah aback. It was full of anger and hate.

"It's all your fault!" Laura cried. "If he hadn't involved himself with your disgusting—"

Immediately, Tony took Laura by the shoulders and thrust her back.

"Watch what you say," he said softly. "You are an old friend, but it gives you no right to talk about me or my business...and Sarah is my business."

Laura's eyes glittered angrily. "She's nothing, Silk. I have money. More money than I will ever be able to spend. Remember when we used to talk about what we would do if—"

"I was a kid, Laura. I was fifteen years old. And you weren't."

Red spots appeared on her cheeks beneath her perfectly applied makeup.

"So what? You were always older than your years. I was your first, Silk. You loved me then."

Sarah wanted to disappear, but leaving then would make it seem as if she was running away, and she had run for the very last time.

"I loved making love," Tony said. "But I didn't know the meaning of the word."

Laura sneered and looked at Sarah, and as she did, every year of her age suddenly showed on her face.

"And you think you do now?"

Tony stepped in front of Sarah, putting himself between her and the venom of Laura's behavior.

"I know that I do," he said. "I also know that you've outstayed your welcome. Maybe it would be better if you left."

Laura lifted her chin and smiled, but it wasn't a pretty smile, nor was it friendly. She looked at Tony and stepped to one side, fixing her gaze on Sarah's face.

"It's too bad," she drawled, "that—"

"Don't finish that thought."

They all turned around, suddenly aware that Lorett had overheard the incident.

Laura glared as Lorett approached, but it lost much of its intensity when she had to crane her neck to look up.

"You don't threaten my baby," Lorett said. "Go home before you give voice to the ugliness that is in your heart."

Laura took a step back in spite of herself.

"You can't tell me what to do," she said.

"You got rich on your back...and when you got too old for the men to pay what you wanted, you sold your soul to the devil."

All the blood seemed to flow from Laura's face. She wanted to run but was too stunned to move.

"You're lying," she muttered. "You don't know what you're talking about."

"Babies," Lorett said. "You sold babies."

Laura gasped. There was no one still living who knew that.

"You're a witch," she snapped.

Tony was too stunned to speak, but the truth was there in the fear on Laura's face.

"You go now," Lorett said. "Do not speak my Sarah's name. Do not even think of her face. If you do, I will know. And you will be sorrier than you can imagine."

Laura squeaked. It was the only word that fit the sound coming out of her throat. One moment she was fumbling for her purse, and the next she was gone.

"Good God!" Tony said, and looked at Lorett in disbelief. "How did you know that?"

"I saw it in her heart," Lorett said.

"You can't really know what she's thinking...can you?"

Lorett smiled. "She doesn't know that, though...does she?"

"Well," Sarah said, "at least that's one name we can remove from the suspect list."

"What do you mean?" Tony said.

"Now that we know she didn't rob a bank for her money...figure it out for yourself."

"Oh. Right."

"Someone else comes," Lorett said.

Tony looked at Lorett again, half expecting to see flames coming out of her mouth.

"How do you know?" he asked.

She pointed toward the window. "I saw them drive up."

Sarah burst into laughter as Tony grinned sheepishly.

"See what I mean?" she said. "As children, we never knew when she was serious and when she was teasing."

Moments later, Maury Overstreet was in the house. He took one look at Lorett and started grinning.

"Silk, my man...your taste in women gets better and better. Can she cook as good as the other one?"

"Shut up," Tony muttered. "You don't know who you're messing with."

"Haven't had the pleasure," he said, and held out his hand to Lorett. "Maury Overstreet, at your service."

To their surprise, Lorett not only shook his hand but grinned as she did it.

"I am Lorett Boudreaux."

She said it in the manner of a queen addressing a subject, but Maury took no offense. Instead, he squinted curiously, studying the symmetry of her features and the tilt of her head atop a long, elegant neck. The jade-green sweater she was wearing was the perfect foil for the black silk pants that covered her extremely long legs. She wore her hair naturally, letting it fall in thick, heavy ringlets about her face and then to the top of her shoulders, using two ivory combs for decoration.

"Bantu, by way of New Orleans," Maury said.

It was the first time Sarah had ever seen Lorett at a loss for words. Finally, she nodded.

"Yes...my ancestors were Bantu. How do you know this?"

"I been to Africa a time or two in my youth. You had the same look as this woman I knew there. She was some sort of a bigwig of her tribe. As for the New Orleans part...it's in your voice, don't you know?"

"Have you eaten, little man?" she asked.

It was all Maury could do not to cry. "Not lately," he said, and then looked at Tony. "Could we talk over whatever it is she's gonna feed me?"

Sarah started to grin. "A fair-weather suitor if I ever saw one. And here I thought he'd been pining away for me."

Tony rolled his eyes at Maury and led the way to the kitchen.

It wasn't until Maury's second bowl of soup that he started to talk.

"Miss Whitman, it was like you said. Your old man went to his lodge meetings real regular. He was well-thought-of by all concerned until him and the money went missing. Now...before you get all huffy at me, I know that's because they both disappeared at the same time.''

"So what are you going to do? That notation on the calendar has to mean something.''

He tipped his soup bowl and poured what was left in his spoon, then slurped it into his mouth.

Lorett beamed. There was nothing she liked better than to see someone enjoying her food.

"Oh, I didn't say I was through. Not by a long shot," he said. "I'm still on the move. Don't count Maury out yet.''

Then he leaned forward and took a notepad from his pocket.

"What can you tell me about your mother? Like...did she belong to any clubs? What did she do on a regular basis?''

Sarah frowned. It had been so long ago, and she'd tried to block the biggest part of it from her memory.

"I remember a few things...like she belonged to Friends of the Library and the Garden Club. I went with her to the Garden Club sometimes during the summer when school was out.''

"Anything else?'' Maury asked. "Did she have a special friend?''

"You mean a female friend?''

"Whatever," Maury said.

Sarah glared. "If you're trying to insinuate that my mother was cheating on my father, then you can—"

"She was not," Lorett said briefly.

Maury looked up. "Did you live here at the time?"

"I did not."

"Where did you live?" he asked.

"New Orleans."

"And you know for a fact that Sarah's mother was on the up-and-up?"

"I know."

He stared at her for a few seconds more and then nodded. "Okay."

"Why do you believe her and not me?" Sarah asked.

Maury looked at Sarah as if she were a silly child who'd asked a silly question. Still he answered.

"That Bantu woman I knew in Africa...she had the sight, too."

"Oh."

"Next question," Tony muttered, trying hard to assimilate the fact that he was actually sitting in on a conversation where everyone believed in ESP and voodoo but him.

"Think back," Maury said, addressing his question to Sarah. "What did your mother do on a regular basis that was outside the house?"

It was as if a light came on in Sarah's memory. She sat up and leaned forward, her voice excited and light.

"She used to come to my school. Every Wednesday. She was the helper for the day, and I loved it."

"Like a teacher's aide kind of thing?" Maury asked.

"Yes. Marmet is small. There was never any funding for it, so parents volunteered their time."

"So every Wednesday afternoon your mother was at your school, and every other Wednesday night, your father was at his lodge meetings."

"Yes, unless they were sick, or something like that."

He nodded, then pecked on his notepad where he'd written "Moose—1:00 p.m."

"And we know your father was in the bank during this time every day, because I've checked with a couple of people who worked there then. They said he always took the early lunch from eleven to twelve so that he could be in the bank for the customers who needed to see him on their own lunch breaks."

"Then what does this mean?" Tony asked.

"Don't know yet, but I'm gonna find out," Maury said. "Don't guess there's any more goodies in that box of yours that would help me?"

"It's too late now," Sarah said. "It was stolen last night when Tony was attacked."

Maury glanced at the stitches on Tony's head. "Sorry about that," he said. "I didn't mention it earlier 'cause I figured that woman of yours probably dented it with one of her pans."

There was a moment of stunned silence, and then everyone laughed.

"I'm not violent," Sarah said.

Maury looked at her and shook his head. "But you could be," he said, then added, "If you was provoked."

"Well, I never," Sarah said, then leaned back in her chair, for once in her life too stunned to retaliate.

As Tony escorted the little man to the door, Sarah had to ask, "Aunt Lorett?"

"What?"

"Do you think I could be violent?"

Lorett turned from the sink where she was standing, and for once didn't answer as quickly as Sarah expected.

"Aunt Lorett?"

Lorett exhaled a sigh. "It doesn't matter what I think," she said. "Go about your business, child."

Sarah stood up, suddenly afraid to hear the rest of this sitting down.

"I want to know," she said. "Tell me."

Lorett looked away once, then met Sarah's gaze.

"If you had to, you would kill."

Sarah staggered as if she'd been punched. "I don't understand."

"You don't have to," Lorett said. "All that means is you have the strength to protect those you love. Now go away. I have food to prepare."

"I promised Tony I'd make him an angel pie."

"It is too damp for such a thing," she said. "The meringue would fall."

"I guess you're right."

"Of course I am," Lorett said. "You make him such a thing next summer, when it is dry."

Next summer? That was so far away. Did that mean they would be together next summer, or was that Lorett's way of getting her out of her hair?

The killer was going through the belongings that had been in Whitman's box. Except for the daily calendar, it contained nothing but trinkets and pictures of no consequence. Leafing through the pages of the calendar, at first the killer saw nothing to set off an alarm—until… It took a few minutes for the realization to dawn as to why such a thing would be on Whitman's calendar.

The killer looked, then looked again, for the first time seeing the handwriting on the pages, rather than what had been written.

"Oh my God."

The calendar dropped unnoticed onto the floor.

It wasn't Whitman's writing.

And in that moment, the killer knew that if anyone else saw the truth, it would be the end of everything.

There hadn't been a fire in the fireplace since the previous night, but one was soon started, and the killer began feeding the pages of the calendar into the flames until they were gone.

The next morning, Tiny Bartlett came running into her house, tossing her purse aside as she raced for the phone. She had a cell phone in her purse, but this wasn't the kind of news one passed on within earshot of others. She wanted the privacy of her room, with her feet up and a drink in her hand.

She poured a glass of red wine, then kicked off her shoes as she sat down on the sofa. Annabeth's number was on her speed dial. Since it was Saturday, Annabeth would be home instead of at work.

She hit the number quickly, then took a sip of her wine and a deep, calming breath.

Annabeth answered on the second ring.

"Hello."

"Annabeth, it's me, Tiny. You'll never guess what I heard."

"What?"

"Laura Hilliard left town."

"No!"

"Yes. I heard it at the post office. Thelma was saying how Laura had left an address for her mail to be forwarded to."

"But she just bought that fancy house on the lake and all."

"I know. And that's not all," Tiny said.

"Well tell me, girl, before I die of old age," Annabeth said.

"Someone broke into Tony DeMarco's house. He went to the hospital in Portland by ambulance and came home the next day by helicopter! Can you believe it? Henry Taylor—he's one of the deputies, you know—said the thing set down right in the front yard."

"Well, my Lord," Annabeth gasped. "A helicopter."

"And that's not all. That woman is back...the one who took Sarah away as a child."

Annabeth shuddered. "That voodoo woman?"

"Oh, hush! I don't believe in such things. Do you?"

"I don't suppose," Annabeth said. "But still, she's got eyes that look right through you."

"That's because you were mean to Catherine Whitman," Tiny said shortly. She didn't like having her word disputed.

"It wasn't my decision to remove her from the Fall Festival committee. I was just doing what I was told."

"Never mind," Tiny said. "What are you doing today? Want to go calling on Tony?"

"Do we dare?"

"Of course," Tiny said. "I mean...he's a friend and he was injured. It's only neighborly to visit. I'll stop by the bakery and pick up a coffee cake."

"I don't mind. Want to call the others?"

"I'll call Marcia. You call Moira."

"Okay," Annabeth said.

"We'll meet at Moira's and then go together."

"At one?"

"Sounds good to me."

Within an hour, the four women had a plan and an excuse to find out more about the gossip that was flying around their little town. Between the FBI investigating anyone with a bank account and the private investigator who Tony DeMarco had hired, Marmet was a riot just waiting to happen.

They arrived without calling ahead, afraid they would be told not to come, and pasted on smiles as they adjusted their hair and their baked goods and started toward the door, only to be met by an armed guard on the steps.

"We're friends of Mr. DeMarco," Moira said. "I live just down the road."

"I'm sorry, ma'am, but you'll have to wait."

He disappeared inside, leaving the four women on the steps with cake in their hands and indignation on their faces. Before they could break into a disagreeable hiss, the door opened again and Tony ushered them in.

"I didn't expect all this," he said.

"Oh, I know we should have called," Moira said, "but as soon as we heard what had happened to you, we just had to come pay our respects."

"That's quite considerate of you, although the food was really unnecessary. I didn't die."

"And thank goodness for that," Tiny squeaked, and thrust a coffee cake into his hands. "Cinnamon raisin. It's my favorite."

He looked at the offerings the others had brought and decided to get it done all at once.

"Maybe you'd all better follow me to the

kitchen. We'll cut this coffee cake, have a cup of coffee, and you can say hello to Sarah in the bargain.''

"Oh...goody," Tiny added. Last night she'd been spared most of Sarah's antagonism, but she was wary, just the same. Matching wits was something at which she sucked, and she hated being made to look foolish.

Sarah looked up from the roast she was preparing as they trooped into the kitchen single file.

"Well. I see we have visitors," she said.

"We came to see how Tony was doing," Moira said quickly, then offered her cheek for Sarah to kiss.

Sarah was saved from the task by waving her hands in front of Moira's face.

"I'm all messy," she said. "Excuse me while I wash up."

"Oh. Yes. Certainly," Moira said, eyeing the rib roast Sarah had been stuffing. "This roast looks marvelous."

"Thank you," Sarah said. "I see you four have been busy, as well. You brought Tony some goodies."

"They're just bakery goods," Marcia said, and set her pie down on the counter. "Nothing as fancy as your homemade things, I'm sure."

"It's the thought that counts," Tony said, and seated the women at the kitchen table.

Sarah grinned to herself as she took plates from the cabinets, then handed them to Tony, who proceeded to serve the coffee cake. Never had she seen four women more out of place in a kitchen.

Tiny was wearing cashmere, and her wool coat had a mink collar. When Marcia took off her coat, Sarah would have bet a month's profits from Ma Chère that her clothes were pure silk. Annabeth was wearing a soft plum wool suit, while Moira's pantsuit was a slinky beige. Their hair was plastered down with hair spray, and their makeup made her think of war paint, rather than an adornment for their faces. Between the jewels in their ears and those on their fingers and around their necks, they could most likely have fed a small country for a year.

"Coffee, anyone?"

They nodded absently, completely absorbed in the story Tony was telling them of his encounter with the intruder.

Marcia was taking her second bite of cake and Annabeth was stirring sugar into her coffee when Lorett entered the kitchen. She eyed the women with a mixture of curiosity and disdain, regally waiting for an introduction.

Tony knew from their expressions that Lorett had arrived. It was all he could do not to laugh. He turned and held out his hand, quickly pulling Lorett into the fold.

"Everyone...this is Sarah's aunt Lorett Boudreaux, from New Orleans. Lorett, from your left, Tiny Bartlett, Marcia Farrell, Moira Blake and Annabeth Harold."

"We're so pleased to meet you...again," Tiny said, and then giggled for lack of anything else to say.

"So you've met before?" Tony asked.

"Years ago," Lorett said. "At Catherine's funeral."

"Aunt Lorett, would you care for a piece of cake?"

Lorett eyed the bakery confectionary askance and then shook her head once.

"I think not...but thank you, of course."

Sarah turned away to keep from letting the women see her smile, but this was doing her more good than a full-page apology in the local paper would have. To see these four silly women put in their place by nothing more than a look was priceless. Before anyone could comment further, Tony's cell phone rang. He excused himself and answered it. It was Maury.

"Tony, here's the deal," Maury said. "I've been running down this 'moose' thing, trying to find anything in the area that had 'moose' as part of the name. I'm on my way south right now. There's supposed to be an old tavern called the Moose and Duck on the way back to Portland, as well as a Christmas tree farm called Moose Tracks. Ever heard of them?"

"Actually, I have, though they don't mean anything special to me."

"Right. Also, there was one other lead, but the old man I talked to couldn't remember where the place was, only that it had once existed. Ever heard of an old motel called Moose Landing?"

Tony frowned, trying to remember back twenty years, but nothing rang a bell.

"I haven't," he said. "But hang on a minute, will you? There are some locals here who might be able to help."

"You got it," Maury said.

Tony returned to the kitchen. "Excuse me, ladies, but I'd like to pick your brains for a moment."

"Certainly," Annabeth said. "How can we help?"

"My private investigator is looking for an old

motel called Moose Landing. Have any of you ever heard of it, or know where it is?''

Moira looked blank. Annabeth leaned over toward Marcia and whispered an aside. Tiny was blushing.

''What?'' Tony asked.

''Well,'' Tiny said, ''it's not there anymore.''

''You mean it's gone?'' Tony asked.

''Not exactly,'' she said. ''I think the buildings are still there, but it closed down years ago. The owners lived behind one of the units. They might still be in residence, but I couldn't say for sure.''

Marcia punched Tiny on the arm and grinned.

''Tiny Bartlett, you sly thing. I can't believe you ever frequented the Landing. It's not quite up to your usual style.''

Tiny blushed a little brighter. ''Well...when we were kids, Charlie and I had to have somewhere to meet. I mean, Daddy was so against our marriage and—''

''Never mind,'' Tony said. ''I don't need the details of your personal life. Just the location of the place.''

''Take the highway north out of Marmet and follow the signs to Canada. It's just across the border,'' Marcia said.

Moira looked aghast. "You mean you've been there, too?"

"Oh, shut up, Moira," Marcia said. "You know where it is. I even saw your car there once."

"You didn't!" Moira gasped.

Marcia shrugged. "One that looked just like it, then, right down to that handicapped parking sticker on the windshield."

Tony rolled his eyes at Sarah, as if to say, "This is now in your hands," and stepped back into the hallway to pass the information on to Maury.

"Which way are you headed?" he asked, after the little man had taken down the information.

"South, I reckon. Then I'll check out this Landing place sometime early tomorrow."

"Keep me posted."

"You know it," Maury said, and disconnected.

Tony dropped the phone back in his pocket and reentered the kitchen just as Annabeth and Tiny began to square off.

"Ladies," Tony drawled, reminding them that they were supposed to be just that.

There was a moment of shocked silence, and then Tiny giggled. Annabeth followed with a sigh. Marcia managed a wry grin. But Moira wasn't smiling. She drew her indignation about her like a winter coat and stood.

"I think it's time we were going," she said. "After all, dear Tony was just released from the hospital, and here we are, letting him wait on us. It's a disgrace. That's what it is."

She looked at Sarah disparagingly, as if laying the blame at her feet, then patted her on the cheek before heading to the door.

"Thank you for coming," Sarah called.

Tony looked back at her and grinned. She was taunting them, and he knew it. He kept thinking about the years that lay ahead of them and knew that no matter what else, he would never be bored.

Seventeen

Maury's visits to the Moose and Duck, as well as the Moose Tracks farm, turned up nothing that gave him a clue as to what had happened to Franklin Whitman.

It was almost nine o'clock in the evening when he pulled up at his motel room and parked. It was unhandy as hell not having a motel in Marmet. The only bed-and-breakfast was shut down because of some family illness. This little ski lodge above the Sugarloaf Mountain ski area had been the closest he could find. It was too early in the season for skiers, and except for the owners, Tom and Morris Fenton, he was the only resident. The dining room wasn't open after eight in the evening, which not only made for quiet nights, it was also a little boring.

Tomorrow he would check out Moose Landing. For now, he wanted nothing more than some food and a good night's sleep. He thought about Silk, living out there in that fine house with two of the best cooks he'd ever encountered. Some men had all the luck.

Sighing wearily, he got out of the car, picked up his box of rapidly cooling pizza and warming six-pack of beer, and hurried to his room.

It had been years since the killer had been anywhere near Moose Landing. The sign that had indicated where to turn was long gone, but the road was as familiar now as it had been then. Twice a month, the trip here had been vital in keeping sanity intact. So many plans had been made. So many dreams had been lived under the gray shake shingles of Cabin Ten.

When the killer finally pulled up at the motel and parked, the glare of headlights highlighted what the ensuing years had done to the Landing. Once, neat green shutters had adorned small white cabins, built in two long rows facing one another. Time had not been kind.

Although it was difficult to tell in the dark, it appeared as if three cabins had burned. What remained of the blackened two-by-four boards in the walls now pointed skyward like charred bones. The other cabins had sagging roofs, missing shutters and stoops, and were badly in need of paint. But in the dark, it was easy to look past the decay. For a moment time slid backward as memories came rushing back.

Then, suddenly, the porch light came on in the very first cabin, and an elderly man stepped out on the stoop.

"Can I help you?" he asked.

The killer got out.

The old man peered into the night, trying to see past the headlights of the car, and saw nothing but a silhouette.

"Are you lost?" he asked.

"No."

"We ain't open for business no more," the old man said.

The killer walked closer. If the old man's memory was as bad as these buildings, then this trip might not be necessary.

But fate was not on the old man's side.

The killer came closer, then closer still, until they were standing face-to-face. The old man squinted, then started to smile.

"Why...I know you, don't I?" he said.

The killer sighed. "I was afraid you'd say that."

The gunshot was sudden and loud. The old man's face crumpled in disbelief as he staggered backward into his little home. He died on the floor with his hands to his chest, as if trying to stem the rapid exit of his blood.

Angrily shoving the body the rest of the way into the cabin, the killer made a brief scan of the room, taking in the jumble of furniture and books and, finally, the old man.

"Sorry, but it was a matter of life and death…namely mine."

Moments later, the car was gone and, the seclusion and silence that had always been the Landing's draw resumed.

It was just after eight in the morning when Maury Overstreet pulled up in front of what was left of Moose Landing. He didn't think much of his chances of finding anyone on the premises as he got out of the car, but he'd come this far. The least he could do was look around.

There was a porch light burning at the first little cabin. He took his coffee cup from the holder on the dash, dropped what was left of his cigarette onto the ground and started to crush it with his shoe when he realized he was looking at fresh tracks, both tire and human.

Suddenly the hair rose on the back of his neck, and he set the cup down on the hood of the car and pulled his gun instead. There was no reason why such ordinary things should give him pause to worry, but he had survived Vietnam and the ensuing years because he'd listened to that inner voice, and he wasn't about to ignore it now.

"Hello the house," he called.

No one answered.

He was on the small stoop when he saw the first of the blood. Then he looked up. There was more on the door. He stared at the doorknob, knowing that if he opened the door in the usual way, he might destroy any lingering prints. So he walked off the stoop and began circling the small cabin, looking for another way in. He found it almost immediately as he reached the back. A screened-in porch had been added, and both the screen and the door to the house were unlocked.

The moment he walked inside, he knew that death was there, too. The scent of someone's last meal had been fouled by the stench of feces and blood. His tiny body curled in on itself as he moved through the small kitchen, past the hodgepodge assortment of old furniture and books to where he could see into the living room.

And then he saw the body—an old man, lying in a pool of his own blood. A cat sat nearby, lapping at the blood, and before he thought, Maury grabbed it, raced through the kitchen and flung it outside.

The cat squalled in protest as it hit the ground running, then hunkered under a bush, a few feet away. Once, in 'Nam, Maury and two of his buddies had come upon the partially eaten body of a young soldier lying in the mud. A half-dozen pigs had encircled what was left of the boy, grunting and tearing at his flesh.

They'd killed the pigs and then reclaimed the soldier's dog tags. It was all they'd been able to do. But Maury had never gotten over the sight. Now, seeing that cat had brought back the nightmare and all that accompanied it. Cursing in three languages with his head between his knees, Maury trembled and cursed until he was out of breath. He was still shaking when he finally reached for his phone.

He made the call to the authorities, then sat down to wait, knowing this was going to take time he hadn't planned. But he would do for the old man what they hadn't been able to do for that boy back in 'Nam. He would wait for someone to take away the body and make sure the tire tracks and footprints out front were not accidentally obscured before the Royal Canadian Mounted Police had time to investigate.

"And why were you here?" the Mountie asked Maury again, and again Maury took out his Private

Investigator License and started explaining about
the discovery of Franklin Whitman's body in Flagstaff Lake and the FBI who'd come to Marmet, as
well as the attempt that had been made on Sarah
Whitman's life.

"And you are working for Miss Whitman?" the
Mountie asked.

"In a roundabout way," Maury said. "I was
hired by her friend, but on her behalf."

"I see. And what was it you were trying to accomplish here...? Link some notation on a desk
calendar to Moose Landing?"

"I don't know that this 'moose' was the one
mentioned, but I've been checking out every business, old and new, with 'moose' as part of the
name."

"Who else knew you were doing this?"

Maury sighed. "About half of Marmet, maybe
more."

"That isn't going to be of much help," the
Mountie said.

"Tell me 'bout it," Maury muttered, then looked
up as someone in a blue minivan pulled up at the
scene.

"That would be Mr. Havenworth's daughter,
Claudia. Please excuse me a moment. There are a

few more questions I'd like to ask before you leave.''

Maury nodded, in no hurry to leave, because then he would have to face the fact that his leads had come to a dead end.

He watched the woman receiving the news of her father's demise and regretted her sorrow as she covered her face and cried. A few moments later she was led into the building to identify the body, then back out again. She was pale and shaking as she stumbled to the side of the building and threw up.

Maury waited until she was a bit more herself then went to his car, took a flask of whiskey from the glove box and headed to the old picnic table where she was sitting. He thrust it in her face without introduction.

''Have a swig,'' he said gruffly. ''It'll help.''

To his surprise, she took the flask, and a drink, without even bothering to see who had offered it. Not until she handed it back did she look up.

''Who are you?'' she asked.

Maury sat down beside her. ''I'm the man who found the body,'' he said. ''He was your father?''

She nodded, her face still blotchy and swollen from crying.

Maury noted absently that she was one of those

women who didn't cry pretty. Some did. Some didn't. She was one of the latter.

"Real sorry for your loss," he added.

"I have to say, I'm not all that surprised that it happened, although we expected it years ago, while the Landing was in full swing. Not now. It's been over for years."

It was the last thing Maury had expected her to say. "Why do you say that?" he asked.

She shrugged. "In the old days, the Landing was a hangout for people having affairs and the place where the local hookers took their men. You know. The family tried to get Dad to give it up more than once, but he liked the drama of it all, I think."

Maury nodded. "Yeah, it can get that way for a fella. Sort of like an addiction, I guess."

She looked at Maury more closely. "You're not a cop, are you?"

"Private investigator."

"Why did you come here? Did you get lost?"

"No. I was looking for this place, only I got here a little too late."

"Why on earth would anyone want to look here? There's nothing left."

"Maybe memories… I wanted to ask your father some questions…see if he remembered the people who came here."

She rolled her eyes. "Oh, he would have remembered, all right. He still talked about the regulars. I used to clean the rooms out here and—"

Maury grabbed her by the arm. "You worked here?"

She shrugged out of his grasp to blow her nose, then nodded.

"For more than ten years. My ex-husband left me with two babies to raise. I had no skills, and Dad let me set my own hours."

"If I showed you some pictures, do you think you might recognize the faces?"

She shrugged. "Maybe."

"I'll be right back."

A few minutes later, Maury had the few pictures Sarah Whitman had given him spread out on the tabletop.

"Ever hear the name Franklin Whitman?" he asked.

Her mouth dropped. "Isn't that the name of the guy they fished out of Flagstaff Lake the other day?"

"Yes, but did you know him before?"

She frowned, then shook her head. "It doesn't ring any bells, other than what I just said."

Maury pointed to the pictures. The first one was the one from Whitman's desk. It was of him, his wife Catherine, and Sarah as a child, wearing their Christmas outfits. The other was the group picture of the bank's employees, taken for the celebration of the seventy-fifth anniversary.

He slid the family picture toward her.

"Recognize anyone in this picture?"

She stared, finally shaking her head. "Nice family, though."

Damn. Another dead end. He pushed the bank picture toward her.

"This is another picture of the same man. Here he's not smiling. Maybe he looks different to you."

"Where is he?" she asked.

Maury pointed.

She leaned closer, peering intently at the face he indicated, then let her gaze slide to the others beside him. Suddenly she pointed.

"I recognize him!" she cried. "A regular. Used to see his car every couple of weeks."

Maury picked up the picture, checking the names on the back against the faces, then frowned, trying to fit the pieces of this ever-widening puzzle together.

"I recognize her, too," she said, tapping the glass on the front of the frame.

Maury turned the picture around.

"They were quite a couple in those days," Claudia said.

"They came together?" Maury asked.

"No, in separate cars. And the reason I remember is they always came in the daytime, when I was at work. Not at night, like most of the others."

"What time of day?" Maury asked.

"I'm not sure. It was so long ago. But it would have to be after ten and before three, because that's when I left work. I had to get home before my kids got out of school, you see."

"Well, I'll be damned," Maury said, and then looked up at the woman. "You know...you might have just pointed out your father's killer."

She gasped.

"You don't mean it?"

"We'll see," he said softly. "We'll definitely see." Then he stood abruptly. "Ma'am, it's been real nice knowing you. I'm sorry your father is dead."

He raced to the car and pulled out his notes, comparing them against the identifications that had just been made.

Larry Romfield, casually known as Sonny, father of two children, husband to Eloise, had died two days after the robbery.

Moira Blake, retired a couple of years ago after

a lifetime of devotion to the bank. Husband was paralyzed from the waist down after a hunting accident. Died six years ago after more than twenty-five years in a wheelchair.

So Sonny and Moira were having a white-hot affair. How did that link them to what had happened to Whitman?

Sonny was dead. Moira stayed on at the bank and lived quietly in the same house she was married in. No outward show of money or instant wealth. No sudden accumulation of things out of their financial realm. So why did Franklin Whitman's calendar have their assignations on it?

And then something occurred to him. What if it wasn't Whitman's calendar? Hadn't Sarah Whitman said something about an old man named Harmon Weatherly clearing out both desks at the same time? What if he'd mixed up the calendars by mistake? On the surface, it wouldn't have mattered. But then Whitman's body was discovered, and his only surviving relative had to come back to claim it. The case was automatically reopened by the local police, and since Whitman obviously hadn't run off with the money after all, the Feds were back in the area, looking for the thief.

And then out comes Harmon Weatherly with a

box of Whitman's belongings, gives them to Sarah, and the shit hits the fan. Somehow the killer discovered that the calendars had been mixed up and knew that if someone started questioning the notations, the years of freedom were over.

And since Sonny Romfield had been dead and buried all these long years ago, there was only one person who had any stake in making sure the truth never came to light.

His lover. Moira Blake.

Maury didn't know how they'd done it, or how Whitman had come to die, but he would bet his sorry ass that he'd just solved a bank robbery and a twenty-year-old homicide. He grinned to himself. Damn, he was good. He was going to have to up his going rate.

He bolted out of the car and headed back to the lodge and the Mounties. They had a stake in what he'd just found out—as much, if not more, than Sarah. Unlike this poor old man, she, at least, was still alive.

Once he'd given them the information, he raced to his car and peeled out of the driveway, leaving the Landing and all its secrets in the dust. He dialed Tony's number as he drove, then cursed beneath his breath as the screen light indicated a failing battery. He tossed the phone in the seat beside him and pressed on the accelerator. It was less than an hour to DeMarco's house. He could tell him face-to-face.

"They've arrested Charles Bartlett!" Sarah cried, as Tony walked back into the house.

"What?"

"It's Ron Gallagher," she said, her voice shaking with relief. "He'll tell you himself."

Tony took the phone from Sarah, then pulled her close, hugging her as he spoke.

"Ron? Is this true?"

Gallagher was all but laughing. The relief of catching the man was like a chemical high.

"We got an anonymous tip last night. I got a search warrant early this morning, and we went to the Bartlett house. I showed him the warrant, and he looked surprised but agreeable. I asked if he owned any hunting rifles. He said yes. When we asked to see them, he handed them over, cool as can be. One had been shot very recently and hadn't been cleaned. I asked if he'd been hunting. He vehemently denied it, but we took the guns in for testing and him in for questioning. Tests came back that the gun was a match for the shell and slug we took out of your house. We arrested him on the spot."

"Are you saying he's also the one who robbed the bank and killed Frank Whitman?"

"The Feds are happy with the case. So am I. Why else would he want Sarah dead?" Ron asked. "If he'd managed to shut her up soon enough, the investigation would probably have died of its own accord for lack of evidence. It was her constant presence in Marmet that kept everything stirred up."

"I can't believe it," Tony said. "He's just a few years older than me. Maybe four, at the most. He pulled off a million-dollar bank robbery, framed Franklin Whitman and married the richest girl in town—and no one ever suspected him?"

"Seems like it," Gallagher said.

"I guess," Tony said. "Well, thanks for calling."

He hung up the phone, turned and gave Sarah a huge hug.

"It's over!" Sarah cried. "Thank God, it's over."

Tony smiled and rejoiced along with her, but all the time he kept thinking that something wasn't right. He'd known Charlie Bartlett his whole life, and even in his worst days running with the gangs, he just hadn't seemed smart enough to pull all that off, especially alone.

"The guards can go home. Everyone can go home," Sarah said.

"Even you?"

The tension in his voice tempered her elation.

"I didn't mean that the way it came out," she said. "I'm not trying to get away from you."

He smiled but didn't comment. The pain of separation was already becoming a reality, and he didn't like the way it felt.

"I guess I'd better alert my security team to pack up," he said.

"Dunn and Farley are already packing," she said. "They were with me when I got the news."

"Fat lot of good they were," he said.

"It wasn't their fault they were drugged. There are women getting drugged all the time, only they usually wind up being raped, as well, and never remember a thing about where they were or who did it."

He grimaced. "I know. I know. So I owe them an apology."

Sarah smiled. "One of the things I like best about you is your sense of fair play." Then she added, "Except in the bedroom. You don't play fair there at all."

Tony nuzzled the side of her neck. "That's because making love isn't play, Sarah Jane. It's serious business.''

"Right. What was I thinking?'' she said, and then sighed as he continued to trace the length of her neck with his lips.

Tony kissed her, making her head reel and her heart break rhythm.

"Hold that thought. I've got to talk to the men.''

Sarah was still smiling as her aunt entered the room.

"What is all the fuss?'' Lorett asked.

"It's over, Aunt Lorett! It's over! They arrested the man who tried to kill me. Now Daddy can rest in peace.''

Lorett stood quietly, studying Sarah and then the surrounding rooms.

"It doesn't feel over,'' she said.

Sarah groaned and threw herself into Lorett's arms.

"Don't, Aunt Lorett. Don't start second-guessing this now. Be happy for me. Be happy the criminal is behind bars.''

The expression on Lorett's face softened. "Of course I am happy for you, child.'' She hugged Sarah fiercely, as if she was reluctant to let her go. But Sarah spun out of her arms and began pacing the floor, counting off the things to be done.

"I don't know what to do next," Sarah said. "Oh. Yes, I do. I already made the funeral arrangements for Daddy to be buried beside Mother. That has to come first."

"I will leave tomorrow," Lorett said. "You do not need me to do these things."

Sarah's elation slipped, but only for a moment. "Yes, of course. I just thought—"

Lorett put a hand on either side of Sarah's face and then held her until Sarah stopped talking and looked—really looked—into her eyes.

"You have some hard decisions to make now, and you must make them as your own woman. You do not need me or anyone else's persuasive presence. What you do must come from your own heart."

Sarah blinked rapidly, overcome by a quick set of tears she wouldn't let fall.

"I'll be fine, Aunt Lorett. Never worry about me."

Lorett shook her head, then bent down and kissed Sarah's forehead as she'd done so many times in Sarah's youth.

"Do not be simple, child. Of course I will worry. It is a parent's prerogative."

Sarah threw her arms around Lorett's neck. "I may not have said it often enough, but I love you very much. You are the best parent I could ever have had. I thank my mother every day of my life for her foresight in making sure my care was left in your hands.''

Lorett frowned, then tugged gently at Sarah's hair. ''You need a cut. Want me to get the scissors?''

''No.''

They looked at each other and burst out laughing.

The only time Lorett had ever tried to cut Sarah's hair, it had been a disaster.

''We will talk later,'' Lorett said. ''I will call the airport now and schedule my flight.''

Sarah nodded reluctantly, then allowed them both some dignity by leaving the room before either one of them started to cry.

Sarah was torn between going back to New Orleans and not wanting to leave Tony. Even then, nothing was certain. Tony had hinted more than once at wanting her, at loving her, but there had been no formal declaration of love or commitment, let alone marriage.

Sarah glanced out the library windows. Tony was in deep discussion with the head of his security team. A little at loose ends, but elated that she was no longer under guard, she meandered through the house, imprinting each of the rooms in her mind for the time when she would no longer be here.

Lorett was still on the phone in the living room as she passed by. Dunn and Farley were coming down the hall with their suitcases in their hands.

"Guys, thank you."

They nodded soberly as she shook their hands.

"Are you leaving now?" she asked.

"Yes, ma'am," they echoed.

"Safe trip...wherever you're going," she said. "Oh...when you see Tony outside, tell him I walked down to the dock."

"Yes, ma'am," they said in unison again.

She smiled to herself as she exited the kitchen, then stopped on the deck, fingering the hole in the wall where they'd dug out the slug that had nearly killed her.

"But it didn't," she said, and turned toward the lake.

The view from the deck was magnificent and the clear, sunny day, although cool, was a perfect backdrop for the calm, shining waters. If Sarah squinted just right, she could almost convince herself that the lake was exactly what it had been built to be— the power source for a hydroelectric plant, as well as a place meant for relaxation and fun.

On an impulse, she started toward the dock. She

wanted to see the water up close, to find a way to make peace with the dark, murky depths. The last thing she needed was another level of fear. Still locked into "go nowhere without me" mode, she started to go back into the house and wait for Tony to come with her, then scoffed at herself and took the steps off the deck. Charles Bartlett was in jail. There was no one left who could hurt her.

The sunlight was warm upon her face. Her red flat-knit turtleneck molded itself to her body as she walked. She had on her tennis shoes and her favorite pair of jeans, and as she moved closer toward the boat dock, she made a mental reminder to herself to ask the sheriff to return her black loafers. He'd told her yesterday that the only prints on them were hers. Bartlett had been smart, all right, but not smart enough.

She paused at the beginning of the pier and looked out at the water. Almost immediately, her toes curled and the muscles in her belly began to knot. It was almost as if her heart knew something her mind had yet to accept.

"Don't be silly," she said sharply, and took that first step.

After that, it wasn't so bad. The pier itself appeared to be somewhere between thirty and forty feet long. The sound of lapping water against the

poles below the walkway was almost soothing.
Nothing ominous. Just a ramp and a dock where
boats could be tied.

Every so often she stepped on a board that would
groan and then creak, and she would automatically
flinch and then laugh. It was only the old dock saying hello.

When she reached the end, she stood at the edge
and looked outward. The sun was bright against the
water, and she lowered her head in a brief moment
of prayer and thanksgiving. When she looked up, a
flock of wild geese had just taken off from the lake.
Briefly they circled in the air and then, in a flurry
of unfettered honking, took flight to the south.

"See you in the spring," she said softly, then
wondered if she was fooling herself into thinking
she had any real part in Silk DeMarco's future.

She looked back toward the house. No one else
was in sight. Reluctant to go back and face Tony
and the impending separation, she sat down on the
edge of the dock instead. Her feet were only inches
from the water. The sun was warm upon her skin.
She leaned back on her hands and lifted her face to
the sun.

Ron Gallagher pulled up at the DeMarco house
as the security team was in the act of loading up

their gear.

Gallagher took a deep breath and started toward Tony. As much as he regretted it, it had to be said.

"Tony...we need to talk," he said.

Tony clapped him on the back. "Congratulations, Sheriff. You did it."

"Hold the congratulations," Ron muttered. "We got a problem."

Tony froze. "Like what?"

"Like the fact that Charles Bartlett was in Portland the night someone took a shot at Sarah."

"Oh Jesus," Tony said. "Are you sure?"

"About as sure as I can be, considering he was at a podium in front of almost four hundred witnesses."

"Christ," Tony muttered, then spun toward the van. "Wait," he said. "We're not through yet."

Before he could elaborate, Maury Overstreet drove up and got out on the run. He was grinning from ear to ear.

"Sheriff, you're just the man we need to see."

"What's going on?" Tony asked.

Maury whipped out the picture, slapped it on the hood of the sheriff's car and then got out his notes.

"I went to Moose Landing this morning, early. Found myself a dead man, only this one was fresh, not like the one you boys pulled out of the lake. At first I viewed it as a big setback to my case…as well as to the old fellow, of course. No offense.''

''None taken,'' Gallagher said. ''Please continue.''

''Anyway, I'm sitting there, waiting for the RCMP to show, 'cause I know I'll have to explain why I'm there, and I'm bemoaning the fact that my only potential witness to what went on at that motel is dead, when up drives the old man's daughter. Long story short, she used to work there as a maid. And, get this, she doesn't recognize Whitman at all, but she IDs two other employees of Marmet National Bank.''

''Who?'' Tony asked.

''Sonny Romfield and Moira Blake. It seems they had a thing going hot and heavy. Then Romfield dies a couple days after the money goes missing. At first I couldn't figure out the connection between an affair and missing money and someone trying to kill Sarah, so I started backtracking. When you get blocked on a case, always backtrack.''

''Good to know,'' Gallagher said. ''I'll remember that.''

''For God's sake, Maury, spit it out,'' Tony said.

''Okay, consider this. Sarah was just a curiosity,

nothing worth killing, until she got hold of something that could reveal the truth.''

''Like what?'' Gallagher asked.

''It's the calendar, isn't it?'' Tony asked.

Maury pointed. ''The man wins the big bucks! Right, it's the calendar.''

''But I have a copy, and I saw nothing to indicate anyone's culpability. Not even the 'moose' notations.''

''But that's just it,'' Maury said. ''It wasn't Whitman who was frequenting the Landing. It was Moira and Sonny. And didn't you tell me that Harmon Weatherly mentioned clearing out both their desks at once? What if he accidentally mixed up the calendars? And what if Moira discovered that mix-up? Not only would it reveal their affair, but it would also reveal their connection.''

''Son of a bitch,'' Tony said. ''What was it Moira said about him at her dinner party? Oh yes! I remember. She said he'd been going to get a divorce. Who would know that better than the other woman?''

Maury was almost dancing, he was so pumped.

''So they were going to make a getaway with the money. Somehow Whitman discovered their plan, and they had to kill him to hide what they'd done. Only Sonny's getting killed wasn't part of the plan, and Moira was left with not only one but *two* dead men on her conscience.''

''What happened to the money?'' Gallagher asked.

''I think that's a question we should ask Moira Blake,'' Tony said.

''Hey! Mr. DeMarco!''

Tony turned just as Dunn and Farley came out of the house.

''Miss Whitman said to tell you she was going for a walk.''

Oh God. Oh no. ''Where did she go?''

''Down to the dock.''

''Christ,'' Tony muttered, and started to run, with Gallagher and Maury not far behind.

He ran through the house, yelling her name. Lorett came out in the hall, and the expression on her face stilled Tony's heart.

''Where is she?'' he asked.

''Something bad is going to happen,'' she moaned. ''The water. It's trying to take my baby.''

''What the hell is she—''

''Don't ask,'' Tony said, then pointed at Gallagher. ''Just help me find her.''

Lorett tried to run after them, but it was as if her legs wouldn't obey her thoughts. She was frozen inside the horror unfolding in her head.

* * *

Sarah heard Tony calling her name. She turned with a smile, waving that she'd heard, as he came off the deck on the run. A brief moment of panic shot through her. Something was wrong. But before she could stand up, something took hold of her feet and yanked her into the lake.

She didn't have time for anything but a quick, indrawn breath before the waters engulfed her. Struggling against the almost superhuman grasp someone had on her body, she felt herself being dragged farther from shore, deeper into the lake.

Eighteen

Tony saw her go under and screamed out her name, but it was a futile waste of energy and air. She was gone with little more than a splash.

Behind him, Gallagher was barking orders into a hand-held radio, while Maury was kicking off his shoes and shedding his coat. Tony kicked off his loafers as he ran. When he reached the end of the dock, he went headfirst into the water, surfacing moments later to scan for a sign of where she had gone. Maury was in the water behind him, bobbing up and down like a float on a fishing line.

"Any sign of her?" he yelled.

"No!" Tony shouted.

Not only was the water without turmoil, there wasn't even a trail of bubbles that he could see. He dived again, and then again, each time surfacing with less hope that she would be found.

There was no thought in Sarah's mind save the frantic need for air. The water was dark and cold and engulfing, pressing on her eardrums and pushing up her nose, wanting into that place in her body where oxygen persisted and life still pulsed.

She kicked and she thrashed, clawing at the arms around her waist and pulling backward with all her might, trying to break free. She reached for her captor, trying to feel skin or hair or some modicum of humanity on which she could gain hold, but her hands kept sliding off. It took a moment for her to realize her abductor was wearing a wet suit, and with that knowledge came power. If she couldn't see under the water, then he couldn't, either. And if she could tear loose the mask or the oxygen tank the man was sure to be wearing, then he, too, would be unable to breathe. Only then might she have a chance.

She twisted abruptly, using every ounce of her strength to turn within the abductor's grasp, and found herself face-to-face with her killer. In desperation, she began ripping at the mask. In the process, she tore loose a hose connected to the air tank.

There was a moment when she felt his shock and then panic, and in that brief span of time, she kicked free. With her last ounces of strength and her lungs all but collapsing, she swam upward toward light and safety. By the time she popped to the surface, she was gasping and choking and afraid to look back.

Tony saw her almost at the moment she surfaced, and screamed out her name. When he saw a large trail of bubbles not far behind her, he knew she was still in danger.

The moment she saw Tony, she began to swim. With every stroke of her arms and kick of her legs, she imagined those gloved hands encircling an ankle or grabbing a wrist and pulling her down again. And she knew if that happened, she would die, just as her father had died—alone and in dark water.

Just when she thought she was too tired to swim another stroke, Tony caught her up into his arms.

Not until Tony touched her face and pulled her tight against his body did he let himself believe she was alive.

Treading water, his arm around her waist, he heard himself yelling above the thunder of his own heartbeat.

"You need to get to the shore. Can you swim to the shore?"

"I think so," Sarah said, and then gasped and screamed when something touched her back.

"It's me," Maury said. "Easy, Sarah girl. We've got you now."

Sarah wanted to throw her arms up in the air and let them take over, but the danger wasn't gone, not until she was on dry land. She looked toward the shore and saw her aunt Lorett wading into the water, and in that moment, she knew she was going to be all right.

Tony slid his arm around her neck. "Rest on me, Sarah. I'll get you to shore."

Fear colored her expression. "He might get me again."

"It isn't a he, it's a she," he said. "And I won't let that happen."

"What are you talking about?"

"Just get to shore. We'll talk then."

She started to swim, with Maury on one side and Tony on the other, matching her stroke for stroke. It was patently clear that they'd celebrated too soon. Charles Bartlett must not have acted alone.

By the time they were at the end of the pier, Lorett was waist high in the lake and reaching for Sarah. When her fingers curled around Sarah's arms, she began frantically dragging her toward dry land.

"Get her out!" Lorett screamed. "Get her all the way out of the water."

As soon as Tony's feet touched bottom, he lifted

Sarah into his arms and started carrying her toward the house.

Gallagher was there, along with his deputies.

"I've got people in the air," he said. "She won't get away."

Sarah struggled in Tony's arms. "Put me down. Put me down! I can walk."

But when Tony set her down, her legs crumpled. He scooped her back up and started toward the house.

"Tony, I—"

"Shut up, Sarah Jane. Just shut the hell up."

She was unprepared for such unexpected anger.

"Why are you mad at me?" she asked.

It was the quiver in her voice that made him come undone. The back deck of his house blurred before him as he stumbled slightly; suddenly he stopped and sat down on the grass with her in his lap.

"Tony?"

"Oh God," he mumbled. "Oh God, oh God." And he buried his face against her neck and started to cry.

Shock spread through her in waves. For the first time, she felt the cold on her skin, the weight of her clothes, the water squelching in her shoes. Her eyes were still burning and her vision blurry. She had yet to take the ability to draw breath for granted again. And because she suspected there was more hell yet to come, she just held him, because she didn't know what else to do.

Maury stopped a distance away to collect his shoes and his coat, and then went into the house without looking at them. Lorett approached, moving swiftly—touching Sarah's head to assure herself that her baby still lived, and then putting her hands on Tony's back.

"You must get up," she coaxed gently. "You must get her out of the open."

The warning moved Tony as nothing else might. He struggled to his feet and grabbed Sarah close.

"I am with you," Lorett said. "Just hurry."

As they moved toward the house, Lorett couldn't help but look over her shoulder. The danger she'd sensed was still there, lurking beneath the surface of the dark, shining water.

Lorett was in Sarah's bathroom, stripping her of her clothes, much as she'd done when she was a child.

"We've got to get you warm and then into some dry clothes," she said. "The shower is ready. Wash it off, baby girl. Wash off all the ugliness and let Aunt Lorett rub you dry."

Sarah was shivering so hard she wasn't sure she would ever be able to stop. Coming down from the surge of adrenaline that had helped free her from her captor was giving her a giant-size case of the shakes. When she coupled that with the knowledge that Moira Blake might be behind everything, it was too much to take in.

"Why her, Aunt Lorett?"

"Get in the shower, Sarah Jane."

Sarah stepped beneath the spray of warm water as Lorett pulled the door shut behind her. She squirted a dollop of shampoo in her hand and started scrubbing her hair. The door to the bathroom opened, then closed again, but Sarah didn't look up. It wasn't until she felt Tony's hand on her back that she flinched.

"Tony! Aunt Lorett is out there."

"Not anymore," he said, then shed his clothes and stepped into the shower with her. "Here, let me," he said gently, and began rinsing the shampoo from her hair. Then he handed her a washcloth and soap, and together, they washed themselves clean.

They dressed without speaking or touching, both watching each other as if they would never get enough. Finally Tony sat down on the side of the bed.

"I thought you were dead." His voice broke

again, as he struggled with the fear of believing she had drowned. "Sarah, I know this isn't the most romantic moment in our lives, but I've got to say this. I love you. I do not want to spend the rest of my life without you in it. You have become the most important person in my life, and I need to know if you feel the same way."

"Oh, Tony!" she cried, and crawled into his lap. "I love you, too. I don't care if we did this too fast and for all the wrong reasons. I've been sick at heart, just trying to figure out how I'd ever learn to live without you when this was over."

"I'll move to New Orleans. We can start a third nightclub there. It's time I expanded out of Chicago, anyway. I'll do whatever it takes to hear you say you'll be my wife."

Sarah put her arms around him, her heart soaring with joy.

"Yes, yes, a thousand times yes, I will marry you."

"Now all I have to do is get you out of here," Tony said.

"But—"

"They know who did this, Sarah. And so do we. She can't hide forever. Sooner or later she'll surface, and when she does, they'll arrest her."

"I don't know," Sarah said. "I still can't believe Moira was responsible."

"Gallagher is searching her house now."

"But how did she get Charles Bartlett's gun?"

"She and Tiny are friends. It was probably a simple matter of knowing their habits and getting in and out of the house while they were gone."

"Why would she and Sonny Romfield kill Daddy? Why didn't they just take the money and run?"

"Who knows? Maybe he caught them in the act, or maybe they wanted to use him for a fall guy so they could live without always looking over their shoulders. Whatever their plan was, Romfield's death changed everything."

"This is all still supposition, though, isn't it?"

The phone rang before Tony could answer her. He leaned back and reached for the receiver without letting her go.

"Hello."

"Tony…Gallagher here…we found the money."

"You're kidding! Where?"

"Of all damned places, in a trunk in Moira Blake's attic."

"Then this clinches it, right?"

"As tight as a drum. She's going down for so

many crimes that her lawyers won't know what to fight first."

"Any sign of her yet?" Tony asked.

"No, but we're working on it. Her car's here. Her belongings and all her identification are here. She can't get far in a wet suit."

"Right," Tony said. "Let us know when you pick her up."

"What?" Sarah asked, as Tony hung up the phone.

"They found the money in her attic. It pretty much clinches the case. They're scouring the woods and the lake now. It's only a matter of time before she's picked up."

"My poor daddy," Sarah said. "He liked her...really liked her. I remember him and Mother talking about her circumstances."

"What circumstances?"

"Looking back, I'm guessing that her husband was abusive, which explains the affair with Sonny Romfield, but it doesn't explain how she could kill."

Tony touched her face, then her mouth, tracing the shape of her features with his fingers, then putting his lips where his hand had just been. Sarah's head fell back against his arm as she gave herself up to the magic of the man.

"Do you feel the passion?"

Sarah moaned. "Yes…oh, yes."

His hands slid up her back, encircling her and then cupping her breasts.

"Do you feel my need? Can you feel the love from me to you?"

"Yes…dear God, yes," Sarah said.

"It's that simple, sweet Sarah. Moira killed once for love, and I'd wager a profiler would agree with me that, when Sonny died, the only way she could keep that love alive was to protect the secret they'd shared. Even if it meant killing again."

"That's sick," Sarah said.

"Yes, it is, and so is she, but they'll stop her. However, I want you away from here until they catch her, okay?"

"But my father—"

"We'll lay him to rest, sweet baby, I promise. But I don't want the task of having to bury you there beside him."

"Surely there's no reason to kill me now," Sarah argued. "Not now that she knows the secret is out."

"Now more than ever," Tony said.

"But why?"

"Because she can't let you win."

"Dear God."

He stood up, his focus already on the things to be done.

"Pack your things, Sarah. I'm going to talk to Lorett...tell her what we've planned, then make a few calls. We'll be out of here before dark."

"Yes," Sarah said, suddenly anxious to get as far away from this place as quickly as she could.

Tony kissed her once more, then left her with a wink.

She moved to the window and looked out to the lake, reliving the feeling of being pulled under. Then she lifted her chin and turned away. The truth of Moira Blake's guilt and her father's innocence would be all over the news before morning. She'd almost paid the ultimate price for the truth, but there was satisfaction in knowing that she'd accomplished what she'd set out to do.

It was time to go home.

Moira Blake surfaced just under the dock at Tony's house, floating in the shadows, out of sight. She watched them carrying Sarah into the house and knew that she had only moments before the place was crawling with armed men. Quickly she took off her mask and flippers, fastened them to her air tank and dropped them into the water. They sank to the bottom beneath the pier as she got out of the water and started through the woods toward her house.

She had always known this day would come. She'd known when Sonny had bashed in Franklin Whitman's skull with the crystal paperweight on Paul Sorenson's desk. She'd known, even as she was sobbing hysterically and helping stuff Franklin's body into the trunk, that God was going to make her pay. She'd known when the trunk went into the water, floating for a few moments on the surface of the lake and then bubbling slowly as it began to sink. She'd known when the first shovelful of dirt had landed on Sonny's coffin that it was only a matter of time before she wound up the same way.

And then the waiting had begun. Year after year, until twenty long, lonely years with a cripple for a husband had come and gone and she was too riddled with guilt to spend the ill-gotten gains. Then some idiot had robbed an armored car and kidnapped a woman. After that, it began coming undone.

She'd tried. So desperately, she'd tried, but she was tired of running and tired of the lies. It would be simple to just turn herself in and wait for the hand of God to strike her down.

She was almost out of breath by the time she got to the edge of her property, but the caution that had served her so well all these years saved her once again. She paused for a moment to scan the yard around her house and saw the tail end of a police car in front. In that moment, she knew it was over. Somehow they'd discovered the truth. She was going to be revealed as a thief and a killer. If she was lucky, she would spend the rest of her life behind bars. That knowledge was almost her undoing. There was a part of her that wanted to march up to the house and turn herself in, but not just yet, not before Sarah Whitman knew what it felt like to lose the man she loved.

Instead of going to the house, she moved quickly to the right and slipped into the barn, where her husband used to keep his sheep, before he'd gone and crippled himself. She ran to the old granary at the end of the barn, grabbed the sawed-off shotgun he'd used to kill rats and ran back into the woods. If they were already searching her house, they would be in the woods within minutes. She didn't have much time.

Tony had just told the head of the security team to continue packing, that they would all be leaving soon. Dunn and Farley were still packing their things into their car and Maury Overstreet was already on his way home. Sheriff Gallagher had gone off with one of the search teams, but not before coordinating another one to search by air.

Tony stood in the foyer, thinking that the house seemed empty, although he could hear Lorett humming down the hallway as she packed up her things, and the intermittent creak on the floor above told him Sarah was doing the same. Now there was nothing left but for him to pack, too, load the car and put the memories behind them.

He'd already made up his mind to put this house on the market. Not even the passage of time would be able to erase the images of Sarah being yanked into the water, nor would he be able to stand out on the deck and not remember the echo of the gunshot or Sarah's screams. The place was haunted with too many ugly memories. It was time to lay them all to rest.

He started toward the stairs, then remembered he'd forgotten to lock the storage shed out back. Fingering the keys in his pocket, he headed for the kitchen. It wouldn't take a minute to put the padlock in place.

He paused on the deck, searching the area until he recognized one of the deputies walking through the trees, and knew the sheriff and his men were on the job. Satisfied that all was as it should be, he hastened down the steps and then moved toward the storage shed at a jog.

Sarah was coming down the stairs as she heard Tony go out the back. She was at the last step when Lorett came running from her room. Sarah took one look at her face and knew something was wrong.

"She's going to kill him," she said, then staggered, as if overwhelmed by the vision.

Sarah's heart stopped. "No...no...this is supposed to be over." She raced to Lorett, grabbed her by the shoulders and shook her.

"What are you saying, Aunt Lorett?"

"She will kill him."

"The security guards! They're still out front. Hurry, Aunt Lorett. Tell them to hurry!"

Lorett blinked and then jerked as she looked at Sarah's face. She went one way as Sarah went another. Sarah ran through the kitchen and out onto the deck, just as Tony disappeared into the storage shed. She had no way of knowing exactly what Lorett had seen, but the horror of it had been there in her aunt's expression. That was enough for her.

She flew down the steps without thought for her own safety and dashed toward the shed. She was reaching for the doorknob when she heard a woman's voice. Before she could open the door, there was a loud shout and then a gunshot.

''No!'' Sarah screamed, and gave the door a yank.

Sunlight flooded the opening as Moira spun at the sound. Her face was a caricature of its former elegance. Still wearing parts of the wet suit, she screamed an obscenity at Sarah as she swung the sawed-off shotgun toward her.

After that, it seemed to Sarah as if everything happened in slow motion.

Tony's body was falling against a workbench. There was blood on his shirt, and Sarah was reaching for the ax on the wall by the door. Then the images became a series of stills.

Moira's lips curled over her teeth, her thumb cocking the hammer on the still-loaded barrel.

The scent of chain-saw oil.

The scrape of sawdust beneath their feet.

The weight of the ax pulling hard against Sarah's elbow as she swung it sideways, like a baseball bat.

The earsplitting scream as steel connected with flesh.

The echo of the second gunshot as the pellets hit the roof.

Then the blood, spraying in a neat little pattern on the sawdust like a sprinkler in the grass.

The frantic heaving of lungs tortured for air.

And then the silence.

"You've killed me," Moira whispered.

A moment of panic flew across Sarah's face, and then she gritted her teeth.

"You killed yourself," she said.

Moira Blake died on the way to the ground.

Sarah dropped the ax, then staggered, and she would have fallen but for the pair of strong arms that caught her.

"I've got you, baby girl," Lorett said, as a half-dozen armed men swarmed through the door. They went straight to Tony, who was lying on the floor beneath the bench.

Sarah's expression was haunted. "I was too late. She shot him. Oh God…Aunt Lorett…I was too late."

"He's not dead, Miss Whitman. Some of the shot caught him across the forehead, but his pulse is strong and steady. He'll have a headache and some scars, and that's about it," the guard said.

Sarah rushed to Tony, dropped to her knees beside him and slid her hands beneath his head.

"Tony?"

He moaned, then opened his eyes.

"This is getting to be a habit," he said, as he touched his fingers to his forehead. "Damn. That hurts." Then he remembered Moira and sat up with a jerk. "She has a gun."

"Not anymore," Sarah said.

Tony looked over Sarah's shoulder. His eyes widened in shock as he saw what was left of Moira Blake. He drew a deep breath and looked at Sarah. He didn't know what to say, but he knew what she'd done.

"You saved my life."

"No, I saved mine," Sarah said. "Because if anything had happened to you, it would have killed me." Struggling with the urge not to scream, she put her arms around him and closed her eyes.

"Sarah…can you tell me what happened?"

Sarah shuddered as she recognized the voice. It was Ron Gallagher, and as she pulled away from Tony to look up, she had a strong sensation of déjà vu. It took a bit for her to remember that she'd seen Gallagher at this angle before—at the cemetery, the day of her mother's funeral. That day he'd bent down and touched her face, and there had been tears in his eyes. But today there was nothing but concern.

"She tried to kill Tony," Sarah said. "Then she tried to kill me. I stopped her. That's all. I just wanted it to stop."

Gallagher looked at Tony.

"What can I say? Moira caught me unaware. I came in to get the padlock, and she was waiting inside. She kept screaming something about Sarah needing to know what it felt like to live the rest of her life without the man she loved, and before I could stop her, she pulled the trigger. I jumped backward as she shot. A couple of pellets grazed me. I don't know what happened afterward, but I will say that if it hadn't been for Sarah opening that door, I would be dead.''

The explanation was good enough for Gallagher. He pointed to one of his deputies.

''Call an ambulance, and call the coroner, too.''

''I don't need an ambulance, just another damned Band-Aid.''

Gallagher grinned. ''Good thing your head is so hard.''

''That's not funny,'' Sarah said, while she struggled to her feet. The coppery scent of Moira's blood was in her nostrils. She felt she was going to throw up.

Gallagher helped Tony to his feet as Sarah bolted for the door.

By the time they got outside, she was sitting against the side of the building with her head between her knees. Lorett was kneeling beside her.

Gallagher knew what Sarah had been forced to do. He also knew she would be a long time forgetting it. Then he turned to Tony.

"I understand you were leaving. You can fill out a report on your way out of town. If we have any other questions, I know where to find you."

Sarah stood, her face pale and expressionless, but her voice was strong with determination.

"We won't be leaving yet. Now that the danger is over, I will bury my father tomorrow...next to Mother. The arrangements have already been made."

"I understand," Ron said. "But if you'd rather take some time, I can hold his remains until—"

"I don't want to come back—ever," Sarah said.

Gallagher nodded in understanding. "You did good, Sarah. Never doubt that."

Sarah looked at her aunt, then at Tony. Besides the love, she saw something in his eyes that she'd never seen before, and it scared her. Quickly she looked away, unwilling to see that far inside herself. Then he took her by the hand, and together, they started toward the house.

Only once, as they reached the deck, did Sarah look behind her. She looked past the turmoil at the storage shed to the serenity of Flagstaff Lake. The beauty of the sunlight on the surface and the bird singing from a nearby tree seemed sacrilegious in the face of what she'd done.

Dark water.

Dark deeds.

But it was over.

The rest of her life had just begun.

The weather was as somber as the mood of the day. It had dawned gray and overcast, threatening rain. Every road leading into the cemetery was lined with parked cars as people waited for the hearse to arrive. It was hard to judge what they were thinking, but few spoke. It was as if they were too ashamed to look one another in the eyes.

The whole town was still in shock. That they had harbored such a heinous criminal as Moira Blake, without realizing her true nature, seemed impossible. Tiny Bartlett, Marcia Farrell and Annabeth Harold were suffering something of what Catherine Whitman had endured those many years ago. The citizens of Marmet could not believe that the women would have been such good friends to one another and not known what Moira had been about. And then there was the business of Charles Bartlett's hunting rifle being used to try to kill Sarah Whitman. Even though he had been completely exonerated, there were those who still claimed that "where there's smoke, there's fire."

And so the people waited, shivering and silent, to pay their respects to a man and his daughter, and maybe, just maybe, to give up a quiet little prayer for their own forgiveness.

Within minutes, the crowd began to shift as it became apparent that the hearse had arrived, with one family car and three patrol cars from the sheriff's department directly behind it.

At that point people began to move toward the open mouth of the grave, wanting to be ringside for the biggest show of the year. And then the back door of the hearse was opened, and an ebony casket was pulled forward. At Sarah's request, Ron Gallagher and all four of his deputies stepped up to the casket, as did Harmon Weatherly, dressed formally in his dark business suit, the one he'd always worn to the bank. With three men on one side and three on the other, they gripped the handles of the casket and slid it the rest of the way out of the hearse, then carried it steadily to the grave.

When Silk DeMarco emerged from the family car with Sarah Whitman beside him, there was an audible intake of breath. They knew what she'd done. They knew why she'd done it. And yet they couldn't tear their gazes away from the stricken look on her face.

Sarah swayed on her feet as she stopped at the open grave. Tony steadied her, holding her close against his side. After yesterday's ordeal with Moira, the doctor had wanted to sedate her, but she'd refused. There were no drugs that could make her forget the insanity in Moira's eyes as she'd aimed the shotgun in her face, or the way the ax had felt in her hands as it sliced through sinew and skin.

A pastor from the church that Sarah had attended as a child stepped forward. He'd been asked to read one Bible verse over Franklin Whitman's grave, and he'd readily agreed. His voice was strong and steady as he opened his Bible, then looked up.

"We come here today to lay Franklin James Whitman to a long and overdue rest. His daughter, Sarah Whitman, has asked that I read one verse to you all, and one verse only, after which she will depart."

There were frowns among the people, but no comments, although it was obvious that they were feeling cheated, to have waited all this time in the cold only to learn the burying would be over almost before it began.

The pastor cleared his throat and looked directly at Sarah.

"Miss Whitman, before I begin, I want to apologize to you, on the behalf of every citizen of Marmet, for denying you in your darkest of hours."

Sarah flinched. She hadn't expected him to say that. She hadn't expected the words that she'd waited so long to hear would draw her throat so tight or make her eyes fill with tears.

Tony felt her shock, then saw her shudder. He leaned down, whispering in her ear.

"Stay strong for me, baby...don't let them see you cry."

It was exactly what she needed to hear. She took a slow, deep breath and then, ever so slightly, leaned into his strength as the pastor opened his Bible.

"From the New Testament, the Book of Matthew, seventh chapter, first verse. And the Lord said, 'Judge not, lest ye also be judged.'"

He closed the Bible and looked up. "Remember those words. You are dismissed."

But nobody moved. They were watching Sarah Whitman take an object from her pocket, then lay it on top of the casket. Only the closest could see that it was a small bunch of keys on a ring that said "Number One Dad."

Sheriff Gallagher stepped forward, took off his hat and shook Sarah's hand. His deputies followed suit and then moved to their cars. Harmon Weatherly paused in front of Sarah, and when she would have shaken his hand, he lifted hers to his lips and kissed it instead.

Sarah couldn't look at them without crying, so she fixed her gaze on the small ring of keys lying atop the ebony casket instead. And as she stared, a drop of rain fell on her cheek, and then another.

Tony was worried. Sarah was near the breaking point, and he feared if she gave way, she wouldn't be able to stop.

"Sweetheart..."

She jerked as if she'd been slapped, then looked at him as if he was a stranger.

"It's starting to rain," he said.

The gentleness of his touch as he took her hand steadied the slow but impending hysteria she'd been struggling to deny. She turned toward the crowd. Slowly, slowly, she stared into the faces, seeing Paul Sorenson meet her gaze and then drop his head, watching Annabeth Harold look away—making them see her while denying them all the gift of absolution. She didn't ever want them to forget what their lack of Christian kindness had done.

Then she looked at Tony, letting his love wash over her, cleaning the last of the bitterness from her soul.

"It's over?" she asked, as he led her to the car.

"Yes, baby, it's over. It's time to go home."

Epilogue

New Orleans, Louisiana
Six months later

"Ooh, *chère*... you better watch out for your man. He's smiling at that Bonet woman," Michelle said.

The grand opening of Très Silk was in full swing and was, by all accounts, a resounding success, just as Sarah had known it would be. She watched the way Tony was working the crowd, then settled back with a grin as she winked at Lorett's youngest and patted her stomach.

"No way, Michelle, you don't know my man so good, or you wouldn't say what you said. I've got something in here that he'll never let go." Then she moved her hand from her belly to her heart. "And something in here that won't let me go."

Michelle leaned against Sarah's shoulder and giggled intimately, as sisters often do, then blew her

a kiss and went to rejoin her own husband, Francois, who was attracting far too many female fans
for her liking.

The moment Sarah was alone, Tony appeared at
her side, as if sensing her solitude. He bent over
the chair and lifted her hair, then kissed the curve
behind her ear that he loved so much.

"Mmm, that feels nice," Sarah said, and stood
up with a taunting smile on her face. "Aren't you
going to ask me to dance?"

Tony swung her into his arms just as the music
segued from a rowdy Cajun tune to a slow, sensu-
ous blues melody.

"My Sarah," Tony whispered, as they danced
around the floor.

"Say it again," Sarah begged.

"My Sarah. My Sarah…always mine."

She looked up at him and smiled.

"Tonight is a little bit of paradise, I think."

"Only a little?" he asked, pretending great disappointment.

Sarah slid her hands beneath the jacket of his tux
and leaned back just enough that she could feel his
arousal.

"Ah…my beautiful Silk…paradise is relative.
Out here, in your club, I share you with everyone…and gladly. But in our home, I share you with

none. That's where my paradise lies. With you and the baby we've made.''

Too overcome to speak, Tony pulled her even closer and twirled her across the floor.

Sometimes at night, when the house was in darkness and she lay sleeping in his arms, he still knew the fear of what living without her would be. And then he would remember what had happened, what she'd been forced to endure, and he would get down on his knees and thank God that she had survived.

He swung her under a massive chandelier and then stopped, letting the other couples on the dance floor flow around them.

"Look up, Sarah Jane."

Sarah tilted her head and smiled. "You were right. It's not too large. In fact, it's magnificent."

"The lights are for you," he said softly. "To keep out the dark."

The smile she was wearing tilted, then died. Sarah tried not to let it happen, but she knew she was going to cry. The moment the tears welled, she looked down, then away.

But Tony wouldn't let her retreat. Not back to that place where he'd seen her go so many times in the past six months.

''Sarah, don't go there anymore. The past is over. From this day forward, we live in the light.''

And then they began to twirl beneath the glitter of the Italian chandelier until Sarah was laughing aloud and hanging on to his arms to steady herself.

He was right. The past was over. The future was them and the baby and the love that they shared.